PURGATERRY

BY
CELIA CLEAVELAND

Copyright © 2023 Celia Cleaveland
All rights reserved.

The characters and events portrayed in this book are fictitious. Any similarity to real persons, living or dead, is coincidental and not intended by the author.

No part of this book may be reproduced, or stored in a retrieval system, or transmitted in any form or by any means, electronic, mechanical, photocopying, recording, or otherwise, without express written permission of the publisher.

ISBN: 979-8-9887977-1-5

Interior art by Canva Pro
Author photo by Rob Batey

Printed in the United States of America.

Please be aware that PurgaTerry includes mentions of suicide, depression/mental health problems, and (alluded to) transphobia.

To those who need to hear it;
as long as you're breathing,
it's not too late.

Prologue

Dean wasn't prepared to go through this today or any day. He was too late.

It took him forever to track down the girl's file, and by the time he got there, the damage had been done.

He should have seen the signs; he might have caught Dels in the act, and he might have saved this poor kid.

As he ducked his head through the playhouse door, there were hardly two steps between his feet and the girl's body.

Was she really twenty-three? He would have guessed younger. But who under eighty wasn't a kid to him? He carefully stepped over the body and focused on the shivering soul in the corner.

It was cold stepping into death for the first time, like being dropped into icy water. He wondered just how long Dels had been targeting her. He could remember vividly when he'd been in this same scenario—when someone had taken advantage of his own mental instability.

He also remembered the one who had come to him, who had found his soul all alone with no idea what to do next. They'd taken his hand and helped him make the best of things, helped him make some sense of his situation. Dean guessed now it was his turn to do however much he could for this girl. He moved his black shoes into her line of sight, and she lifted her eyes up from the floor to meet his.

The fear in them, the confusion, Dean could see it all. This girl had already been on the edge, and Dels had pushed her over. Mentally cursing the whole ordeal, he gave her a reassuring smile, and he made a silent promise that he would do his best to make things better for her. Or at least, better than what he'd had to deal with in his own situation.

"Hi, I'm Dean. Sorry I'm late. But in my defense, you're far too early." He crouched down lower, closer to her, and held out his hand. There would be so much he couldn't tell her, so much that she wouldn't understand right away. But Dean thought he should keep things as simple as possible for her right now. "Wanna get out of here?" he asked.

Dean couldn't tell if she had nodded, but her hand trembled out to meet his, and he gently guided her over her body and maneuvered her out the small door.

This was supposed to be the part where he gave her the choice, but the truth was that, now, she didn't have one. All he could do was bring her back with him.

It could make things even worse if she ever found out just how extensively she had been screwed over.

1. Terry Was Dead, to Begin With

Terry had no memory of how she died. At first, she had thought this was all a dream, but that didn't last long. Her dreams didn't tend to be this vivid or include places she didn't know.

She remembered a hand. A comforting hand took hers and helped her up. She remembered walking what felt like a very long time and yet no time at all. Then, suddenly, Terry woke up in the weird white room with no memory of getting there.

All she had to go on was the name tag sticker stuck to a shirt that was far too loose. The sticker peeled off in one smooth motion. She gazed down at the words, reading them over several times, but still wasn't able to absorb any more information than the first time.

The words "Hi, I'm Terry" were there in big, friendly letters. The word "Terry" was handwritten in the big white space and scribbled near the bottom were the words "recently deceased."

That was just one of the things that didn't make sense about what was happening or what she saw. Was she "Terry"? Part of her scoffed at herself, because of course she was. She must be, otherwise, why would it be on her name tag? But a larger part of her felt the label of "Terry" fit her awkwardly. It was a name that draped over her, hastily painted over something else—a name that would have felt more comfortable.

She sat up in what looked like a dentist's chair and observed that the room she was in was not only starkly, blindingly white, but it appeared to curve around her with no discernible corners or edges.

She eased herself out of the chair. It was a bit high for her height, and she had to drop the last few inches. The tile of the floor was smooth under her bare feet, and she wondered why she wasn't wearing shoes. Her large shirt fell almost to her knees, well past the hem of her unzipped gray hoodie. Her soft, fleecy, mint-colored pants were comfortable but not exactly a look she would have expected to be wearing in the afterlife. If she was indeed actually dead, which she still doubted, because, really, why would the first thing she saw in the afterlife be some futuristic dentist's office?

She walked toward the walls and slid her hand along them, looking for some sort of seam that would denote an exit of some kind. But no exit was to be found.

The light source above her looked like standard drop ceiling fluorescent lights, but there wasn't the usual buzzing noise coming from them. In fact, there was no sound at all after the squeaking, sliding noises Terry made as she climbed down from the chair.

She circled the room again, searching for clues of any kind and coming up with absolutely nothing. She found the pockets on her hoodie and felt something wadded up in one of them. Terry pulled it out to find a crinkled silver wrapper. The shiny side was unremarkable, but the white side caught her by surprise. A single word was scrawled there in pen:

"Hatori"

She had no idea who or what that was, but it was the first thing she discovered in this place that felt in any way familiar. She

PurgaTerry

was going to inspect it further when a television screen suddenly appeared. Terry startled and crammed it back into her pocket.

The screen flashed to life on the far side of the wall as the sounds of a calming saxophone filled the air. The screen showed the words "Welcome Message 3" for a brief second before being replaced by a man standing in front of what looked like a whiteboard.

The music lowered in volume as he began speaking.

"Greetings, friend, and welcome to your first day here in Purgatory."

The man on the screen had a pleasant voice, but with some seriously outdated clothing choices. It almost looked like he was wearing a robe, or maybe even a toga. As he spoke, the words "Cato: Chief Ambassador of Purgatory" appeared at the bottom of the screen in a curly, cursive font.

"Upon entering the afterlife, our judges determined that your soul's purity levels were not up to the standards that would have secured you an automatic ticket to what we call 'Upstairs.' This could be for several reasons, including but not limited to: a high amount of low-level sins, repentance of mid- to higher-level sins before death, and suicide."

Okay... Terry thought. *So, this is some sort of afterlife, but I'm not in Heaven?*

"The good news is that if you have been placed here in Purgatory, you still have a chance to avoid the opposite fate to Upstairs. That being what we call 'Downstairs.'"

The scene on the screen changed angles. The man was now sitting closer to the whiteboard and turned to his left, leaning in slightly toward the camera.

"The bad news is, if you are seeing this particular welcome message, it means that you are one of the individuals who died by suicide."

Suicide? Terry's mind flinched at the word, poking at it but not wanting to get too close. Processing and absorbing the word in relationship to herself was something she was having difficulty with.

The man on the television did not pause to explain further, continuing with his speech as if that word were not the heavy, sobering thing that it was.

"As that is the case, your options for residence here in Purgatory are limited—"

As the man continued speaking on the screen, a section of the solid-looking wall to Terry's left parted, and in walked a different man—this one wearing a more modern suit that still looked a couple of decades out of style, but at least he was wearing pants.

He sauntered over as the man on the screen spoke, chewing gum and sarcastically speaking the dialogue along with him as if he had heard it a dozen or more times.

"—to the facilities of Level Eight, unless you are placed in a service that requires you to blah blah blah, thank you very much, Mr. Toga, I think I can take it from here." He tapped the monitor, and the screen went silent, the word "mute" hovered in the bottom left corner of the screen in large yellow block letters.

He then turned to Terry, gesturing to the monitor as he approached a few feet from where she stood.

"Sorry about that. We usually let everybody at least finish the video, but I've been forced to hear that thing so often, I could kill myself... if that were even possible to do here."

He chuckled, then stopped when he noticed Terry did not join in.

"Sorry. Probably in poor taste, considering," he muttered. "My name is Dean, and I'll be your manager."

"Manager of what?" Terry asked, raising an eyebrow and looking the man over. He appeared to be in his late thirties or early forties with short brown hair combed to one side and a light-dusty-blue tie. He did look a tad official, but there was just something slightly rumpled about his appearance that made Terry second-guess his qualifications.

"Manager of you, while you're here. So, shut up and listen."

Part of Terry wished he hadn't interrupted; the video was still

PurgaTerry

playing silently over the man's shoulder. Maybe there was some crucial thing she was missing because of this guy's interference.

Dean did not appear to care. "Don't worry, you didn't miss anything. It's all a lot of exposition to basically tell you that not only are you dead, but how you died was... sort of controversial, shall we say."

"And what does that mean?" she asked, finally giving up trying to pay attention to the video and turning fully toward him.

"It means that suicides like yours are a bit of a moral quandary for the big judges Upstairs. They can't exactly send you straight down, but your soul isn't quite clean enough to go straight up, either. That's what Purgatory is for. The souls that need some purging before they can be properly judged."

Terry—still hiding behind her skepticism—did not want to indulge this man with the questions that were now rising in her mind. But her curiosity got the better of her. "So, does everybody who dies like I did come here?"

"Only those who agree to it. There are different jobs at different levels, and you were placed here with me."

"But, why?"

"Because you need looking after, and since I'm with the Soul Shepherd department, what better place for you to be?"

"That seems kind of random."

Dean merely chuckled. "Welcome to the afterlife, kid. Things don't always tend to make sense around here."

Terry watched as he straightened some papers in the manila folder in his hand without opening it. "So, you're, what, an angel?" she asked. To which Dean made a sound of amusement.

"Nah, that's upper management. I'm more middle to lower. I'm your manager, and I've been here a long time, so let's just stick with that."

"How long is 'a long time'?"

"Never you mind, longer than you've been around. Which isn't saying much. You were what, twenty-three when you died?" He glanced down at the folder in his hand, letting out a low whistle.

"Shoot, you're gonna be here a while."

Terry took a second, more skeptical look at the outside of the folder. "Wait, does that file say how long I'll be here? Can I see it?" She reached out to grab it from him, but he pulled away, holding up his other hand to halt her.

"Whoa, whoa. No can do, kid. This is for managers' eyes only. Nobody gets to know exactly how long they'll be here."

"It seems like there are a lot of things around here I don't get to know."

Dean shrugged. "Well, get used to that. You're at the bottom of the pecking order around here. And here on Level Eight, that's like being on the bottom of the bottom. You're lucky you even know what you do. We can't even give you your real name."

"What?" She balked. "This isn't even my name?" She realized she was still holding the name tag. "Then what is it?"

"Weren't you listening to what I just said? I can't tell you. I had to make up a new name for you."

"And you went with 'Terry'?"

"Seemed like a good idea at the time. Most managers have a theme when it comes to naming their new residents. Me, I'm more of a 'first thought' kinda guy."

"What was the first thought that made you think 'Terry'?"

Dean paused a moment, then gestured toward her torso.

"Your shirt. It has a pterodactyl on it." He pointed at the center of her shirt. It depicted a green pterodactyl holding a mug on which were printed the word "Tea-rodactyl."

She gave him a pointed look, once again arching an eyebrow at him. "And that's what you came up with?"

She watched as Dean turned and began to feel his hand up and down the wall in the general area that he had entered.

"Probably not one of my better choices, but it's functional," he said without looking back at her. He continued feeling the wall with one hand and held tight to the folder in his other. "I always lose track of this opening."

"You know pterodactyl starts with a P," she stated.

PurgaTerry

"What, you wanna be 'P-Terry'?" Dean glanced over his shoulder at her.

She shook her head.

"All right, just be glad about what you got, then," he said, finally appearing to have found the opening and swiping some sort of card in a slot Terry couldn't see. "Now, come on, we got a few things to do before you start."

When a doorway appeared, Dean began to walk through, waving for her to follow.

Terry hesitated before leaving the room, feeling the paper still in her pocket. It didn't seem significant, but the fact that she'd found it hidden away gave her pause. This guy didn't appear to know about it, and Terry decided it might be best to keep it that way for now. The video continued playing behind her as she took a shaky step through.

She followed him down a long, featureless hallway that ended in a set of double doors. A dark, foggy night loomed on the outside of the doors as Dean continued sauntering through them, not stopping to see if Terry was following. Which at first, she wasn't.

But after a moment's hesitation, Terry eventually figured that she might get more answers if she did what she was told. Reluctantly, she followed Dean and allowed the eerie fog to swallow her whole.

So, according to this Dean person and that weird video, she was dead. And if they were to be believed, she had done this to herself and, what was more, chose to do community service in some midpoint of the afterlife for who knew how long?

It wasn't as if she had anything to verify that this wasn't a dream or some kind of elaborate hidden camera show, but there was also the fact that she did have some form of memory loss. There was a distinct "before" time that she couldn't quite access. Her memories were as foggy as the oddly not-chilly night surrounding them.

"It's not that cold, so why is it so foggy?" she asked.

CELIA CLEAVELAND

Dean did not pause or turn around as he led her from one streetlamp's pool of light to another. "Not sure," he answered, sounding as if he had never given it much thought before. "It's just always been there. Of course, it's only dark because it's nighttime. Don't ask me how the whole day and night thing is supposed to work here, either. It just does. No idea what time zone we're in. Maybe Purgatory has its own."

Terry was finally able to match Dean's pace by this point; he still looked straight ahead.

She checked her pulse for the fifteenth time since they started walking. Even just this little bit of physical excursion should have made her heartbeat at least somewhat faster. But ignoring the fact that she wasn't feeling any strain from this long of a walk, she still couldn't feel any blood pumping through her.

If this was some kind of prank, whoever was behind it was thorough.

"All I know is that nothing whatsoever gets done when the sun goes down. But anyway, we have to get to the Main Hub to find Cass."

"Who's that?"

"Technically, she's my boss, but she's only slightly senior. She's been watching one of my other residents for me while I came to get you. You'll need to meet them both anyway, so I guess now's the time."

Maybe she would have better luck with this Cass person. Because she was obviously not going to get any help from her new "manager."

"While we're walking, feel free to cycle through those five stages of grief. It makes things so much easier to get them out of the way at the start."

When Terry didn't give any indication she had heard him, Dean continued, "Denial, anger, bargaining, all those, I mean."

"Yeah, I know what the stages of grief are," she answered, hoping that would satisfy him.

"Oh, I see we're at anger already. Well, good for you."

PurgaTerry

"I'm not angry, and the stages won't be necessary since this is clearly a mistake."

"Aaand right back to denial, " Dean mused. Terry could barely see his form in front of her, but it looked as if he had turned his head slightly to make sure she was still following.

"Look, try to understand this. You took a life—granted, it was your own—and however you want to try and rationalize it, the hard truth is you took yourself out of the race before you'd reached the finish line. You still had time, a life to live as you saw fit, but you chose to end it when you still had years to go. Now, I can't give you back those years, but I can make certain that your time here isn't wasted and that you'll have the best possible outcome, so long as you just listen to me. Okay?"

Terry found herself nodding, if only as a reflexive gesture to his raised voice.

"This is supposed to be a kindness, a second chance. And whether you like it or not, you died by your own hand. It happened, and used to be you'd find yourself in one of the albeit nicer rings of Downstairs, but you're not. Do you know why? Because whoever it is who does the judging around here decided that you were worth helping. You accepted the terms, so this is your reality now."

"Okay..." came her short, stilted reply. She was still figuring things out, not only about her situation, but about herself as well. In times of stress, was she the type to fight, fly, or freeze? Terry didn't think she would have pegged herself as the "freezing" type, but here she was, like a deer in headlights, shrinking at Dean's sternness that—even in the short time she'd known him—felt very out of character for him.

"Okay?" he asked. "So, you understand?"

Terry tilted her head in a half-shrug. "About as well as I can, considering I've only been here maybe half an hour."

Dean furrowed his brow and turned from her. "I suppose that's good enough for right now. I suppose I just hoped you'd accept things more quickly than it typically takes folks."

"Can I ask why?" She attempted to come back to his side, pulling her hoodie closer around her, even though she still wasn't at all chilly.

"You can," he answered, "but that doesn't mean I'm going to tell you."

Her shoulders slumped at his quip. At least he seemed to be back to acting like himself, even if that self was irritatingly unhelpful.

Through the fog, she could make out the outlines of some buildings, but it was too dark to get a good look at them. It was almost as if they were temporarily concealed from view, like the details of her past self. Her memory pulled up the map of some video game in her mind's eye, with only the parts she was actively playing visible, the uncharted sections shrouded in clouds. She continued to follow Dean in silence only permeated by his footsteps and his occasional whistling of a tune that echoed in the cavernous dark.

2. Welcome to Level Eight

The Main Hub was indeed not far from the building they had left. In the dark and fog, it was hard to get a sense of what it resembled to Terry, but the inside had the feel of a bank or some sort of city hall.

It was fairly quiet for the moment and not hard to spot the only other people in the large entryway.

A pale woman stood, wearing a dark-mauve skirted business suit and holding a clipboard next to a girl who looked a bit younger than Terry, possibly a teenager.

The woman flipped her light-brown hair out of her face as she noticed their approach, green eyes narrowing.

The girl began to bounce on her heels like a puppy being told to heel. When nobody told her verbally to do so, she bounded the rest of the way to meet them.

"Dean!" the girl called as she met them in three strides.

"Is this her? Oh my gosh, she looks so young!" She whipped her focus to Terry. "How old are you? Or like, how old were you? Because I was seventeen when I died, but technically, I'm twenty-four. I don't feel like I'm that old, though. You stop visibly aging when you come here."

Before Terry could answer the girl's question, she continued firing off one after another, appraising her as she circled excitedly. "So, where are you from? Or do you remember? I dunno how much you're going to remember. It's weird, because there's stuff everybody gets to remember like how to talk and walk and the normal stuff. But then there's the things specifically about you and your life, and remembering all of that's, like, a big no-no here."

"Terry, this is Willow, our resident ball of energy. Wills, this is Terry," said Dean.

Willow immediately grabbed Terry's hand to shake.

"Hi, so nice to meet you," she said, flashing a very large but very sincere grin. "You're so pretty! But... did you die in your pajamas?"

Terry looked back down at her clothes yet again. That actually made a lot of sense.

"Uh, I think so."

The halo of curls atop Willow's head bounced with her every wide gesture, and the skirt of her sunflower-yellow dress swished with every movement. The color stood out well on her dark skin; Terry was almost envious. Her only spots of color were the green of her fleece pants and the pterodactyl on her shirt that had given Dean her name.

"You know you can change your clothes just by thinking about it here, right?" Willow asked.

Terry shook her head with a side glance at Dean. "No, but that would have been nice information to have before I walked outside barefoot."

"What, you afraid of getting sick or hurting your feet? You're dead, remember?" Dean said, sounding a bit too defensive to go unnoticed.

"That is still up for debate," Terry said. Although the evidence was becoming more and more evident. "How do I even do that, the clothes thing?"

PurgaTerry

"Oh, I can show you later," Willow chirped. "For right now, you might be comfier with these."

Willow handed her some simple gray high-tops for Terry to take, which she did with not a small amount of bemusement.

As she was slipping her feet into the shoes, the woman began rhythmically drumming her nails on the clipboard. This got Dean's attention, and he turned toward her.

"And this is Cass." He gestured to the woman, who smiled a polite dark-lipsticked smile. It might have been too dark for her light complexion, but then again, what did Terry know about fashion? She was one to talk.

"Cassiopeia," the woman corrected him. She turned her gaze back to Terry. "And you're Dean's new resident. How are you finding Level Eight, Terry?"

"Haven't seen much of it yet, I'm afraid," Terry answered with a shrug.

"That's all right, as there isn't much to see," she said. She juggled the clipboard to pull a folder from underneath it, waving away Dean's hand as an offer to help. Setting the folder at the top of her small stack, Cassiopeia opened it and slid out a small laminated card, which she promptly handed to Terry.

It looked exactly like a driver's license. She hadn't seen herself in a mirror yet, so it was nice to finally get a look at what she, or her soul, looked like.

A short dark-brown—almost black—bob of hair framed her round face, and her green eyes stared back without a smile. It looked as if the picture had been taken unexpectedly, and possibly when Terry had been in the middle of speaking.

Next to her picture were various stats. Her afterlife name, birthday, her death day, hair and eye color, the words "Shepherd Trainee," and a group of letters and numbers:

DCR-129—Px7

Before she could ask, Cassiopeia appeared to read her mind. "That is your identification number. It helps us keep track of you. Hang on to your ID card—it serves as your identification as well as your bus pass, and it helps us to know precisely where you are supposed to be and what you are supposed to be doing at all times."

"If you lose it, then you won't be able to get another one for a really long time. It's like, a whole process," Willow chimed in.

"The higher-ups do love their long bureaucratic processes," Dean added.

"Let me show you mine." Willow took her own ID out of the small purse that dangled from her shoulder by a gold-colored strap.

Terry took it when Willow offered, comparing it to hers. Willow was—obviously, since they had the same manager—part of the same department. A "Soul Shepherd," whatever that was. Her eyes flicked between the two nearly identical cards, noticing the slight differences beyond the obvious ones like their pictures. Willow's ID read AGS-821—Px6, and one other key difference caught her attention.

"Your last name is 'Warren'? How do you know that?"

Willow blinked at her, going still for the first time Terry had seen her.

She snatched her ID back and stuffed it inside her bag before answering with a more awkward smile. "It's nothing, really. It's just—um—something I know."

Terry raised an eyebrow. "Okay..." Before she could ask more about it, Willow began talking again, pointing to the jumble of letters and numbers on Terry's card.

"And that's your ID number, see the part at the end with the P? That number'll go down like mine as you work off the years you're supposed to be here. It doesn't mean you only have seven years to go or anything, only the managers know how many years you have to work off—but I dunno why the number is seven."

"It's a holdover from an older system," Dean added. "Used to be you had to go through all the levels, but nowadays, each level has a different purpose, and we can't have each one of you traipsing around all of them."

PurgaTerry

"Is anyone really 'supposed' to be here?" Terry asked, more to the entire group.

Willow screwed up her face, giving her question a thought before speaking. "Hmm, I guess not, but we're here now, right? Wherever we're meant to be next, we'll get there when we're supposed to."

This was getting to be too much for Terry. There appeared to be some form of rules in this place, but then there was stuff like this that felt random. Well, if nobody was truly meant to be here—if she wasn't—then why couldn't she simply find a way out?

"Maybe you will," Terry replied, "but I think I'll just find my own way to wherever the next step is."

She turned from the three of them and marched for the doors of the bank-like building.

"Wait, you can't just leave," she heard the woman, Cassiopeia, call after her.

"Watch me," she muttered as she pulled open the door and stepped back out into the fog.

As she grew farther and farther from the close crop of buildings, Terry noticed that the overcast sky gave way to more and more cloud cover. The fog that was barely noticeable before was now thick enough to almost feel, leaving wet spots on her clothes.

As she continued to walk determinedly in the general direction of "away," she wasn't quite sure what she would find outside of their little campus. The fog was now far too thick, as if someone had erased the landscape around her, leaving her in a pure-white void.

Soon, though, she thought she saw something in the distance—hard as it was to make out through the fog—and she headed toward it. She was feeling pretty pleased with herself—that was, until she got a good look at the building growing closer and closer as the fog dissipated.

It was the same building she had just left. Dean and Willow were still there, standing in front of it, Dean looking mildly impatient as he glanced down at his watch. Willow seemed wary, much more concerned than Dean.

"Have a good walk? Are you ready to listen now?" Dean asked as Terry approached them. She stopped directly in front of him, her frustrated frown quite apparent even from far away.

"Okay, what sort of trick are you pulling?"

"No tricks. I told you everything you need to know. You can't leave this level until you've served your time. Unless you're on official business with me, of course."

"And how am I supposed to know when that is?" she asked, growing more than exasperated.

"You don't, but I do. I'll let you know when, don't you worry."

Terry was already growing frustrated by Dean's non-answers. If he was supposed to be her "new boss," shouldn't there be some element of trust? If there was, Terry wasn't feeling it yet, and she doubted if she ever would.

"Now, if you'll excuse me, ladies, I've got some managerial things to do," he said as he walked between Terry and Willow, gesturing but not looking back at either of them. "Wills, show her to your room. You'll be roommates."

Willow gasped, her face brightening into the smile she had worn for most of the maybe ten-minutes-or-so Terry had known her.

"Oh my goodness, we are gonna have so much fun!" Willow cheered, grasping hold of both of Terry's hands and bouncing on the balls of her feet. "It'll be so great to have a girl around again!"

"Again?" Terry asked.

Willow made a sharp squeak before cheering again. "Yay!"

Terry gave an uneasy smile in return, not certain if she was what Willow might categorize as a typical example of a "girl."

"Yay..." She tried to sound enthused to appease the younger girl and let Willow lead her off toward wherever it was that the souls who came to "Level Eight" called home.

They headed off down the block, and as they walked from one streetlamp's pool of light to the next, each light seemed to come up out of nowhere and disappear back into the misty void.

PurgaTerry

For a while, there was nothing else to see as Terry followed her new roommate. Willow stayed two steps ahead of her, swaying and humming a tune Terry found familiar. A song about how it's hard to stay awake when you're asleep, because everything was never as it seemed.

"Is that 'Fireflies'?"

Willow halted her humming, stopping mid-sway. "Mmm-hmm. It came out after I died, but I heard it a bunch a few years ago, and it stuck with me," she said in a wistful sigh. "I miss seeing fireflies. They're one of those little things I wish we could have here. They always reminded me of Tinkerbell."

Terry let out a soft chuckle at that. She wasn't certain if it was due to Willow's mention of the fairy or the emphatic way she'd said it, but it made her take more notice of her surroundings and ponder what might make things feel less... "empty" was the only word she could think of.

"I guess if we're talking about bringing ambient bugs into this place, I'd like to hear some crickets. It could use some extra background noise."

"Oh, I agree!" Willow said. "I miss hearing crickets, too. They used to help me sleep."

"Me too," Terry replied without thinking. She was pleased to find it wasn't a guess. She did have memories of the insects and their soothing call. Somehow, she connected it to that word—name?—that remained wadded in her pocket. Hatori. For the second time, she wondered if she should bring it up to someone, but before she could, Willow broke the silence that had fallen between them.

"Look, I know not everything around here is a pink Starburst, but it's not as bad as it could be."

Terry turned back to Willow at that, face contorted with confusion. "A pink what?"

"Starburst. You know, the candy. The pink ones being objectively the best ones," she answered as if it were an obvious comparison to draw. "I know things aren't great here, but if you give it a chance, it's not that bad. Plus, you've got a chance to make things better for yourself."

"That's what I keep hearing, but I still don't understand why I chose this. If I supposedly did."

"Well, you wouldn't be here if you didn't, at least, that's the way it's supposed to go. It's like doing community service, I guess. I wouldn't know though; I've never done community service, or... I don't think so, at least."

"So, which is it? Should I be doing it for myself or the 'community'?" Terry was still not a fan of all this opposing logic.

Willow seemed to think about this for a moment, twisting the strap of her purse in her hand.

"... Both?" she said uncertainly. "I guess you just have to find your reasons for doing it. Because, like it or not, this is your reality now. You should make peace with that."

On some level, Terry knew she was probably right. If she and Dean were to be believed—and she had no real reason to disbelieve them—this was something that she had chosen, and perhaps it would help her in the long run. Her former life was done, and she should probably focus on making this new one meaningful.

It still nagged at her though, the why of it all. Who had she been, and how sad could her life have been for this to have been her only option?

"Do you not think or wonder about it, though? Who you used to be? Why you chose this?"

Willow shook her head, screwing up her face like 'of course not' and shrugging. "I figure, whatever my old life was like, if they erased my memory, it must not have been that great. I just focus on what's ahead of me. My past will come back in time, once I've served all my days."

Terry still wasn't mollified, but she let it slide for the younger girl's sake. Willow wanted to befriend her, and Terry supposed she could use a good friend in this place.

"And are all people in Purgatory like you?" she asked, slightly amused.

PurgaTerry

Willow laughed. "Not that I've seen. I'm one of a kind, baby!"

As they continued on, the fog began to lift as dawn broke over some unseen horizon. Terry took in what looked like a college campus, with sweeping lawns and large ancient-looking arching structures. She had to assume that whoever built the great halls that stood before her had done so a very, very, very long time ago.

She also noticed a theme with these buildings. All were columned and arched in a combination of Roman and Gothic style and made of some purely white, almost pearlescent building material she had never seen before.

"So, the Main Hub is where we came from, and you'd just come from the Welcome Center; that's where everyone arrives since that's where the Lethe Machine is," Willow explained. "The machine that wiped your memories and filed them away. The Hall of Justice is at the top floor of the Main Hub. You'll have to go there at least once eventually. After you've done all of your CS. I haven't been up there myself, but I guess it's your last stop on your way out of Purgatory."

As Terry followed, Willow pointed down a side path that they didn't turn down, and before she could ask, Willow made mention of it. "Down that way is the Hall of Records; that's where everything that's in your file and your memories are stored."

She appeared to walk just a touch faster past the turnoff, but Terry lingered there for a moment, caught in the prospect that the answers to so many of her questions might be down that path.

"Come on." Willow grabbed her hand and pulled her along. "We're about to pass the Library."

"There's an actual library here?" Terry asked.

"Yeah, technically, it's called the Hall of Knowledge, but since it's got a whole bunch of media from Earth, people just call it the Library," Willow answered encouragingly, as if pleased for the change of subject. "It's an offshoot of the Upstairs one, which has all of the books, movies, music—pretty much all media that has ever or will ever exist housed there. Ours isn't quite that well stocked, but it's still a great place to go during your downtime.

But you'd have to get permission from Dean first."

"But what about the Hall of Records?"

Willow grimaced but recovered quickly since Terry was still following her. "It's strictly verboten for all residents without clearance. Trust me, though, you don't need to go there. It's just a big computer or something, I dunno. I haven't been there, either. But I'll bet it's boring. Anyway, we'll pass the bus station, and then we'll get to where we're staying."

There was a very substantial change in style when they stepped just a few blocks down to the transit station.

They seemed to go from some weird alternate ancient Rome right into a Greyhound station from the late eighties.

Of course, the buses weren't actually "Greyhound"—it would be super weird to see such product placement in Purgatory—but the style of the buses was similar: shiny and metallic on the outside, although somewhat rusty and dull in certain areas. She hadn't gotten aboard one yet, but she had a faint memory of what buses looked like and, what was more, smelled like on the inside.

Beyond the transit station and the great halls lay the dorms, or whatever they were called here.

"Are those the living quarters?" Terry asked, pointing out the large, brick, rectangular prisms that all matched in neat rows along the blocks. They seemed to go on forever out into the mist that surrounded all the buildings.

Willow gave a snort of laughter at this, covering her mouth apologetically when Terry looked back at her. "I mean, kind of. I wouldn't exactly call them 'living' quarters of course, though, maybe apartments? Residences?"

Terry nodded. That would do as well as anything could, she supposed. But curiosity still nibbled the edges of her mind. Could this place make an infinite amount of anything that was needed? Was it connected to how she could apparently just conjure up new clothes for herself?

She voiced these questions to her companion, to which Willow shrugged. "I dunno. I guess I've never thought too hard

PurgaTerry

about it. We're here for a while and then we're not; I don't wanna get bogged down by the 'hows' and 'whys' of it all."

That was one thing she and Willow could agree on. The fleetingness of what surrounded them. To Terry, Level Eight was a place that felt temporary, like the out-of-place bus station. It was a place to wait, but not to stay. Not a place one would want to be for long. But she had a sneaking suspicion she would be here longer than she hoped.

3. Hurry Up and Wait

There wasn't much that Terry did remember her first "night" in Purgatory, but she did remember one gem of a saying: "Life sucks, and then you die." She didn't remember where or from whom she heard it, but she found it fairly accurate for her current circumstances.

She didn't subscribe to the philosophy herself, even though the ending of her life might confirm it for some people. She was more of the opinion that life does suck... most of the time. Not always, though. Probably about 90 percent of an average life sucked pretty hard. That other 10 percent, however, crammed just enough remarkable, amazing, juicy goodness into it to make the whole ride worth it for just about everyone.

Then there's the afterlife. Nobody mentioned that it could suck, too. There were all of those religions with their views of a Heaven or a Hell or what have you, but for the most part, since there were only a handful of people to actually come back from the other side, it's sort of hard to get the message back to everybody in the still-living world.

Lying in the dark of her newly-assigned room, looking up at the textured ceiling, Terry tried hard to listen for the rhythmic breathing of Willow, or the hum of an air conditioner, or a barking dog, or anything at all.

This place was far too quiet.

After their little tour of the Level Eight buildings, Willow had brought her to their residence and cheerfully welcomed her to their room, a tiny apartment that felt like a hospital room and a motel room had some sort of bland room baby. Her bed was closest to a wall-length mirror, with a chest of drawers opposite their beds. Willow had the bed closest to the window, curtains drawn, and that was pretty much it. The bathroom—or the vague idea of a bathroom—☐was one big tiled room where the shower and toilet were within feet of each other with no barrier whatsoever. She had more questions about the room—especially the idea of toilets and beds in Purgatory—but an exhaustion Terry had never known came over her the moment she sat down on her bed. It had been a taxing day—or whatever this was—so she tried to tune out the pressing silence and find some sleep.

The first few days of Terry's new afterlife on Level Eight passed in a blur of sleep and the occasional waking by Willow to check on her.

She didn't leave for any meals offered, she didn't rise for the mandatory group sessions, she didn't even rise to go to the bathroom, although she found she didn't need to do that anymore in this place.

Terry knew exactly what she was doing. She was wallowing. Something just felt right about it. About staying in bed for as long as possible to avoid having to face this truth—this mistake. It still didn't make sense to her. Sure, she didn't have her memories to shed some light on the situation, but she just felt like there was something off about this whole thing. She didn't know what else she could do, so refusing to play along seemed like a good enough option.

Every so often during short wakeful periods, she would

PurgaTerry

encounter Willow, bubbly as the first time she met her. On her second day, she had regained consciousness to see her roommate checking herself over in the mirror. Her dress was a short, flippy white number with tiny dark-blue flowers, a pattern Terry could imagine on a china cup.

Willow's reflection smiled at her from the mirror.

"Hey, you're awake. I was just going to the rec room to hang out with some of the others. Do you feel like coming?"

Terry groaned in answer and turned over onto her other side, covering her head with her blankets.

"You know, the group sessions are mandatory for moving forward around here," Terry heard her say. "You probably don't have to go during the downtime, but the managers want to see that you're trying."

That was the last she saw or heard from her roommate for the rest of that day.

On the third day, she was given a much more forceful awakening.

Terry was wrenched from sleep by the sudden swipe of her covers and a sharp bellow from a masculine voice.

"All right, enough moping, up and at 'em!"

Terry scrunched up and shut her eyes tighter, but the tone and volume Dean was using was hard to ignore (not for lack of trying). When she did try to resist, an even louder, more piercing sound ripped through her quiet room. It jolted her up, and she saw Dean standing over her, an air horn in his hand aimed directly at her face.

She shrieked as she bolted up, to which Dean only smiled.

"Oh good, she's up." He lowered the horn and set it on the side table. "Now, get dressed, you've been avoiding things for too long. Time to start work. I get it. This is a big change for you, and you've got to let yourself get adjusted and get all that sleeping and moping and other such living stuff out of your system, but really, two solid days without even stepping foot outside your room? It doesn't look good on you, and it sure as Downstairs doesn't reflect well on me. It makes me look like a manager who can't manage, do you see?"

Through his speech, Terry had managed to crawl out of bed and blearily search for the flimsy comb she had been provided on the dresser. Squinting at herself in the mirror, she could see her short hair needed some taming, but she wasn't quite sure this little comb would do the trick.

"What kind of work?" she asked as she successfully hunted the comb and began to make an effort on her mane.

"What kind of work?" he repeated with a laugh. "Did all that sleeping make you forget? You're here for community service and for self-improvement. Now, I suppose we don't have to start you on Shepherding today, but you at the very least have to go to your group session. In the meantime, you're going to go with Willow to the rec room and play Uno with the other residents of your sector."

It was only then that Terry noticed Willow standing a little way back from Dean, a nervous grimace on her face as she wilted slightly in the corner. She perked up when she realized Terry had seen her.

"Oh yes, definitely!" she answered chipperly. "We've got all sorts of things in the rec room, and I just saw some of the others there. We even have a TV that gets actual cable!"

That did intrigue her, not so much the prospect of watching TV, but the fact that the people in this midway afterlife even had access to TV.

The rec room appeared just as sad to Terry as her own bedroom. It had the feel of both a waiting room and some sort of after-school program. About eight circular tables were placed throughout, with at least four chairs at each. The aforementioned television was bolted to a far corner, at that moment playing some sort of morning talk show. To Terry's left was a large, wide bookshelf

PurgaTerry

not filled with actual books but coloring books. Stacks of loose coloring pages and cups full of markers also sat on the shelves.

Below the art supplies were a few board games, puzzles, and decks of cards. Several of the cards were in fact for the game Uno.

From what Terry could see, the markers didn't work that well, but that apparently hadn't stopped the residents from using them. She could see evidence in the form of dozens of colored pages lining the wall to her right, proof of all the previous souls who had come before.

There were a few ladies over at one table playing Uno and one girl sitting alone with a notebook open and scribbling, her blonde hair falling in her face and slightly obscuring what she was writing.

Willow bounced in from behind Terry (it seemed the girl couldn't help but bounce everywhere she went) and sat down at the table with the blonde girl. Terry followed reluctantly, settling herself in the chair directly across from her.

Willow sat between them, looking back and forth from the girl to herself, probably waiting for one of them to speak. When neither obliged, she took it upon herself to provide the introductions.

"Terry, this is Juliet. She's a resident like us, only she doesn't serve in our department. Jules, this is Terry, Dean's new charge and my new roomie."

Juliet looked up from her notebook through her curtain of thin light hair in Terry's direction. Once she had tucked most of it behind her ear, Terry saw that she was a pretty young thing, with an emphasis on "young." If Willow was indeed "nearly eighteen," this girl had to be a couple of years younger.

Of course, depending on how long Juliet had been there, she might be even older than Terry. It wasn't as if Terry looked her age, either.

Terry went ahead and took the initiative. "Uh, hi," she greeted Juliet. The girl still eyed her warily, but she put her pencil down. "Um, were you drawing something?"

Juliet answered by quickly covering the pages of her still-open notebook. "Only doodles," she answered. "I'm not that good, but it looks better to the heads if we're seen using the notebooks they give us. I'm not much for putting down my thoughts."

"I think I can relate to that," Terry said as Juliet swapped her pencil for one of the markers in the cup at the center of the table.

Willow smiled at this exchange. Terry hoped she would give Dean a good report about her interactions with the other residents. She then remembered something he had mentioned. "Didn't Dean say he wanted me to go to a 'group session' or something?" she asked while watching Juliet's faded purple marker make light squiggles on her paper.

"Oh yeah," Willow answered. "It'll start pretty soon. They bring in the guys in our section from their rec room."

"So, why exactly are we separated by gender?" Terry wondered.

Willow and Juliet exchanged a look, and Willow leaned in closer to Terry. "You've noticed a few things about being alive you haven't managed to stop doing, right? Do you still feel like you have to eat, sleep, and everything? Let's just say there are some other appetites that can carry over after you die."

Terry blinked, unsure for a moment as to what Willow meant.

"She means sex," Terry heard a voice answer her unasked question. She looked up to see a lanky man wearing very large glasses and sporting the brightest blue hair Terry had ever seen. He plopped down in the last unoccupied chair, turning it to straddle it backward.

"Apparently, since we're supposed to be 'purging our sins' and 'making ourselves pure' and everything, that includes not having sex. Even though, one: apparently those urges go away after a while, and two: not everybody is into straight sex. It's a dumb, archaic rule that I'm surprised is even enforced at all."

"Hi, Puck," Juliet greeted him quietly. The man put his arm around her and gave her a friendly, quick side hug.

"Hey there, Jules! And how's my baby sister?" Puck asked.

"He's not really my brother; we just have the same manager,

PurgaTerry

and he likes to call me that," Juliet quickly clarified.

"Least I hope we're not really siblings. Wouldn't that be tragic? Our parents down on Earth losing two kids to suicide? Especially how each of us went."

Juliet shrank back down behind her hair again at this topic, but it intrigued Terry.

"Wait, you two actually know how you died?"

"Of course," Puck answered. "I know how everybody in this section died. I'm great at guessing, you see. Jules here poisoned herself, your buddy Wills was a wrist cutter, and me? I'm so fly, I jumped off a building to prove it."

Terry couldn't help but roll her eyes at that comment and caught Willow in the act as well.

"So, you can guess how I died?" Terry asked.

Puck seemed to deliberate, giving her a once-over, and he was about to answer when she heard Willow make a noise from the other side of the table and a gesture that caught his eye.

"Oh, hey, look. The rest of my lot's shown up. I think we'll be starting group soon." He rose from the table, grabbing Juliet by the arm and moving her to another table where two other young men, similar in age to Puck, were beginning to seat themselves.

"So, wait, does everyone here know how they died? Then why don't I?"

Willow's smile suddenly turned nervous, her eyes averted from Terry's suspicious gaze.

"Willow?" she pressed. "Do you know why I don't remember how I died?"

"Not... as such," she answered, still not meeting her eyes. Then she gestured wildly toward the doorway. "Oh, look, the group leader is here! Time to get ready to share!"

Willow then hopped up from her seat, leaving Terry with her suspicions to sit with Juliet.

All of the men and women moved their chairs to sit in a lopsided circle with the group leader at the head. Only one other person besides Terry had seated themselves somewhat outside the circle—a dark-skinned guy who looked around Terry's age. He also wore a hoodie similar to hers, dark green with a zipper down the front. Although he clearly had died in regular street clothes and not his pajamas.

The leader was a tall, bespectacled man with sandy hair. He held a large box and directed one of Terry's fellow residents to set up a large white board on an easel near the middle of the room facing the circular tables.

The man clapped his hands and scanned the room, smiling at a few of Terry's fellows in turn, Puck and Juliet among them.

"All right," he said, "I can see a few familiar faces, naturally, but for the most part, the majority of you are new to Level Eight and may not have gotten a chance to come together like this yet. My name is Orion, and I'm one of the managers here. Hello everyone."

Most of the group responded with versions of "Hello, Orion."

Puck emphatically called out, "Hi, Daddy!"

Orion narrowed his eyes tiredly as if he should have known he'd do that. "Don't call me that, Puck. Why are you even here? You have more than enough group therapy hours."

"Moral support for Juliet," Puck answered, putting an arm around her again.

Orion shook his head good-naturedly. "Fair enough." Then to the group, he said, "I'm going to be passing out these notebooks for everyone. You may already have one, but I wanted to make sure that each of you had access to something that you can use to vent or express your feelings in however way you choose."

He called one of the residents to assist him in passing out the black-and-white composition notebooks. A few people, including Puck, took one with no small amount of eye-rolling.

"I'll bet we're doing the tree thing," he said, leaning closer to Juliet. "The things I do for you."

He then picked up one of the pencils from the cup on the table and began sketching out the vague image of a tree before Orion had finished handing out the notebooks.

"Now, feel free to keep these notebooks to draw, journal, or keep track of whatever you want."

When she was handed a notebook, Terry gave it a once-over before opening it to the first page. She wasn't exactly sure what they were going to do with them, but they appeared to be average notebooks, as far as she could tell.

"Does everyone have a notebook and a pencil? You'll want to use a pencil for this exercise. I know we have markers, but you might want to be able to erase and adjust your drawing as we go."

Puck gave a sigh. "I know most of you here are fairly new, but I've been here for so long, I know every single group exercise that Orion has up his sleeve. He only has about twenty he cycles through."

"I heard that, Puck," Orion said as he passed by their table. "And I certainly have more than that."

"Oh, of course," he replied, and then once Orion's back was turned, he shook his head to the others at the table, mouthing *no*.

"As I said, most of you here will still be fairly new to Level Eight and Purgatory in general. I'm sure you still have a lot of confusion and unanswered questions. Today, I'd like to help guide you through an exercise of the self. We're going to gaze inwardly and possibly unearth some things about you that will help you on your journey here."

Orion began to draw out the outline of a tree on the white board in a very similar shape to what Puck already had on his paper.

"First, I want all of you to begin drawing a tree. It can look however you want, as long as it has all of the parts of a tree. Roots, trunk, branches, leaves, etcetera. Now, the roots are going to represent your past—where you come from. This can be a place, a culture, or just something you feel has shaped you as a person."

While the others at her table and around her were following Orion's instructions, Terry was already beginning to zone out. How could she label a tree's roots with things from her past when she barely remembered her life? All around her though, she could hear the scribbling and sketching of her fellow residents, and even at her table, her companions were already setting to work on their drawings, Puck being the fastest among them.

As Orion walked everyone through the other parts of the trees they had drawn and what they represented, Terry felt more out of place and frustrated than ever. Even if she wanted to do the stupid exercise, she didn't have very much to work with. How would she even begin? There must be something else she could be doing to better spend her time. Something like finding a way to access her lost memories instead of waiting for answers she was realizing more and more probably weren't going to come.

Grabbing her pencil, she stood and acted as if she were going to sharpen it at the pencil sharpener that sat near the entryway to the rec room. Most people had their attention on Orion, and, thankfully, he wasn't facing her either, so it was easy to slip out of the room and down the hall unseen.

Not knowing where exactly she wanted to go, Terry began to meander down the hallway until she rounded a corner and saw the familiar green hoodie of someone else who had skipped out on the group.

He gave her an appraising look, raising one eyebrow at her clothes, and Terry became even more keenly aware that she was still wearing the pajamas and hoodie she'd died in. At least she had shoes on this time.

"So, what kind of tree did you say you were?" he said in lieu of a greeting.

"I didn't," she answered. "I don't really get how this therapy or exercise is supposed to do anything."

"It's just busy work," he replied, and Terry caught a small note of disdain in his tone as he shrugged. "They spout a lot of bullshit about the whole 'process' helping us in the 'grand scheme' or something, but I've been here long enough to figure out that whoever these managers are, they just want us to fill our quotas and make room for the next crop of dead folks."

"Aren't you just the optimist?" she said. It certainly was a different take on things around here, a lot more cynical. But then again, she might have been hanging around Willow too much. That girl could find sunshine in a black hole.

"I'm a realist," he corrected her, and as he stepped closer, she turned her head to take in his features more clearly.

He was tall—well, taller than her, anyway—with dark eyes and a dark hoodie, all seeming to match his more dark outlook. Terry wondered if his clothes were a conscious choice, as hers had not been.

"So, what, you don't think they're here to help us, or that we're here for the reasons they say?"

A quick glance back toward the group on the other side of the window, and the loner shrugged again. He could probably be taller if he wasn't slouching so much. Terry wasn't sure why, but posture was beginning to feel like something of a pet peeve of hers.

"I don't think they really care either way. They've never been human, never been alive to know how our world really works. All they care about is numbers and stats and quotas."

"That hasn't really been my experience," Terry said honestly, unsure if she was truly missing something. Maybe this guy was just as full of bull as he thought this place was.

"Huh, maybe your manager's better at acting like he cares. But you can't tell me he's told you everything you wanna know."

She blinked at him. "No, he hasn't. He's dodged almost every question I've asked. Does yours do that, too?"

"Oh, hell yeah," he answered. "And we're just supposed to accept it and not question anything? It's a good thing I'm stationed where I am, or I'd never learn anything I want to know."

"Where are you stationed?" she asked.

"Where are *you* stationed?" he asked instead of answering.

"Um, something about 'Shepherding'?" She hadn't been fully paying attention when Willow had given her the basics of what a Soul Shepherd did.

He smiled for the first time since she'd seen him. "I think we could help each other out, Pajama Girl. I'm Asher."

"Terry," she said, now feeling like all the questions she had been wanting to ask were fighting for the chance to be the first out of her mouth. "But what do you mean? Could you get me information about my status, or my file?"

Asher held up a hand to silence her. "Slow down. Don't worry, I can get you what you want, or I can find a way for you to. My assignment is sort of perfect for stuff like that. But there's a few things we've got to work out first."

"Like what?" Terry asked.

"Lemme see how far I can get around here with what I got, and I'll let you know."

He chuckled at her visible deflation. But what did he expect? What did she expect? Terry had been hitting a wall with her search for answers since she arrived in this place.

"Not what you wanted to hear, huh?" he said. "It sucks, I know. But patience is an essential trait around here. No matter how bad you want things to hurry up and change. We all have things we wanna do, and we know we'll get there eventually, but me, I'd rather not be kept waiting any longer than I have to."

Terry was going to ask Asher what he meant by that when a fumbling, tripping sound alerted her to Willow stumbling around the corner, finding her footing only by holding onto the wall to balance herself with one hand, the other holding two of the notebooks Orion had handed out.

"Terry!" she called once she'd recovered. "I'm so glad I found you! Why did you disappear? You forgot your notebook." She held it out, and Terry spotted that Willow had taken the liberty of writing her name on it in a faded green marker.

Terry took it, but mostly to appease her. She had no real intention of using it and would probably stuff it under her bed once they returned to their room.

"I think it could really help you if you did some journaling in it," Willow said, then her eyes found Asher still standing behind them. "Oh, hi there!"

"Hey." Asher nodded from behind her. Terry saw some

PURGATERRY

recognition on Willow's face, but her expression changed as she looked from him to Terry.

"So, what were you two up to?" she asked with an implication in her tone that Terry didn't quite understand, but that she didn't like, regardless.

"I just found him out here when I left the rec room."

"But you should have stayed; it was a neat exercise," Willow said.

"I made an appearance," Terry replied. "The manager guy saw me there. Do you think we can—I don't know—ease me into this whole thing a little more slowly?"

Terry could tell that was not what Willow wanted to hear, but she nodded reluctantly. "I don't think Dean will like it, but I guess if it makes you feel better about participating."

"It does. Really, it does," she said. If she absolutely had to do these things that were required of her around here, Terry was going to attempt to do them as slowly or as little as was allowed.

While Cassiopeia appeared standoffish and Orion had the air of an elementary school teacher, she hadn't yet met any of the upper management Terry might call "unattached from the human experience" until she had an encounter with her case therapist.

When she entered the room, Terry took note that the woman did not stand to greet her. Instead, she continued to pore over several files at once, only acknowledging Terry when she closed the door.

"Right then, DCR-129—Px7, also known as Terry. My name is Lyra, I am your case-appointed therapist. You may come to me if you are feeling that the group sessions are not adequately helping you with your mental state as you transition from your previous life to the next."

Lyra spoke in a monotonous, rehearsed way, as if she had made this speech many, many times before. She barely gave

Terry a cursory glance as she continued to give her only the barest attention.

"So, if you could just sign these papers allowing Level Eight upper management clearance to view any revelations you divulge here that are prudent to your well-being in Purgatory, you can be on your way."

Terry frowned at the paper, looking back up to Lyra skeptically.

"If you're supposed to be my therapist, aren't you going to evaluate me and—I don't know—ask me some questions?"

Lyra looked up at the ceiling before sparing a glance Terry's way.

"Do you feel like you need some active listening and evaluation?" she asked.

Terry blinked at her tone. This manager sounded like she was finding Terry to be bothersome and like it wasn't her job to actually interact with her.

"I mean, isn't that why you've been appointed to me?"

Lyra sighed. "I'm appointed to nearly twelve-thousand souls on the various levels, at least three hundred on Level Eight alone. I have to balance the evaluations of every single one of them, including you. Do you really think that I have time to listen to your every thought?"

Terry didn't want to say that, yes, she did indeed think that. If her job was to provide therapy, of course.

"I am here to evaluate your mental state as you transition here. I only need to know the bare minimum of how you're feeling. These meetings are not going to be more than five minutes in total. Otherwise, as long as you don't have some form of breakdown or violent outburst, you and I don't need to see each other. So, just sign those papers, and we can each be on our way."

Terry didn't really know what she was supposed to expect. Did she think that each manager or upper manager was going to give her the same amount of attention and interest as Dean? No, she shouldn't. She was merely just one departed soul in a sea of others in Purgatory also on the road to redemption. And there

PurgaTerry

were more people dying every day, so at least some of them were arriving here just as quickly. Terry didn't think that she should receive as much individualized attention as she had been getting. Still, the whole encounter made her feel more insignificant than she could ever recall feeling. It was a lot to process from one five-minute interaction. She'd have to make a note to observe others in upper management—if she were to meet any others—to gauge how they felt about this whole fairly impersonal system.

She didn't expect anything extravagant, but Terry thought that they would at least call her by her name as opposed to her number, or look her in the eye and fake interest in her at the very least.

But once she had indeed signed the papers, Terry was practically shooed out of Lyra's office and back out into the hallway.

She wouldn't admit it out loud to him, but it honestly made her miss Dean—a little.

4. Soul Shepherding 101

Terry wasn't sure exactly why the bus station on Level Eight needed to have a smell at all, but the scents that she was picking up were all too reminiscent of the stations she could vaguely remember on Earth. The outside where the buses pulled in and out had the crispness of an autumn day mixed with the harsh smell of gasoline. For added authenticity, the inside smelled of pine-scented cleaning products and—like the rest of what she'd experienced of Purgatory so far—felt like a nebulous, transitory space.

With not much to see inside the station, her eyes drifted to Willow walking beside her behind Dean, hands wrapped around and nose nearly pressed against a cellphone. Of all the very strange things that Terry had seen here in the afterlife, a dead teen using a phone felt both surprising and really, really not surprising at all.

"Why do you have a phone, and *how* do you have a phone?" she asked incredulously, which made Willow un-bury her nose to find her.

"Well, it's kind of a long story, but the short version is that they gave Dean one—managers are supposed to keep in contact with each other for reasons, I dunno—but he's too attached to his pager, so he gave it to me."

"But how do you even get reception here? And why do the managers need cell phones?"

Willow merely shrugged. "That's Purgatory. Sometimes, there's just no explanation. It's just weird."

As they made it to the wall where the large LED screens flashed with the various bus schedules, Terry noticed that they weren't only displaying destinations and times, but names of people.

An attendant stood at a desk below the screens and waved to Dean when she spotted them.

"Angie!" Dean called to her, waving back as he approached. He tapped out a short rhythm on her desk before asking her, "How are we doing, Angie? What do ya got for me today?"

"I'm the same as ever, Dean," she answered with a tired but genuine smile. "And I got y'all some nice easy cases today. Great for your newbie to cut her teeth on."

Now leaning an arm on the desk, Terry could have sworn Dean's eyes flicked in her direction before he leaned in closer to Angie, volume lowered.

"And, uh, how about the, you know?"

Angie gave Terry and Willow a quick glance before leaning closer to Dean.

She shook her head. "Not today, sugar."

Terry saw Dean lean back, eyes falling to the floor, chewing on the inside of his cheek. He tapped another rhythm on the desk before putting his smile back on.

"Well, just keep me posted, huh?"

"You know I will," Angie said with a wink.

"Oh, speaking of my newbie, this is Terry." He took an arm and nudged Terry forward.

Terry waved and smiled awkwardly. "Um, hi."

"Nice to meet you, sweetie, I'm Angie," Angie said. She had a

PurgaTerry

look about her that wouldn't be out of place sitting in a rocking chair on a porch somewhere in the southern United States. Her accent sounded about right for that area, too. It felt pleasantly familiar and eased some of Terry's apprehension.

"I'll be here every time y'all come to the station for your duties. I've got everybody's schedules, and I send them on their way."

"And she's about to give us ours, so we can get on our bus and start our day," Dean said.

Angie seemed to have taken the hint, because she quickly pulled out a printed copy of the schedule that was still flashing above them, grabbing a pink highlighter to mark one whole section of the paper.

"There you go, and I've marked where y'all will be going so Terry can start getting used to how things work." She handed the paper to Dean.

"Thanks, Angie." He gave another nod and then turned for the sliding doors that led to where the buses were parked. Angie gave them a wave, and then Terry and Willow were back to following Dean like little ducklings again.

"Okay, so step one was to get our schedule from Angie, step two will be to find the right bus to board, and step three will be the interesting part." Dean led them past several buses as he consulted the schedule in his hand, trying to find the correct vehicle.

"And step three would be?" Terry asked, gently guiding Willow away from walking into a steel pillar.

"That's when we start showing you how to Shepherd souls," Willow answered, looking completely unsurprised that she'd almost met the pillar face first.

"Right you are, Wills. Today, we show Terry how it's done, and right now what needs to be done is to get on the bus that'll take us to our target soul on Earth."

Terry had heard them mention their assigned service of Soul Shepherd—which she supposed was hers now too—but she hadn't yet figured out where the buses came in. Now she guessed she knew. The buses themselves didn't look particularly otherworldly, either. At least Terry understood why this part of the whole Purgatory thing looked the way it did. Buses were such commonplace things that they could very easily go unnoticed by a living person. They were indeed so ordinary-looking, Terry wondered what would stop someone in the living world from hopping on the wrong mode of transportation.

She was about to ask this, but then decided against it. Maybe she should take Willow's words at face value and just embrace the weirdness of Purgatory. If she asked about everything that didn't make sense to her, this might be a very long however-long-she-had here.

Instead, she read what she could from the schedule in Dean's hand and started looking out for the correct bus. Eventually, they passed an old-timey looking one with faux-wood paneling and a green-based paint job. It looked to have been modeled after an old-fashioned trolley car, but with wheels that made the end result look like some sort of hybrid vehicle.

Terry paused, a strange feeling tickling the back of her brain. She blinked and pointed it out to Dean.

"Is this it?"

Dean checked the schedule again, matching up the numbers.

"Looks like it. Good job, T."

The three of them appeared to be the first ones on board, so they made their way closer to the back, Dean taking a seat and Terry taking the one behind him. Willow—naturally—planted herself next to Terry. Really, this girl was taking this whole trainee helping position very seriously. At least Terry didn't completely mind the company. Willow was an odd duck, in her opinion, but Terry had to admit she was entertaining.

"Ooh, this one's a little bit fancy," Willow acknowledged as she plopped down next to Terry. She thought her companion easily impressed, but maybe it was because she felt like she'd seen all of this before. As the cabin of the bus quickly began to fill up, Terry took a moment to really take in her surroundings. Brass bars

PurgaTerry

lined the ceiling and the backs of the seats, the ones suspended from the ceiling lined with leather straps for commuters to hold on to. The seats themselves reminded her of park benches, not the most cushy places to sit. But Terry found she liked the inside of these buses, or at least this one. There was something about the old-fashioned wood paneling and the shiny, polished metal accents that she found comforting, even familiar.

She had barely noticed when the bus pulled away from its spot at the station and was jolted momentarily from her observations by the weird flash outside the windows. No one else reacted or seemed to care. Once the flash had faded away, they were suddenly on a strip of road surrounded by other cars and vehicles, without any of their passengers appearing to notice. Rolling down whatever street they suddenly manifested on, Terry sat with Willow on the wooden bench with Dean standing beside them holding onto the leather strap connected to the polished bar above them. There were still a few open seats closer to the back, but Dean did not appear to mind standing for the ride. That, or he might have still been unsure if Terry was going to try and make a break for it.

When they had begun their travel, the round overhead lights filled the inside of the bus with warm, yellowed light, but soon after they had reached the roads of the 'living world,' the harsh sunlight from outside took over, and the overhead lights were extinguished.

"So, how many residents have jobs on Earth? How will we know when our stop is?" she whispered to Willow.

"Not sure about the first thing," Willow answered. "You'll notice everyone around here is a Shepherd, but just maybe from different regions. You might start recognizing some after a while."

"And as for the other—"

"As for the other question, I know, and I'll let you know when it's our stop," Dean answered for her.

It was hard to gauge exactly where they were as the landscape outside whipped by. Once Terry got a good look at one street, the bus would sputter or bump and suddenly they were on a completely different one, or on a dirt road, or passing by a field.

She also took notice that at every stop, very few passengers were getting on. Most everyone was getting off, and some Terry recognized as having boarded at the same time as they had.

When the bus finally came to their stop, Dean tapped on her shoulder and began to make his way toward the front, obviously expecting Terry and Willow to follow.

With Willow behind her and Dean in front, Terry was sandwiched in and had no choice but to go with the flow.

Dean clapped the bus driver on the shoulder and gave him a brief thanks before leading Terry and Willow off the bus. The doors closed behind them, and the bus took off again, only going about a block before disappearing into thin air. Had Terry not seen a hundred other unbelievable things in the last twenty-four hours, there's no way she would have believed in vanishing buses.

Willow must have seen her looking for it. "Oh, don't worry, it'll be back. They've got other stops to make."

"A lot of other stops to make," Dean added. "A lot of people to Shepherd today."

"There's a lot of people every day," Willow added.

"Yes, but we only have to worry about who's on our schedule today." Dean pulled it out to look over. It was the hard copy of what had been flashing over Angie earlier, a folded sheet of old printer paper with perforated edges on each side.

"This stop, we've just got the one, but the bus will be here to pick us up to take us to the next three. So long as we're done here in about forty minutes or so."

Dean looked at his watch, and Willow turned on the screen on her phone.

"It's almost noon right now," Willow said. "Do you think we're close to the soul?"

"If we're not, it shouldn't be hard to find them."

They appeared to have been dropped off in a public park

PurgaTerry

somewhere. Terry could tell from the snippets of conversations she was catching that they were at least still either in the United States or some English-speaking country.

"Is this Ohio? It feels like Ohio," Willow said, apparently trying to guess where they had landed as well.

"Close, it's Michigan, the peninsula. Close to Northville. We're looking for James Phillip Hembree. Thirty-four, five-nine, white, brown hair, blue eyes, black glasses."

"So, we're mostly going to stay in the US?" Terry asked.

"Yup, well, North America. Although I don't think we've done many in Mexico yet. At least Dean hasn't picked up any schedules for me from there."

"That's because your Spanish is terrible," Dean said. "Doesn't that phone have a language app or something?"

Willow gave him a 'pfft' sound. "Like I'd waste precious storage space on educational apps."

They walked down the concrete walkway past a running track and toward a large pond where several children and older people were feeding a flock of ducks. They were wandering pretty aimlessly from what Terry could surmise. Eventually—since that was so often the case with Dean ever since she'd met him—she took it upon herself to ask, since information was not being shared.

"So, how do you know who this guy is?" Terry scanned the area, but there didn't appear to be any indication of the person they were looking for.

"It's not hard. They give us a description on the schedule. Then we just have to confirm he has his ticket to make sure it's him, and then we punch it, and his soul is marked for extraction," Willow explained.

Willow held out her hand to Dean, and he obliged by handing her the schedule with the page folded open to their current Shepherding target.

"Now, you're gonna have to help track him down; there are a lot of pasty white dudes here today," Willow said as she shared the page with Terry.

Terry now skimmed over the man's information, her mind slowly registering that in about forty minutes, this man was most likely going to be dead. And they were the ones who had to make sure that happened.

"So, we don't have to actually be there when the person dies?" Terry asked.

"Not always," Dean said, "but the system usually gets backed up, so more often than not, we reach them just in the nick of time. Managers get the pagers, and they delegate who should go where and when. We don't always work in a group like this. For instance, I can trust Willow by now to handle her own cases, but I'm still supposed to be the one assigning them to her."

"Is that why she has a cell phone?"

"Officially, yeah."

"But unofficially, it's because Dean loves me and wants me to be happy." Willow looked up from said phone and beamed with a knowing smile at him.

"So... do I get a phone?" Terry asked.

Dean shrugged. "Maybe someday, once I know I can trust you."

Terry was going to voice another question that she assumed was not going to be answered when his pocket began to buzz.

Whatever his pager read, his face paled. His eyes read the text over a couple times before shifting his gaze between the two girls.

"Wills, I gotta go. Manager business. All hands on deck. You think you can take this from here?"

Willow nodded. "Sure, Dean. No problem."

"I'd say you've got a little time to find him. Take Terry with you, and when you locate him, show her what we do. Make sure his soul is or gets marked." He started moving back toward the bus stop. "Might be back a little later than scheduled, maybe one-fifteen or one-twenty. Get some ice cream or something while you wait if things don't take too long."

He then handed Willow some money, which she snatched up with a smile.

PurgaTerry

"You got it."

Willow grabbed Terry by the hand and began skipping off toward the large playground.

"Ice cream only after you do the job!" Dean called to them, to which Willow only waved her hand without looking back.

Instead of a bus appearing for him, as Terry had expected, a pair of elevator doors opened out of nowhere to swallow Dean up, closing and vanishing as quickly as they had come.

With Dean gone, Willow appeared to relax. "Let's get that ice cream." She grasped Terry's hand and yanked her toward a cart selling ice cream.

"I thought nobody was supposed to notice us."

"Not noticing and not seeing are two different things," she replied. "It's not like we're invisible, we're just not important to anyone except the marks."

Willow demonstrated by clearing her throat to get the vendor's attention.

The man glanced up for a split second and then his attention quickly drew his eyes downward, away from Willow's face.

"Can I help you?" he asked, in a stilted, autopilot response.

"Two cones, please. Two scoops each. Cookies and cream for me and—" She turned to Terry. "What do you want?"

Terry watched as the man began filling the order almost robotically.

Willow raised her eyebrows expectantly, and Terry piped up.

"Uh, mint chocolate, if you have it."

"Mint chocolate chip okay?" the man asked, eyes looking past her, glazed over.

Terry nodded, then, unsure if a nod would cut it, said, "That's fine."

He handed the cones to Willow, and she pulled a couple of dollars out of her tiny purse.

"Where do you get the money?" she asked as Willow handed Terry her cone. "I mean where does it come from when you or Dean get it?"

"Well, we don't exactly get a paycheck since this is a community service type gig."

"And because we're dead," Terry added.

"Yeah, that too." Willow giggled. Terry was going to have to get used to the flippant way her new acquaintance appeared to look at death.

"But Dean gets some managerial perks, and a small allowance is one of them. Only to be used in service of our work, of course."

Terry smirked, biting into the top scoop of her cone.

"Right, because ice cream is vital to our duties."

Willow crinkled her nose in response. "Hey, the Upstairs people don't really mind, so long as we meet our quotas and don't use it to buy Lamborghinis or anything else that could massively affect the economy. I don't think a couple of frozen treats are gonna exactly break the bank."

Terry supposed not, especially since she was already enjoying the fruits of this little loophole.

"So, what do they mean when they say we have to 'mark his soul'?"

"Mmm," Willow said, swallowing her latest lick. "They mean the tickets. We have to make sure their ticket gets stamped so they can board the bus when it comes for them. We also have to make sure their bodies are prepared for the soul to leave it. This is usually when we have to numb them. Or, like, make sure they don't feel any unnecessary pain when they aren't supposed to."

"And you do that how?"

"It can take a couple of days, but once they've been scheduled, you're supposed to locate them and influence their senses and emotions. Make them numb or peaceful or something. It's a courtesy, and it helps the body and soul not freak out as much when they're separated."

"So, does the person know they're going to die?"

Willow shook her head.

"No, no, no. Nothing like that—well, most of the time—but their soul needs to be prepared for what's about to happen.

PurgaTerry

If they're not, it can be really bad. A soul that isn't prepared right can have trouble leaving the body or have a serious case of separation anxiety. They might get stuck and not be able to go anywhere."

"Like a ghost?"

"Yeah, kinda."

They had gone almost the entire way around the pond. Terry was starting to recognize the ducks as they passed them.

"So, how do we find this soul?"

"They'll sorta call out to us. They'll be the only ones who really take notice of us."

The trail they walked down passed by a large waterfall that spilled into a man-made lake below, and Willow nearly knocked Terry's ice cream out of her hand as the girl tugged her toward the edge of a lake to point out the ducks. Several of the green-and-brown-headed mallards were using the waterfall as a slide from one level to the next. After probably a little too long watching the ducks enjoy their little ride, Terry noticed that her ice cream cone was gone and figured they should probably keep searching for their soul.

Not too far from the lake full of ducks, they came upon a woodchip-covered expanse of ground with several slides, swings, and various playground structures. It was earlier in the morning, so only a few children were on the playground. One was climbing up a slide, and two were attempting to launch themselves out of the swings, while their parents sat on benches nearby, only looking up from their phones occasionally to check on them.

Neither of the parents on the bench looked like James Hembree from where Terry stood, and Willow appeared to have noticed this, too. She was only just now finishing off her cone and gestured with the end of it to another bench not far from the walkway.

"Maybe if we stay in one spot, he'll come to us," she said with a shrug.

"Are you really suggesting we sit down on the job?" Terry

asked. Willow—already sitting on the bench—crinkled her nose at Terry. "No— I mean yes, a little, but for real, though. If we keep moving around, and he keeps moving around, what are the chances we'll actually run into him?"

"It's a big park," she said, resigning herself already to having a seat next to Willow.

"Yeah, but at least this way, we can watch everybody go by, and we won't be possibly missing him."

Terry wasn't sure if that was actually a good argument or if she, too, just wanted to sit for a while, but she went with Willow's idea and began scoping out all of the passersby.

"We should at least look like we're talking and face away from the playground," Terry said with a glance toward where the parents of the kids sat, a blonde woman with what Terry could only describe as a helmet-like 'mom' haircut looking in their direction with suspicion.

"That mom over there might think we're shady."

"You got it." Willow gave her a thumbs up and pulled out her phone again, and Terry felt like she should have something to pretend to look at, too.

"Doesn't your phone have some kind of extra info on this guy?" she asked. "Maybe a picture or something?"

Willow looked up for a moment and appeared to consider something, then went back to tapping and swiping the phone screen.

"I don't think so, however—" She paused as she appeared to find what she was looking for. "Dean sent me a whole PDF of the procedures when he gave me the phone. It has everything there is to know about the Shepherding process in it. Do you wanna look at that?"

The fact that Willow needed to dig through the depths of her phone's files to pull up the PDF suggested she had not found it very helpful. When she handed Terry the phone, Terry skimmed through the first few pages, feeling like she, too, might not be able to get through it. The contents read like the terms and

PURGATERRY

conditions agreement when signing up for an Apple account. But she thought she was getting the gist of one section after a few minutes, nearly forgetting that they were supposed to be looking out for the shepherdee. She was relying on Willow to be her eyes and point out anyone who came close to James Hembree's description.

"Ooh, Terry, look at that girl's shoes!" Willow said while tapping her shoulder enthusiastically.

"Is the girl with the shoes with Mr. Hembree?" she asked, not bothering to look up.

Willow deflated beside her. "No."

After a couple more false alarms, one where Terry had to chase Willow down from running up to pet an (arguably cute) Boston Terrier, Terry took a break from trying to make heads or tails of the PDF and considered her fellow Shepherd-in-training.

"Look, Willow, I'm all for taking as much time as possible on this assignment—you know how I feel about being here—but it kinda seems like you're avoiding looking for our mark on purpose."

"Dean leaving kinda threw me off, you know?" Willow replied, avoiding Terry's gaze. "And it's your first time, too. That makes things even more complicated."

"Still, you've been at this longer than I have. I didn't think I'd have to be the responsible one on my first outing."

Willow frowned, looping one of her curls around her finger and watching it spring back when she let go.

"You're right." She sighed. "But it's just... I've been here almost ten years—I'm pretty sure—and Dean's never left me to do one of these on my own before. What if I mess up?"

"It's been nearly ten years, and he's only just now left you on your own? Jeez, how long does Shepherd training take?"

Willow's frown turned sadder. "Not as long as it's taken me."

Her heart went out to Willow as Terry took in what she'd said. She pulled her lips into a line, unsure of what to say to her. Terry felt like she should say something encouraging and friendly—even big-sisterly—but she was coming up short. She settled for a light yet awkward fist bump to Willow's shoulder and a "Well, you know…" letting it trail off, because she honestly didn't know.

She was spared the necessity of trying to come up with a follow-up for that non-response when Willow brightened, pointing to the other side of the playground and another bench, where a man fitting James Hembree's description had just sat down. He looked rattled, but Terry observed him calm himself as he pulled out his phone, every now and then looking up toward the playground in a similar fashion to the parents from earlier.

"I think that's our guy!" Willow said a bit too loudly. Terry shushed her, and she quickly apologized.

Terry's stomach dropped at the thought that their mark was at the park with his child, and she followed his eyes to the play structures, wondering which of them was his kid. But there were still only the same three kids playing, as far as she could see, and the same two parents on the other side.

"Did you see if he came here with a kid?" she asked.

Willow shook her head. "I don't think so."

They watched him for a few more minutes, Terry growing wary, as every so often, James Hembree would move his phone up closer to his eyes for a second, tap the screen, and then covertly lower it back down.

"Wait, is he taking pictures of the kids?"

Willow blinked, her eyes going from furrowed with uncertainty to wide open. "No… no way. He couldn't be."

But as they scrutinized him, Terry saw him make the same suspicious motion again, and a sour pang of disgust began to form. She was suddenly not as sorry about Shepherding this guy today.

"That's creepy," Willow said with a look to Terry. "I'm not wrong, right? That's creepy?"

Terry nodded, her surprise and disgust giving way to a kind of resolve. She tilted her head toward Willow, looking away from

PurgaTerry

the man and his objectively sketchy behavior.

"Well, even if what he's doing isn't exactly right, we're still supposed to Shepherd him."

"I think we should tell those moms," Willow said, getting to her feet and already striding toward the parents of the children.

Terry sprang to her own feet and chased after her, grasping for Willow's arm. "Willow, you can't. What about the whole not noticing us thing?"

"They've already noticed us," Willow replied. "And besides, they deserve to know if some creep is creeping on their kids."

"But that creep is about to die," Terry tried to reason.

"Oh, so that means he gets a free pass?" Willow shook her head and kept walking, dragging Terry along. "Nuh-uh. Even if we lose track of him, this is the right thing to do, T."

Terry couldn't blame her, but as she had said to Willow earlier, she really hadn't expected to be the responsible one on this first Shepherding excursion.

"Maybe you can get closer to him in case he makes a break for it," Willow said. "I'm still telling them."

It appeared her friend couldn't be stopped, so she went ahead and did as Willow suggested. Terry still felt that, however they may feel about the man's actions, bringing unneeded attention to the man whose soul they were supposed to be Shepherding in a short while didn't feel like a smart move.

As she rounded a small crop of saplings growing outside of the woodchipped area, she saw Willow farther away, too far for her to hear, talking to the children's moms. She watched Willow point Mr. Hembree out to them, and one of them called the children's names while the other made a beeline for him, brandishing her child's Hello Kitty umbrella like a weapon to club him with.

James Hembree saw her approaching, and he made a break for it, heading past where Terry stood. Willow dashed in the same direction, passing the mother and calling to her that they'd handle this. Terry followed Willow's pursuit, knowing that they probably didn't have much time to 'handle' the situation before the man's bus arrived.

She was afraid that people might be starting to notice as he dashed across the grass like his life depended on it (which it sort of did), and his gait began to wobble, the rhythm of his strides interrupted by frequent hard breaths as he started to stumble toward a large ornate fountain close to the walking path. Before either of them could catch up to him, he dove headfirst into the water.

The man flopped around in the water almost like a fish as he appeared to try and keep his head under the water. When Terry finally reached the edge of the fountain, it was to find James Hembree face down in the water, a tiny trail of bubbles escaping from his mouth.

Willow met up with her, and they both grabbed hold of him to pull him out of the fountain. Now soaking wet, the man couldn't seem to stand on his own. Not wanting to bring any more attention, Terry and Willow tried to find somewhere farther from the walking path to do what needed to be done.

They had only managed to drag him to the other side of the fountain—mostly obscuring them from the path—when Mr. Hembree collapsed to the ground.

They gave him a moment as his breathing slowed. Terry was unsure if he was just exhausted or if he was actually dying right in front of them.

"Should we try to move him somewhere else, not out in the open?" she asked.

Willow didn't answer. She was still watching the man on the ground, eyes wider than they had been earlier and frozen to the spot.

"Willow," she called to her to try and snap her out of it. "Willow, what do we do now?"

Terry bent down close to where the man lay, jumping back and nearly losing her balance when the man started seizing, shaking uncontrollably. His mouth began to foam as they could

PurgaTerry

clearly see something within him pulsing, trying to escape without a way to do so.

Her patience with Willow wearing thin, Terry jammed her hand out toward her.

"Gimme the phone again."

Willow handed the phone out to her shakily, the PDF file opened up on the screen. Terry took it in both hands and fired off a few quick texts to Dean. She wasn't sure how much space she had to work with, as he only had the pager, but '911' felt like it would get her point across.

She then began to skim through the document. As long and wordy as it was, she thought she could figure out the basic gist. With her fellow Shepherd anxiously raking her hands through her curly hair, Terry decided to start reading the file out loud, if only for something to do and something for the two of them to focus on.

"Once the target has been identified," she read, "it is imperative that the assigned Shepherd mark their soul for collecting within twenty-four hours of their appearance on the schedule."

"That's his ticket, right?" she asked Willow. When she received no response, Terry knelt down and began to search the now-twitching body for his ticket.

"Once the soul has been placed on the schedule, the assigned Shepherd must acquire their ticket for stamping, applying any necessary adjustments to the soul's emotional state or other senses."

"So, what? He's supposed to have the ticket on him when we find him?"

"I mean, I guess?" Willow answered, looking over their mark with growing wariness. "It comes from the Ticket Repository; it usually just appears."

"You guess?"

"I told you I haven't done this by myself before! We should call Dean. This guy's having a bad reaction."

"I texted him, but I don't know how fast he'll respond." Terry's eyes snapped up to Willow's. "Wait, what do you mean?"

"I mean I think we didn't get to him in time and his soul is freaking out."

"But you said that wouldn't happen!"

"I didn't think it would, now stop yelling at me!" Willow yelled back, ignoring her own volume. "You're gonna cause a scene"

"I thought everyone else would ignore us."

"Not if we're yelling over a dead body. Even that tends to draw attention for us," she stammered through her panic.

"Oh, what a helpful on-the-job trainer you are."

"That was mean, but I'll forgive you since I'm freaking out too, because... this shouldn't be happening!"

Not finding anything helpful for their specific predicament in the PDF, Terry gave the phone back to Willow. Her fingers were shaking as Terry saw her dial the number for Dean's pager to try to reach him again. "I don't know what's going on, but Dean will."

"You mean Dean didn't tell us something that was probably important for us to know? Well, there's a shocker." Terry rolled her eyes. But her attitude dropped when she noticed the panic in Willow's eyes. Her hands were still shaking, and she began pacing around the body. Clearly, Terry's own hangups about Dean's managerial tact would not be helpful at the moment.

Almost on instinct, Terry put a hand on Willow's shoulder, which halted her and caused her to look up from her phone.

"Hey, hey," she said calmly. "I'm sorry, okay? I don't blame you. We'll be okay, and this guy will be okay. We'll just wait here for Dean, and it'll all be fine, okay?"

Terry used her free hand to gently pry Willow's fingers from the death grip they had on her phone.

"Let me hold that, and how about you take a big, deep breath?"

After a moment of hesitation, Willow consented and relinquished the phone, inhaling deeply and then exhaling slowly.

"Good," Terry said. "Now do that a couple more times until you feel calmer."

As Willow continued her breathing, Terry knelt down beside

the still-twitching, seizing body. She waited a couple seconds for the seizing to slow and hesitantly reached to his neck to check his pulse. She found none, but the man's eyes still darted in every direction, his soul still pulling at his body, pinging around inside him, searching for a way out.

Terry had no idea whether or not he was in pain throughout this, but it didn't exactly look like it tickled. She found herself hoping that Dean would hurry up and get there. No matter how much weird camouflage they had as Shepherds, Willow was definitely right—the longer they stayed around a twitching dead body, the more interest that might draw.

"Can you... can you do that feeling numbing thing you were talking about?" she asked, pleased to see that Willow had at least calmed down enough to not need the deep breathing anymore.

"I've never done it after they'd died before," Willow replied, voice tightening as her eyes began filling with tears.

Terry held up her hands again. "Shh, it's okay, you can do it. I'll use the phone and keep trying Dean. Just do what you can."

Willow's lip trembled. "But his ticket is already punched! If the bus comes and his soul's not there, he'll get left behind."

"If the bus comes, we just explain the situation. If his ticket is punched, then they're expecting him. Now just put something under his head to make it look like he's sleeping and do whatever you need to do to get the soul out."

Willow nodded, glancing still shakily toward the now disturbingly-still man.

Terry waved a hand in her eyeline to get her attention, a strange sense of determination coming over her.

"You can do this."

That caused some of Willow's tears to fall, but she knelt down next to the man just as Terry had. As Terry continued to message Dean's pager—no doubt blowing the thing up—Willow held her hands over the man's body, closing her eyes as if praying over him.

After a few shaky breaths, she heard Willow take another

long, big inhale, exhaling just as slowly. Terry then began to hear Willow humming a soothing lullaby-like tune. She wasn't sure if it was more to calm herself down or the man. Terry didn't dare disturb her, but she could tell Willow was "in the zone."

She stepped away from them toward the bench at the walking path, looking out toward the edge of the park and where she presumed the bus would stop. She turned back toward Willow as she was doing her—what—soul whispering? She still didn't quite understand, but from where she stood, Terry could at least see the man's eyes had stopped rolling around in every direction.

She watched as Willow gently closed his eyes then rested a palm on his forehead. As she saw Willow take another deep breath, she thought she saw the man take one in as well. Then when Willow exhaled one final time, so, too, did the man. In a fluid, sweeping motion, Willow removed her hand from his head, bringing with it a trail of light.

Then—just like that—there were two James Phillip Hembrees on the grass. One—the body—growing cold and losing color on the ground. The other—the soul—standing next to Willow, who stood up from the body as she noticed him.

Her face lit up at the sight of him, even though he looked exhausted and confused.

Terry could tell what was coming next, and sadly for James, she was just far enough to not be able to stop it. Willow launched herself at him, wrapping him in a hug that he found evidently very strange. All revulsion for his pre-demise activities evidently forgotten.

When she finally let go of the decidedly unreceptive-to-hugs soul, she addressed him with a relieved smile.

"James Phillip Hembree?"

"Uh… yeah," he answered.

"We've got some things to tell you."

And none too soon, for as Willow was beginning her explanation, Terry heard the distinct sound of a large vehicle's brakes from behind her. She turned to see the exact same bus that had

PurgaTerry

brought them to this park. Same build, same driver, but new destination above the windshield.

She rushed up to Willow and James in two long strides.

"Give him the condensed version, Willow. His ride's here." She pointed toward the bus behind her.

Willow did a double take as she saw it, then she quickly looped her arm through his and started half-dragging him toward the waiting bus.

It was as Willow was fast-walking and fast-talking the man's soul toward his destiny that Dean finally showed up.

The elevator doors from nowhere appeared just behind her, and Terry could hear Dean jogging up to her. He was strangely out of breath for somebody who she was pretty sure didn't need to breathe.

"All right, I'm here, I'm here! What's the emergency?"

He rested his hands on his knees, leaning over a moment to catch his breath. When he stood back up, Terry met him with crossed arms.

"What the heck took you so long? I kept typing '911.' What part of that did not evoke 'emergency'?"

"Well, excuse me, but I believe I told you it was important manager things," he said, straightening his tie. "It was all hands on deck, nothing I could do to get out of it."

"Well, your team here really could have used some managing."

"Doesn't look like it to me," he responded, gesturing toward the bus where Willow was waving James goodbye. The door closed, and the bus began to pull away into nothingness once again. To wherever it was that Terry wasn't allowed to know about yet.

Spotting Dean with Terry, Willow skipped up to them as fast as one can skip, already excitedly recapping what had happened to him.

She was going a mile a minute, and Terry couldn't blame Dean for holding up his hands as if she might jump to hug him as well.

"Whoa, whoa, slow down. You sound like a chipmunk."

"Sorry, sorry, but Dean, you will not believe what Terry did!"

Terry blinked. "What I did? You did all the work; I just calmed you down like I would a skittish horse."

"Yeah, exactly. I was freaking out!" she shouted, turning back to Dean. "I was freaking out, Dean. This guy had not been prepped. I dunno who was supposed to do the prepping, but they did a crap job, because we couldn't find his ticket, and then he died! He started seizing something awful!"

Dean's brow furrowed. "What do you mean? And slowly, explain slowly."

"I had no idea what to do, and if Terry hadn't calmed me down, I'd still be flipping out, and he would have missed his bus."

"Yes, but what was that about the seizing?"

Willow shot a glance to Terry, who mimed the breathing technique. Willow followed suit, taking another deep breath in and out before speaking again. She then—much more calmly and succinctly—gave the recap to Dean about what happened.

The line on Dean's furrowed brow deepened. This was the most serious Terry had seen him up to this point.

"It wasn't my fault, Dean," Willow assured him. "We assumed he'd been prepped by somebody. They've always been ready by the time we find them to stamp their ticket. I don't know what happened."

Dean shook his head. "You did fine, Wills. You did exactly what you should have done. I'm just sorry I was gone when it happened, and that I never explained to you what you should do in these types of cases. This is weird, to say the least. I'll talk to Cass about it and see how this could have happened in the first place."

He then dropped the serious face and was back to his old grin.

"You did great though. I don't blame you for freaking out. I'm proud of you."

This made Willow's smile go supernova bright, white teeth shining.

PurgaTerry

He then looked Terry's way and nodded to her.

"I'm proud of both of you. That was some great teamwork, and great calm under pressure. I'm just sorry that you had to do this so soon, and without me."

Just then, a thought came to Terry. It was a little too convenient that Dean just happened to step away when this occurred, and that the bus just happened to show up at the right time.

"Willow, can you go get us a couple more ice creams to celebrate?"

"Ooh, yeah, okay!" Willow said and bounced off to find the vendor they had previously seen.

Terry then scooted closer to Dean's side, eyeing him warily.

"Wait, you... you didn't plan this, did you?"

Dean's face contorted, displaying a level of anger that Terry felt was a bit melodramatic.

"Why, Ms. Pterodactyl, that is a hurtful accusation. To think that my own trainee would think so low of me. I am just ashamed for you."

"Okay, you're straight up calling me 'pterodactyl' now?" she asked then remembered her initial point. "But you left us on purpose? How much of that was your doing?"

Dean leaned in, looking back toward Willow as if she might still be able to hear them. At least he had the decency to look somewhat sheepish.

"Okay, so I left you two on purpose. Willow was way overdue for some solo Shepherding. But no, Little Miss Skeptic, I didn't plan this whole thing."

"Hmm, why am I finding that hard to believe?"

"Believe what you want, but I would never stress Wills out like that intentionally. She's had a rough time as it is."

"Haven't all of the residents had a 'rough time'?"

"It's... a little different for you girls," he admitted reluctantly. But before she could ask him, he held up his hand again. "And no, I will not elaborate on that."

Terry's face fell. "Okay, fine," she grumbled. "But I still think it was super shifty that you decided to give Willow and I some solo Shepherd time on the day something happens neither of us knew how to deal with."

"Don't worry," he assured her as he started to follow where Willow had gone, Terry trailing behind. "I'll talk to Cass, and we'll get to the bottom of that. Don't tell Wills, but she didn't know how to handle that kind of situation before because—as far as I know anyway—it's almost never happened before. Souls have missed their buses before, or not gotten their ticket stamped, or, sure, some have even refused to get on the bus. But I don't think I've seen one stuck inside his own body like that. Not during my time here, anyway."

Terry didn't answer, mostly because she was certain she would get no more answers about it from Dean. But it gave her a strange pit in her stomach that this hadn't all been his plan, and that there were things about this whole Purgatory thing that even the great Dean didn't know.

"But seriously, thanks for helping her out. Wills can get anxious if she doesn't have somebody with her to help."

Terry eyed him curiously. "Would this be a good enough deed to get access to my files?"

Dean laughed. "Ha, nice try. But no."

5. Terry is a 'Special Case', Whatever That Means

The bus ride going back was uneventful, besides the fact that this one looked different on the inside than the one they had arrived in. This was larger, with padded seats closer in Terry's mind to a charter bus than the cozy feel of the trolley-like bus they rode before.

They got off at the Main Hub, which was a surprise to Terry. She didn't think that they would stop anywhere but back at the bus station. But she supposed that made things easier for Dean.

Their shoes echoed on the all-white marble as they crossed to another waiting woman with a clipboard and a tablet. "Ah, Cassiopeia, I've got some kiddos to brag about to you today!"

"'Kiddos'?" Terry asked, cocking an eyebrow. "I'm in my twenties."

"And I'm nearly one hundred, making you a kiddo by default," Dean replied with a smirk. "And you're a newbie to boot."

"And is she named Cassiopeia, too? Are all upper-management people called that?"

Dean gave her a puzzled look before looking back toward the

woman. This woman was just as severe-looking as the Cassiopeia she had met, but this one had light-brown skin and long, straight black hair in some form of half updo. She looked down her long nose past the spectacles she wore at Terry, eyeing her with vague distaste.

Next to her was someone Terry did recognize—Asher. He was occupied with something on his phone (*did everyone in Purgatory get one but her?*) and didn't immediately acknowledge them.

"Oh, my mistake," Dean said, drawing Terry's attention back to him. "I didn't tell you. This *is* the Cass you met the other day. She just likes to change things up on her appearance every so often."

"Wait, she can do that?" Terry asked. "You're a manager; can you do that?"

"How about we save that question for another time," Dean said in an avoidant tone Terry was starting to recognize. "Right now, I've got to tell Cass here what a great job my trainees did."

"I think I'll be the judge of how 'great' their job was," Cassiopeia said. "Ms. Terry, this is my charge, Asher. You may have met already, but I wanted to introduce him properly."

Asher then looked up from his phone at Cassiopeia's voice. "Yeah, I know her. Pajama Girl."

"Good to know that nickname is sticking," Terry said, only partly sarcastic.

Dean then recounted what Willow had told him about Terry jumping in and helping when Willow was uncertain about her abilities. He made her sound a lot more in control than she had felt at the time, but she supposed she appreciated Dean's attempts to make her look good.

"Well, it would appear that you did indeed have a successful first outing," Cassiopeia said to her. Then to Dean, she said, "I commend you on the well-executed management."

Terry noticed that Dean left out the fact that he had planned the "interruption" leading to his absence. She didn't say anything, however. She had an inkling of an idea that, if Dean wouldn't

PURGATERRY

allow her access to her file, perhaps if she asked his superior, she might allow it.

"I'll mark your progress today when I put in your hours in the log. I'll be keeping track of all of your work hours and your social hours. You'll need to fill your quota on both to be able to move forward."

"Ms. Cassiopeia?" Terry asked. Cassiopeia looked annoyed to be interrupted, but Terry took her pause to mean she was free to continue.

"Um, would there be any way to have just a little access to my file? Not even a lot, just a page or so."

"Out of the question," Cassiopeia replied in a clipped tone. "Residents are not allowed to access their files in any capacity."

"But I thought you might have some authority over these things."

"You thought right; however, I must repeat that it is absolutely out of the question."

"But Dean let Willow—"

Dean coughed loudly, interrupting her and muffling her reply slightly. "You heard her, Ter. Out of the question, no exceptions."

Cassiopeia narrowed her eyes at Dean. "Indeed. Don't press your luck, Ms. Terry. You've had a good day, but that doesn't equate to special treatment." Then Terry could barely hear her saying under her breath, "You ought not to get credit for today in any case, as you're still in training, but Dean made a case for you."

"But don't I need today to count toward my 'community service'?" she asked, not hiding the fact that she could hear Cassiopeia.

The administrator clicked her pen and jotted something down, now speaking clearly to Terry. "What you *need* to do is start taking this place seriously. You should be more focused on improving yourself and your attitude toward Purgatory instead of badgering your superiors for information on your past life. That way, you can actually progress here."

"Who says I'm not taking this seriously?"

"I do," she said. "I have been keeping my eye on you, and rest assured, I will continue to do so. And I don't allow back talk, either. You should also work on your attitude problem in your group sessions."

"Maybe I wouldn't have an attitude problem if I could get a straight answer in this place," Terry mumbled.

She noticed Cassiopeia's eyes go wide with indignation before Dean whistled—literally whistled—to get Terry's attention.

"O-kay," he said, pulling the syllables of the word out into two separate words. "I think we've heard about enough from Terry today. Maybe you two can take her somewhere else to cool down?" He gestured to Willow and Asher.

Willow's eyes flicked between the four others, attempting to smile, but it came off as more of a cringe. Asher only shrugged.

"That's a splendid idea," Cassiopeia agreed. "Why don't the three of you start toward your residence? I have things to discuss with Dean," Cassiopeia said. "You should have a group session coming up, in any case. You don't want to miss that."

"Yeah, gotta let the grown-ups talk," Asher said with a smirk. "We can head back to the rec room. Don't worry, they won't say anything interesting while we're gone."

Terry wasn't entirely sure about that, but despite her hesitation, she trailed along behind Asher as Willow led them off toward the door.

Asher leaned in a little closer than Terry was comfortable with as they walked. "Hey, don't worry about Cassiopeia. She's a manager, remember, they've never really been alive. They don't know what it's like."

Terry recalled their previous topic of conversation.

"Especially in her case," Asher said. "For what it's worth, they do keep way too much from us. But they don't get it; there's enough unfair about this place without adding on that we don't have memories either."

"Nice to know somebody gets it," Terry said. She found herself smiling at his sly grin. She still felt a little uneasy about his

PurgaTerry

proximity, but she meant what she'd said.

Behind them, Willow cleared her throat.

"Ahem, anything you'd like to share, Terry?"

Terry did not like the way Willow was smirking at them, like she was in on some kind of secret that she and Terry shared.

"Nothing," she stated. "How about you two go on ahead? I'll be along soon."

"But Terry, I don't want to go without you," Willow said.

"It's a'ight, Willow. Pajama Girl's got some business to take care of, right?" Asher then gave her a pointed look.

"Yeah," Terry agreed, thankful he was quick to catch on. "Don't worry, I won't be long."

Willow looked unsure, but she allowed Asher to lead her away. "Okay, but don't get into trouble. We had a really good day today."

"I won't," she said in a tone she hoped was reassuring.

"See you later, Pj's," Asher said with a wink, somehow giving her nickname a nickname. Then, in a low voice, he added, "And I'd check that Welcome Building if I were you. That's where I found a couple things out about myself."

"Thanks," she whispered back.

Terry then waved Willow on and walked around to the side of the building. She was pleased to see there was a side entrance. The floor of the hallway—unlike the grand entrance—was carpeted, muffling her footsteps and those of other people, so Terry nearly missed spotting Dean and Cassiopeia cross into a room off to the side in the same hallway. She hid behind a corner, hoping that she was fast enough not to be noticed by either of them. When she heard the sound of the door closing, she crept up to it to listen.

"So, we're just letting them look through their files now?" she heard Cassiopeia on the other side of the door.

"It was just one thing, not even a whole page," Dean answered, attempting to defuse the situation and quell his superior's anger. "I had to give her something."

"No, Dean, no you didn't. Any information that could lead

them back to their former lives could cause them to backslide into what caused them to end up here in the first place."

"Don't worry about that. Willow only wanted that one thing because she remembered her brother. She's not interested in digging up the rest of her past."

"For now," Cass said. "And what about Terry, hmm? Will you cave to her as well? She's been wanting to access her memories since she got here. You need to keep her under control, make her see that her past life is only relevant here as far as what she did to get here and how long she is expected to remain."

Terry heard Dean lower his voice, and she shrunk back when the door was eased shut. Although Terry could still hear the two of them, it wasn't as easy.

"Look, I know Terry's a special case, but she's only going to keep asking questions, especially after she's been comparing how things are for everyone else but her. It's only a matter of time before she stops asking and starts taking things into her own hands," Dean said.

"You of all people know precisely why she is a special case and why things had to be altered for her. I don't want a repeat of Delilah, and I know you don't, either."

"Terry could never do what Dels did," Dean replied with a flat sort of defensiveness. Though Terry had no context for this conversation, she smiled a little when he said that.

"And how can you be sure?" Cass asked. "You haven't been a supervisor as long as I have. You have no idea. I've seen every sort of human soul there ever could be, and I know what a soul on the edge looks like."

Dean chuckled without humor. "Funny, then why didn't you see what Dels was up to before I did?"

"That was not my job," Cass answered, a haughty defensiveness filling the short sentence. "But we've been over this. No matter whose job it fell to watch her, what befell Delilah was of her own doing. She was uncooperative, unwilling to focus on her tasks, all too concerned about trying to somehow 'get back' to her old standard of normalcy. Does that sound in any way familiar?"

There was a pause, and for a few seconds, Terry only heard the rhythmic tapping of Cassiopeia's fingernails on some flat surface.

"It won't be the same as before, Cass, I promise. Terry's too smart for that. She'll come around."

"See that she does."

Terry heard Cassiopeia's shoes clacking across the floor, and she scurried down the hall and around a corner. She braved one peek around it to see Cass and Dean exit.

"I'm only looking out for you, Dean," Cassiopea said. "Two souls under your watch getting sent Downstairs for infractions won't look good on your record. You might be forced to stay on your post longer than you anticipate."

"What, you think being stuck in the middle with you is a chore?" he asked, his normal tone returning. "You've gotta have more confidence in yourself, Cass."

Cassiopea narrowed her eyes at him. She was obviously not joking.

"But I got it, I'm watching out for Terry. But you also gotta let me do that in my own way."

"As long as you aren't violating protocol, then that's fine."

A brief second of Dean turning toward the cracked door was all she saw before Terry made a break for the hall just around the corner, hoping that Cassiopeia would exit the other direction.

As Cassiopeia exited down the hall and around a corner, Dean cleared his throat more loudly than was necessary.

"You can come out now, Terry-dactyl," Dean called after a few more minutes. He must have been waiting for Cassiopeia to leave. How had he known she was there? She'd tried to be as covert as she could. She moved out of her hiding place to be greeted by a smile that told her Dean was not surprised in the slightest to find her there.

"That was all classified information you just eavesdropped on," he said. "But I don't have to say anything. I didn't find you here. No eaves were dropped as far as I can tell. So long as none of what was said gets out."

Terry nodded. "Understood. But Dean, I still want answers."

"What do you need those answers for, huh?" he asked, winding an arm around her shoulders and leading her back the way she came. "You died by suicide, and then you came here. That's all you really need to know, isn't it?"

"But you don't understand, Dean, I need them," she said. "I don't think I can 'move forward' or whatever without them."

"You know, Ter, 'want' and 'need' are two different things."

"I know that. But in this case, it's both."

"Well, you won't get anywhere looking at the past. I keep telling you that your memories are in your file, and you'll get them back when you complete your time here."

"You say that, but how am I supposed to progress and make myself better if I'm not allowed to remember what I did? How is that fair?"

"Life isn't fair, kid. What'd you think the afterlife would be?"

He went quiet for a few steps after that. Terry could almost see the cogs turning in his head.

"But I suppose you do have a point. I could be more forthcoming on some of the details. But really, you know everything you need to. They call this a courtesy, or whatever. Suicide is serious business, and I understand that… in all that it entails, but it was still a violent act against yourself, so someone needs to pay for it."

"I guess, but aren't there underlying causes that got me to that point? Am I not allowed to know about those, or is that part of the 'courtesy'?"

That appeared to stump him momentarily, but he recovered with his usual vagueness.

"You keep poking around, Ter, and you might find you don't like the things you uncover."

She didn't respond to that. She wished she had a rock to kick along as they walked to get her frustrations out.

PurgaTerry

"When the time comes, you'll get your answers. But that's just not what this place is about."

"But then how do I know when I'm improving?"

Dean smiled. "I'll let you know."

Terry guessed that was about as good as she was going to get for the moment, but then she remembered something else that didn't make sense.

"But what about the others? Most of them know exactly how they died. Why don't I?"

Dean's eyes moved down to his shoes as they continued to walk, his silence proof that he really was keeping something from her. She decided to let it go for now and began forming another plan she hoped might bear some fruit.

6. Making Deals Over Crispy Bacon

Terry was experiencing a rare moment of freedom. The morning's mandatory meeting was over, and she had not heard anything about Shepherding duties for the day. And for the first time, she was not being watched. So, Terry took the opportunity to attempt something that had been weighing on her mind.

The Welcome Building where she woke up was most likely the place where she had had her memories taken from her. Unlike some of the other buildings, the Welcome Building didn't require any permission from a manager to access. All Terry needed to do was walk in without seeming suspicious.

She hoped it was a good sign that there didn't appear to be any security, but she proceeded with caution as she tried to retrace her steps from that night. The entrance was just as cool and echoey as she remembered, and she headed down a hallway she thought was the right one, taking a left that probably should have been a right and then backtracking to correct herself.

Terry felt pretty good about herself, not having run into an yone yet. Either this really was an empty space most of the time, or she really was just that good at sneaking. When the carpeted hallways gave way to tile ones, she felt as if she were getting close.

At last, she found a wall with one distinguishing feature that she could recognize, a card swiping lock next to a doorknob that did not appear to be attached to a door. She pulled from her pocket the only two items she carried, the gum wrapper and her ID card. Terry was skeptical that her card would even let her access the room, but she had gone this far, she figured she might as well try it.

There was no indication to show her which way to face her card as she swiped, but it turned out not to matter, because it swiped, beeped, and the light above the indicator turned green. Amazingly, she had done it.

Pumping her fist in quiet triumph, she watched as the door carved itself into the wall. She then tapped the knob and the door gave way, melting into nothing as it had before.

Her sense of triumph was short-lived, however, for on the other side of the door, leaning on one of the arms of the chair at the center of the white room, was Dean.

"Oh, hello, Terry," he greeted her as if he'd been expecting her. "Fancy seeing you here. What brings you over to this neck of Purgatory?"

Terry groaned, the wind leaving her sails as fast as it came. Of course he was here, of course he was. He was always several steps ahead of her. "Dean, come on. You know why I'm here."

"Yes, I do, but I would like to hear your thought process."

"I figured... I thought that if my memories were stored here at some point, they might still be here somewhere, so I wanted to see what I could find."

Dean shook his head, rising from his leaning posture and tutting. "It was a good idea, I'll give you that. But do you think after we take the memories we don't send them off immediately? No, no, they're shipped off to the Hall of Records within twenty-four Earth hours of a soul's arrival."

PurgaTerry

Crap, so she wasn't even close to getting to them here. That must have been why it was so easy to get into this building.

"Again, nice try, Kiddo. But we're not gonna make it that easy for you. You gave up those memories for us to keep safe for you, you trusted us with them to keep them out of the wrong hands."

"The wrong hands being my own?" she asked.

"If they're going to be harmful to your progress, yes," Dean said. "You still don't get it, do you? It's a courtesy, not a punishment. We're helping you have a clean slate to do your service here."

"A clean slate?" she repeated.

Dean waved his hand in a 'so-so' gesture. "Well, clean-ish. I promise, kid, your memories are safe in the Hall, and they'll be returned to you as soon as you finish up here."

"But what about what I can remember?" she asked, teetering on the edge of giving away the only clue she had still hiding in her pocket. "If... if I already know something, can you tell me about that thing?"

Dean seemed to mull this over, nodding slowly. "Sure, of course. Within reason, I could. Is there something you need cleared up?"

Terry observed his face, trying to read any deception in his expression. Any microexpression or tic that might indicate he wasn't genuine. Supposing she might as well go for it, she took a breath and asked, "Who's Hatori?"

She saw his eyes widen for a fraction of a second, long enough to register that he recognized that name. He then sighed through his nose, gaze downcast.

"Of course it would be that."

"So, you can't tell me?" she asked, prepared for the door to be closed once again on her efforts.

Dean scratched the back of his neck, finding her gaze again but still sounding more somber than his usual self. "I didn't say that, but I didn't exactly say I could either."

"If I ask the right questions?"

Dean nodded. "Not here, though," he said, sliding his card

along a barely visible slot to make the doorway appear once again. He led Terry out into the hallway and back down the path that they had taken the night she had arrived through the open, foggy expanse.

The diner Terry saw in front of her when they exited the bus was small but cozy. It was one of those that was either built several decades ago or made to look like it was. White walls with pink trim, dark-pink tables, and a yellow stained glass window at the front. The checkered floor looked worn but not too bad. A sign outside read "Angel's." Terry smiled at the irony. And above the name, "since 1932." So, at least that answered that question. The humidity and the sparse palm trees reminded Terry vaguely of Florida. She presumed that was where they were, but she still had no clue as to why.

"What are we doing here, Dean?" she asked as he led her to a booth and sat her down facing the kitchen doors.

"Taking in the ambience, for now, then, in a minute, getting some of the best damn pancakes in the whole world. Kicks IHOP's tail by a long shot."

Sliding into the seat across from her, Dean began to pull the straw from the neatly wrapped napkin holding the utensils and unwrap it. "Order whatever you want, but we're both having the pancakes. Milkshakes are fairly decent as well, if you're in the mood."

"Well, hey, stranger!" a friendly voice chirped. Their waitress grinned at Dean, tapping his shoulder with her pencil affectionately.

"Edith," he greeted her with a matching fondness. "You know I can't stay away from here when I'm in town. Just haven't had a reason to come down this far lately."

"Are you gonna go visit Nana April while you're here?" she asked. Her voice was musical and held a slight Southern accent

PURGATERRY

at the edges. It was oddly familiar to Terry.

Terry raised her eyebrows. "Nana April?"

Edith patted Dean's shoulder once more before picking up their menus, even though they hadn't yet ordered. "Oh yeah, Floyd comes by every now and again and always pays my grandmother a visit. Her papa saved his grandad's life in—which war was it, Floyd?" Before Dean could answer, Edith waved the question away. "Well, anyhoo, Floyd's grandaddy made him promise to always look out for our family. Don't worry about ordering; I know what Floyd likes."

She then turned her attention to Terry, pointing at her with the pencil in her free hand. "You are new, though. Your lady friends are getting younger, Floyd." She gave him a wink, tapping him on the head with the pencil.

"Now, Edie, you know it's not like that," he said. "Terry is a new hire at my job, and I've been showing her the tricks of the trade."

"She still looks at least ten years younger than your last hire. The big city girl? What happened to her?"

Dean became very focused on crumbling up his straw wrapper. "She didn't work out," he said simply.

"Well, I could have told you that was gonna happen," she said. "She didn't look like a good fit for assisting you. Only time will tell with Miss Terry here." She then backtracked. "I am so sorry, are you fine with 'miss'? You remind me of my nibling, and they keep getting after me about pronouns. They don't wanna be a 'miss' or a 'mister,' you see."

Terry smiled politely. "'Miss' is fine, or just 'Terry,' but... thanks."

"Don't seem so surprised. Some of us hicks are mighty progressive."

"How about those kids? How's the baby?" Dean asked.

"Not gonna be a baby much longer," Edie said. "Molly's 'bout to be three, and Carter will be starting kindergarten this year." She then pointed to another booth near the kitchen. Two young children were coloring on paper place mats while surrounded by various stuffed animals and toys.

"Too fast," Dean mused. "I remember when Carter was born. But why bring them here?"

Edie looked back from her children to Dean. "Couldn't afford a babysitter, and day care is out of the question. I couldn't afford it for them both."

Terry watched Edie roll her eyes as Dean pulled out his wallet. "Now, Floyd, that wasn't me asking for help."

"But you need it," Dean said. "Don't be stubborn. What would my grandaddy say?"

He pulled out several hundred dollar bills and pressed them into Edie's hand. Terry's eyes grew wide as Edie reluctantly took the cash. She had no idea where he could've gotten that much money.

Edie took another look at the bills before stowing them in her apron pocket. "Lemme go get your food. It'll be on the house today. That's nonnegotiable."

Dean nodded. "Sounds fair."

As Edie left toward the doors to the kitchen, Terry noted the softness in his eyes as he watched her leave and as his gaze fell briefly on the two little kids.

"Okay, so spill '*Floyd.*' How do you know that lady?"

"Aren't we here for you to ask questions about you?" Dean responded. "I might just change my mind if you keep pestering me about my business."

"I don't believe that," Terry said. "You're just deflecting. Who is she?"

Dean appeared to mull it over for a second, then sighed, correctly assuming that Terry wouldn't let it go.

"She's my great-granddaughter, and she's the real reason we're here."

Up until this moment, Terry thought someone's mouth dropping open in surprise was a thing that only happened in cartoons. But now, here she was, mouth agape, ready to fire off even more questions when Edie returned with their food.

"Well, that didn't take long," Dean said, probably to draw Edie's attention to him.

"You're a creature of habit, Floyd," Edie said as she placed the plates in front of each of them. "Easy to be quick when I can read your order off in my sleep."

Terry looked down at their identical plates. Chocolate chip pancakes, scrambled eggs with bright-orange cheese mixed in, and bacon much more burned at the edges than Terry could recall ever eating. But it smelled good, at least.

"And you're a peach for remembering," Dean said. "Thanks, Edie."

"You're welcome," she said, patting his shoulder before leaving to check on her children at their table.

Terry made sure she was out of earshot before rounding back on Dean.

"How do you have a great-granddaughter? Does Cassiopeia know about her? I thought you were like her and the other managers, that you'd never been human?"

Dean let Terry rattle off her questions, not looking up at her as he dug into his pancakes.

She waited impatiently for him to swallow his food and give her some answers already. They weren't about her or her past, so, technically, it wasn't against the rules for him to tell her.

He held up a finger while he was chewing. Then, once he'd swallowed, he finally looked up at her again.

"Second question first," he said. "Yes, Cass knows about her, and I s'pose the answer to question number three can explain number one."

"Not all managers are like Cassiopeia?" she offered.

"Most are, but I was a... special case. Some residents can get promoted, and it helps their CS numbers if they become managers."

"So, you were alive at some point?"

"Yup, a long time ago," he answered, now sounding a tad

wistful. "Edie's grandmother is my daughter. I never got to meet her when I was alive, and I just—I like checking on them, being there for her and her family like I couldn't when I was alive."

Terry blinked at his tone. She'd never seen Dean look so serious or sound so sad.

"So, when I tell ya I know what you're going through—wanting to find out about your past—I really mean it."

She didn't know what to say. She had just taken it at face value that he must be like the other managers, that he couldn't relate and therefore didn't actually care.

"Dean, I— I didn't know, I'm sorry I assumed you couldn't understand."

He shook his head, cutting off another bite of his pancakes. "It's fine, you couldn't have known. But just because I know about my family doesn't mean I can tell them who I am or interfere more than I do. That money comes from a trust I left behind. It's all I've got left to give April and the rest of them, but I've got to be covert about it."

After another bite, he continued.

"So, you'll have to be covert with any information I'm able to give you about your life, you got it?"

Terry's heart figuratively skipped a beat, and she sat up straighter. "You mean you're actually going to tell me something?"

"Under some conditions," he replied. "Don't get too excited. We're gonna play a little game. Twenty Questions. Yes or no answers, and you only get five right now."

"What, why only five?" She asked indignantly.

"Because this is the next condition: You have to *try,* Terry. Make an effort in your Shepherd work, go to the group therapy sessions. Participate. I want to see you're really trying to get out of here."

"But you know that's all I want to do—"

"You want your old life back," Dean interrupted. "And that's not something that I can give you. But I can make it so neither of us get investigated for a bad performance review. I'll give you what info I can, and maybe—just maybe—you can figure out an arrangement like mine."

Terry supposed she understood, but that didn't change her irritation concerning her measly five questions upfront. "So, five now, and the rest later?"

"Five now, and five more after you've earned them. Then we'll go like that from there."

He then scooted her plate closer to her. "And while you're thinking of your five questions, eat. You'll thank me."

Dean was right about one thing, the pancakes were delicious. Terry wasn't sure if it was the fact that she hadn't eaten food since she'd died, but she wolfed down every bite to the last chocolate chip. The bacon was crisper than she was used to, but there was something to the slightly burned taste that enhanced the flavor.

Whenever she would start on a question for Dean, he would hold his hand up and point back down to her plate. "Join the Clean Plate Club first."

At last, her plate had indeed been cleaned to the best of her abilities. She gulped down her orange juice and slammed her glass onto the table. "Okay, now can we start the five questions?" Before Dean could answer, she had another thought. "And that shouldn't count as one of my questions, smart aleck."

He chuckled. "Fair enough, but your next words should be question number one."

Terry nodded, sorting through her myriad questions for something to the point that required a straight answer. 'Who or what is Hatori?' would be her first question, but that wouldn't garner a yes or no response. She'd have to pick one and hope she didn't waste a question.

"Is Hatori a person?" she asked after chewing on the question—and the last piece of her bacon—for longer than she felt she should have.

Dean smiled. "Yes," he said. "Glad you started with an easy one. Okay, number two?"

Terry gave it more thought than the first. So, Hatori was a person, and it stood to reason that they were a person she knew and was close with. "Was I close to him?" she asked, trying to gauge Dean's reaction to the pronoun as well as her second query.

"Yes."

"Was he my boyfriend?"

Dean made a face at that. "Absolutely not."

"Ah ha!" she shouted in triumph. "So, I must be related to him, or you wouldn't have reacted that way!"

He nodded, leaning back in his seat, caught off guard by her quick thinking. "I'm impressed. You've got two left, and you weaseled an extra detail out of me, so I'll spot you a reveal. He's your brother."

Terry sat up straighter, the realization that she had a real and solid piece of her life making all the burning inquiries start to overheat her brain. She tried to cool them down, though, as she only had two questions left, and she wanted to make them count. She had a sneaking suspicion that things weren't good for this brother of hers when she'd died. More than a sneaking one, if she were honest.

"Is he dead, too?" she asked, wary of the answer.

"Not exactly," Dean said.

"Okay," she considered that. "Is he here in Purgatory?"

Dean pulled his lips into a fine line, his gaze avoiding hers for a second before finally shaking his head.

"No, and that's your last one until you've earned your next five," he said. "Lose one of those Ps on your ID, or at the very least, step up during Shepherd duties. I wanna hear that you're participating around here, and you'll get the next ones before you know it."

It was easy to agree to that, or really anything Dean said at that moment. Because Terry was riding high on the first real clue to her past. She held onto it like a precious stone. Even if she couldn't remember or picture this brother Hatori, it raised her spirits exponentially anyway. He must have been crucial in her

PurgaTerry

life if he was the one clue she had left for herself.

If she had left it for herself, which she still wasn't sure about. In any case, she was determined to get her next set of questions answered and collect as many clues as she could. It occurred to her that Dean was risking his job for her by doing this. Not only his job, but since he was actually a resident, risking any progress he'd made on his own community service.

She wanted to say thank you, to tell him that she appreciated his efforts more than he could possibly know. Terry didn't quite know how to put it in words though, and just saying so didn't seem like enough.

For now, she settled with asking, "You think Edie can make us a to-go box with just the bacon?"

7. Group Therapy Should Be Outlawed

The day after Terry and Dean agreed on their arrangement, she was determined to do what she was supposed to do when it came to her Shepherding duties. She had even decided not to go snooping around behind his back, at least for the most part.

Participating in the group therapy sessions, however? That was something else. There wasn't much to them, just one of the managers talking to them and trying to 'relate' when she knew now for sure that Dean was an anomaly and one of the only managers that had ever been an actual living person.

So, hearing an otherworldly being who had never even seen a tree, much less felt or climbed one, talk about using them as some form of metaphor for life was more than a touch absurd to her.

Then there were the activities. There were pieces of blank paper and several different coloring pages, but it was the plethora of dried out markers that remained an unsolved mystery of Purgatory.

Then there was Uno. So much Uno. Terry had avoided playing

until this point, content to watch Willow, Juliet, and the other residents play. There were other card games too, but the main event of the rec room appeared to be the Spanish word for number one.

Terry heard there were other activities every so often. Apparently, she had missed karaoke night and some form of craft utilizing old magazines.

"Where do the managers come up with this stuff?" she asked Willow on the third day post her new deal with Dean.

Willow shrugged. "They probably pull from what they see people do in places like this."

Terry raised an eyebrow. "Places like Purgatory?"

"Places like waiting rooms, hospitals, bus stations. Liminal spaces, you know? Places that are meant to be transitional. Nobody is supposed to be in Purgatory forever, so they try and keep us busy with what they think works."

Terry supposed that made sense. She was more surprised at Willow's insight. It made her wonder—much like with Dean—just how long she had been here and how much longer she had to go.

The manager leading the latest group session—Orion again—entered the rec room, and Terry fought the urge to roll her eyes. But as he approached and the rest of the residents began to seat themselves in a semicircle around him, she didn't just hear his words, she tried to actually listen.

"Okay, everyone, today, I'd like to go around the room and have you describe—to the best of your abilities—what you remember your death feeling like, and not just physically, but how it made you feel. Some of you may not have the actual memory of the event, but a residual emotion will still be there. Feelings can linger, even if the memory of what caused them is gone."

Terry perked up at this. It wasn't the sort of thing the managers usually wanted to focus on. Upward and forward momentum was the goal in these parts, and the fact that Terry knew from experience how difficult it was to try and access the past here, Terry was intrigued as to why this manager would

PurgaTerry

bring up their pasts when the rest of the time they wanted the residents to focus solely on their future.

"Now, who'd like to start us off?" Orion scanned the room for volunteers.

Before she knew what she was doing, Terry's hand shot up, surprising Orion, Willow, and herself.

"Terry, well, this is a surprise." Orion sounded pleased, gesturing for her to go on.

The uneasy sensation that accompanied all eyes in a room turning toward her fell upon Terry as she racked her brain for something she could say. She hadn't really thought about it as much as she wanted to admit. What had death felt like to her?

"Go ahead, Terry," Orion encouraged her. "Dig down deep to find those uncovered big feelings. We're here for you if you feel you need to cry."

Terry raised an eyebrow at that. "Hmm? Why? I mean, I get the 'digging up feelings,' sort of, but why would I cry about it?"

"Well, it was a traumatic thing that happened to you, even if you did do it to yourself."

It took Terry aback. Perhaps it was because she hadn't fully and totally accepted her death yet, or perhaps she hadn't fully processed it, but she found the thought of actually shedding tears over it fairly odd.

"I don't think I can, honestly. I mean, I haven't since I got here."

Orion looked much more concerned than Terry thought he ought to be.

"You've been here for almost a month, and you haven't cried yet?"

"I don't— I mean, I don't think I really cry. Not a big crier."

"Terry, it's perfectly natural to cry, especially after a loss."

"Like losing my life?"

"Yes, exactly. You ended it yourself, that's true, but it ended all the same. You lost yourself, and it's normal to feel like you can cry over that loss."

"Like I said, I don't think I'm one who cries a lot." She shrugged with her hands in her pockets.

Orion looked uneasy, but he continued. "Well, let's come back to that later, but for now, if you could simply focus on describing the feelings, the sensations you can remember."

Despite feeling at the moment like she was failing some sort of test, Terry closed her eyes and tried to focus, searching for the right words to describe her death.

"Cold," was what came to her first.

Willow clicked her tongue. "Well, everybody sort of says that first."

"I don't understand," she said.

"Okay, so beyond that initial cold feeling, it's different for everyone. I've never heard the exact same story about death," Willow elaborated. "Like, for me—even though I can't remember everything about it—it felt like I fell asleep on the bank of a river, and the river rose up and carried me away. It was like drifting. Then the next thing I remember is Dean helping me out of that river."

"So, Dean was there to Shepherd you?" Terry asked, a little quieter so as not to catch anyone's ear.

"Yeah, it's usually a manager's job to collect any suicides. Since they're not on the schedule, they're usually unexpected. I mean, *we* were unexpected, I guess."

"Does that mean he was there to collect me?"

"Yeah, of course," Willow said, still at her full volume.

"He must've offered me the whole Purgatory deal then, right?"

Willow blinked at her, eyes darting toward Orion again for the briefest second.

"Let's see what you do remember, huh, Terry? What did death feel like to you?" Orion asked.

If Terry wasn't getting used to Willow's chipperness, she might have thought that was a redirection, much like their ever-avoidant manager was so fond of doing. She gave her friend the benefit of the doubt though, and she tried again to find the words for what the experience had felt like to her.

PurgaTerry

She looked down as she thought, her shoes smoky purple against the contrasting gray tile and walls surrounding them. It was about four or five seconds of mulling before Terry could come up with something.

"You know when you're falling asleep, and sometimes, all of a sudden, your body just jolts you awake for seemingly no reason?"

Willow nodded, and Terry continued.

"I was drifting—sort of like you—but not in water. It was more like falling asleep, and then something jerked inside me, and I was snapped back to reality."

"Ope, there goes gravity," Willow chirped.

"Huh?"

"Never mind."

"Right..." Terry said. As accustomed to Willow's quirks as she was getting, there was still the odd outburst she didn't understand.

"So, was that all? Do you remember anything from when you were snapped back?" Orion piped in, which gave Terry a mild start. Talking to Willow about it had made her almost forget it was he who had given her the question in the first place.

Terry shook her head automatically but gave it more thought. A very small window appeared in her mind's eye, its tiny panes spilling light through a cluster of crystals that hung from a low ceiling, a ceiling too low for her to stand up properly without bumping her head.

She remembered confusion, fear, and an absence, like someone had been there with her as she had drifted off, but now that she was "awake," they were gone. She was alone—had been alone—in the first moments of her afterlife.

"I was alone... I think," she answered. "Does that make sense? I mean, I don't remember Dean finding me."

"Oh, well, that's normal. You don't always remember getting helped out, or the first few minutes."

"But I do remember someone being there, and they left."

Terry tried to watch Willow's expression, but at that moment, Dean's voice sounded from the doorway.

"That's enough reminiscing for today, I think." Terry turned to look back at him. His tone was jovial, but the way he met her and Willow's gazes Terry caught as strangely pointed.

"Apologies, Orion, but I'm gonna have to borrow my two girls for a while. Got some CS duty for them, and they can't very well get their hours if I don't drag them along." He gave Willow a wink.

Willow sat a little straighter as she noticed Dean as well. "Oh, yeah, that's right, Dean."

Seeming a little flustered by the interruption, Orion waved them off, and Terry and Willow rose to follow Dean out of the room, the question of the precise memories she had surrounding her death coming down the hallway along with her.

8. Terry Really Did Drop Her Plate

This newest Shepherd excursion to Earth took place at a skating rink that appeared to have been built somewhere between the seventies and eighties. Terry didn't feel confident enough in her coordination to try the skating part of ice skating, and she wasn't that big of a fan of the ice part, either. But it delighted Willow to no end, and she jumped into the line for the skate rentals the moment they were inside.

The rental line was queued up to the left of the entryway, and Terry could feel the rush of cold air breezing through the doors to the rink proper. She shuddered internally and shivered outwardly. Looking to Dean for direction, she hoped that this particular Shepherding wasn't going to be too messy. There were so many things that could go wrong at an ice rink, from the sharp blades on the skates to the slippery ice they glided on. Terry hoped that it wasn't going to be as bad as she thought it would be.

Dean seemed unfazed by their surroundings, looking, as he so often did, just slightly amused by everything and holding a secret that made his smile just mischievous enough to be annoying.

"So, do we know the target yet on this one?" Terry asked, following Dean over to the concession stand. She took a glance over to the line where Willow had gotten at least five spots closer to the skates. Willow waved and mouthed something like *what's your shoe size?* Terry waved and shook her head, hoping that Willow understood she did not want to skate.

"Not just yet, but we'll be around when whatever it is goes down," Dean said. "In the meantime, I want to grab some popcorn."

Terry raised an eyebrow as she watched him order his snack. "Do you get a kick out of this or something, Dean?"

"Of course not," Dean answered, taking his bag of popcorn from the attendant and turning back toward the other side of the rink lobby, popping a couple kernels into his mouth. "It's a tragic thing every time; it's a human life ending, P-Terry. But it's easy to become a little numb to the tragedy after the first hundred times. You gotta find a way to make it interesting."

"So... popcorn?"

"Not in a 'let's watch the carnage' type of way. I just wanted a snack. Don't be so morbid."

"Right, like I shouldn't be morbid when somebody here is about to die."

"Let's not focus on that part," he said. "Let's focus on the fact that the soul departing today will be going on to the next great adventure."

"That sounds corny enough to be from a greeting card," she said. Dean made a "pfft" sound and shoved her playfully forward.

"Go join Willow in the rental line. I need you both on the rink to be on the lookout."

Terry groaned, rolling her head to look toward the ceiling. "Come on, Dean. If I wasn't already dead, I'd think the person who was going to catch the bus today was me. Me and skating do not go together. I am *going* to fall on my butt, and it will not be pretty."

He gave her another gentle push from the shoulders. "You'll

be fine. Just stick with Wills; she knows what she's doing."

She groaned again, a tad softer this time, but she complied. She shuffled along, dragging her feet to where Willow still stood now two more people ahead in line. Terry joined her, and, thankfully, no one behind them said anything about her joining the line so close to the front. Willow beamed as they got closer and closer. Once they were finally at the front of the line, she told Willow her size. Willow ordered them two pairs of skates. Terry was surprised that they were so close in foot size, since she was shorter and more petite than Willow by a few inches. By "petite," of course, she meant "figure of a twelve-year-old boy," but Terry supposed that didn't have too much bearing on how big her feet were.

Handing the attendant their shoes, Terry and Willow followed the cold air through the doors to the ice rink. At least Terry had her hoodie on; she was not a fan of the cold. She sat with Willow on the benches as they laced up their skates, Willow assisting her by tightening her skates as much as possible.

Terry noticed Willow shiver a bit while she sat tying her own skates, and she wondered why Willow decided to wear such a short babydoll dress to someplace so cold if they could change their clothes with a mere thought.

"I know we didn't know where we were going today, but why don't you—you know—do the thing to change your clothes?"

Willow, her skates securely on, stood on wobbly legs to find her balance. "It only works while we're in Purgatory," she said. "But don't worry. I'm fine."

Willow held out her arms to steady herself and nearly fell over before grabbing hold of a bench on the outside of the rink.

Dean finally emerged from the lobby, a pale-yellow cardigan draped over one arm.

"Look what I found in the lost and found," he said, holding the cardigan out to Willow, which she gratefully accepted once she had regained her footing.

She donned the sweater and pulled it close to her, giving

another shiver but smiling still.

"Thanks, Dean," she said, and he gave her a one-armed side hug before Willow began to carefully step on her skate blades toward the entrance to the rink floor.

Terry had finished standing and finding her balance while this was happening, and she began to wobble after Willow when Dean stopped her, putting a hand on her shoulder.

"All right, I've got the info. The schedule says the bus will be here in about forty-five minutes. So, we're going to have to locate the target before then. Look out for Wilhemina 'Billie' Berkowitz. Female, age thirty-seven, blonde hair, light skin, green eyes."

"And once we find her, then we can leave?" Terry asked.

"Hey, you're supposed to be making an effort and participating and such," Dean said. "Plus, you know Wills won't want to leave yet; she's already got the hang of it." Terry looked in the direction Dean pointed to see Willow already skating laps around the rink floor, trying to do some sort of trick skating move and managing not to fall flat on her face.

Terry sighed. "All right, I'll be on the lookout. I'll tell you when I find them. Just let me know when it's time."

"Ten-four," Dean said. "In the meantime, though, try to have some fun, all right?"

"I'll try," she answered with another sigh and flashed him a strained grin.

She saw him sit down on one of the benches and made her way to the ice floor. Taking a tentative step and holding onto the rink's rail for dear life, Terry started to glide along on the blades. After a few long strides, she felt confident enough to only hold onto the rail with one hand, and she watched as Willow did laps around her, now somehow able to skate backward and on one foot.

After about the fourth or fifth lap around the rink to Terry's second, Willow slowed down to a stop and then tried to match Terry's pace.

"Are you sure you're not too cold?" she asked Willow, whose

PurgaTerry

tiny skirt of her dress fluttered with her movement.

Willow shook her head. "Nah, I was only a little bit cold. I just forget that we can feel it when we're here. It's no big deal. But how about you coming away from the rail?"

Terry considered it with a wary gaze toward the center of the rink; there were small children who had come onto it after Terry gliding along the middle unaided now. It felt like she was the only one who was still sticking to the sides.

"I'll hold your hand for the first lap, how about?" Willow offered, holding out her hand while she tried very hard to keep to Terry's snail speed.

Terry was wary, but she went ahead and took Willow's hand anyway, allowing her friend to pull her away from the relative safety of the rail and out into the wilds of the center.

She tried to match Willow's strides, mimicking her movements as they skated along, gliding past some of the other skaters as they gained speed. Terry hoped that Willow wouldn't go too fast too quickly. She was still new at this, after all.

"So, why haven't you cried yet?" Willow asked. Terry sighed and frowned at the question, shoulders sagging. She had hoped Willow would let this go.

"I don't know. It's like I told Orion, I don't think I really cry."

"That's silly, everybody cries sometimes."

"I don't know what to tell you, Willow. I guess I've been too focused on figuring things out here to feel sad about it."

"But I mean, it's okay to mourn yourself. What you lost."

Terry wasn't sure what Willow wanted her to say or do. Did she want her to burst into tears right this second? Even before she died, Terry could sense that she wasn't one to show big emotions. And maybe she had been too preoccupied with how to get her memories back to really ponder the loss of those memories and the life attached to them.

Maybe it was because—in Terry's mind—she didn't need to mourn it or them. She was determined to figure out a way to get them back, so what would be the point of crying over it?

A small rut in the ice caused her to stumble, but Willow held onto her, appearing to drop the subject for now. "Don't worry, I've got you," she said, pulling her gently just a little bit faster than Terry wanted to go. "Want me to teach you how to spin?"

She reluctantly agreed, and soon, the two of them were in the dead center of the rink, hands joined, spinning in tandem and managing not to get dizzy. Terry wondered if they were just that good or if that was one of the benefits of being dead. The only thing was she was a little afraid of letting go and what would happen once they stopped, but Willow guided her into a slower spin and showed her how to dig her toe pick at the front of the skate into the ice and stop.

They were starting to have a fairly good time, making a game out of gliding across the middle along with the younger kids instead of merely doing laps around the rink. Terry hardly noticed it was time until Dean caught her eye and tapped an imaginary watch on his wrist.

"Crap," she said, now looking around. "Willow, we need to find the target."

Willow was attempting to make a weaving pattern in the ice when she looked up, suddenly reminded she was working.

"Oh, right, what was their name?"

"Wilhemina 'Billie' Berkowitz," she answered.

"Hmm, that's not a common name, but it's not like we can just start shouting for a 'Billie' randomly."

They both looked around, as if Billie would just suddenly jump out and wave her arms around.

Then Willow shot forward, calling back to Terry. "Hang on, I have an idea!"

She slowed down to the entrance of the rink and hopped off to Terry didn't know where, but she went ahead and followed, searching for her or Dean, finding him first.

"Willow said she had an idea. Do you know what she's got in mind?" she asked Dean, who just shrugged.

"Beats me, but Wills will have it covered, I think, then we can locate the target."

A minute or so later, Willow reemerged holding a brown leather wallet, and she made a beeline straight for the rink again, mouthing to Terry *lost and found* before returning to skate, going up to some of the strangers, holding out the wallet, and asking for their names.

After a few tries, Willow smiled again as she skated away from a middle-aged-looking blonde woman, pointing excitedly and giving the thumbs up toward Terry and Dean. She then intentionally tripped over her skates, knocking into Ms. Berkowitz and falling on top of her. Terry watched as Willow apologized and helped the woman up, taking note of how long the physical contact was between them and wondering just how much of it was needed to numb her. But the woman appeared to take the 'accident' in good faith and left Willow with a smile as she made for the rink's entrance.

Willow followed her to the entrance where Terry and Dean waited. She grabbed the rail and gave a small pout.

"Okay, so we did it. Can we stay like... twenty more minutes?"

Terry could tell she was trying to do big puppy dog eyes at Dean, but she didn't think Willow needed to bother. Dean had anticipated this, and Terry was quickly discovering that when it came to Willow, Dean was a pushover. If only he was so accommodating to her in her search for information about her memories.

"Take thirty. Terry and I will do the rest," he said. Willow, it seemed, didn't need to be told twice. She shot off again to try more tricks that Terry wouldn't dare.

"You gonna join her?" Dean asked, turning to Terry as she leaned against the wall and the glass that separated the rink from the rest of the arena-sized room.

She pursed her lips but shook her head. "Nah, I've had my fun, and I participated some. Plus, it sounds like you'll be making sure I do my work, too."

"That I will," Dean said. "I've got you motivated, but every now and then, I gotta use the stick instead of the carrot to keep things even."

He took a few steps closer, leaning against the glass beside her, both of them now taking turns watching their target and watching Willow. Billie Berkowitz was now skating beside two children, and Terry felt a pang of guilt at the sight of such a happy-looking family about to have probably the worst day of their lives.

"She's a mother," Terry said. "She's got kids, at least. How do you stand it, Dean?" she asked. "We're about to take her away from her children."

Dean was quiet for a long time, his eyes watching the family, too. He was right beside Terry, but she could sense that he was far away in that moment. She remembered then what he had told her about his own family—about his daughter—and her guilt only magnified.

"Oh, I'm sorry. I forgot about—"

"It's fine," he cut her off. "I might not have told you, but Angie tends to save me the more interesting cases. There are only so many car accidents and cancer cases one can handle at a time. Well, she also tries to make sure I don't do kids, but sometimes, these things can't be avoided. It's true what you said, we're probably about to ruin skating for those kids forever. But no matter how it happens, I try to remember that we don't make the bad things happen. We don't cause the death. We are Shepherds; we Shepherd them, and that's it. All we have to do is pick up the pieces afterward."

He went quiet again, looking serious for once. "It does get hard to watch sometimes, but you have to focus on the good you're doing, because the bad part has nothing to do with you. Usually."

"Usually?"

"In your case, I mean," he said. "Mine too, and Willow's. We chose to leave the world early; that was the only time we made the death happen. And now, we have to pay for it."

PurgaTerry

"And nobody has to pay for it when the ticket gets punched on time?"

"Nope. That's the natural end point of the life, or at least, the end point this whole universe decided for them. I don't pretend to know everything, but that's what I do know."

"That's where you're wrong," Terry teased, trying to ease the tension. "You pretend to know everything all the time."

He smiled, looking more like himself again. "That I do, Ms. P-Terry," he said with a chuckle.

"So, I really did it, then. I really did kill myself."

Dean nodded, not looking at her, his eyes back on the skaters. "Yup."

"And you're still not going to tell me why I did it?"

He shook his head. "It's personal to you, even if you can't remember it. Why would you want to know the whole story, anyway?"

"Why am I not allowed to? Shouldn't that be my decision?"

"Normally, it is."

"What does that mean?" she asked, trying to prod him again, inspecting his face to see if she could see a tell.

"Nothing," he answered. "It's classified—need-to-know basis—and this is one time when you really don't need to know."

She set her jaw, trying to get into his line of vision so he could see just how frustrating that type of answer was to her. But he was very good at avoiding gazes, just as good, in fact, as he was at avoiding questions.

"I'm not gonna pretend I don't know what you were feeling then or what you're feeling now," he said, "but one of the whole points of Purgatory and its system is to help you move on from your past life. Purge those previous sins so you're ready for whatever comes next."

"Says the guy who is also still clinging to his past," she said.

"That's... that's different," Dean said. "It's something that Cass and the other managers let me do. It's part of my moving on process, I guess. Gotta make sure those I left behind are taken care of. April was part of my unfinished business, I guess."

"Do I have to deal with that?" Terry asked. "My unfinished business?"

"Probably, but that should be what you're doing in your group sessions and the like," he said.

Terry supposed that the whole 'purging' thing was supposed to be her finishing up her unfinished business and letting go of her old life or whatever, but she really did think that there should be a better way of going about it. The system that Purgatory had now… Terry couldn't help but find it flawed at best, rife with unfair contradictions and room for errors at worst. She knew that she didn't have much control at all, being at the bottom of the bottom of the bottom, but Terry sincerely thought she could come up with something better. Something more workable and fair than what Purgatory offered now.

"You don't find this whole thing unfair? she asked.

"Of course it's unfair, Ter," Dean said. "Nobody said that life or death were supposed to be. But no matter what, in the end, you did the unfair thing to yourself; you decided to end your life. That was pretty unfair."

"So did you," she said, a tad defensively. "And why does that mean I have to be punished in the afterlife?"

"Don't think of all of this as a punishment," Dean said. "It's not, P-Terry. It's a chance to fix things, to make amends to that life you had that you robbed yourself of. Your past self needs closure, and this is what was decided would give the living Terry that closure."

"It still seems flawed," she said in a mumble.

Dean sighed. "Don't I know it. But until someone comes up with a better way, this is what we've got. I do have regrets, you know. Not about the Shepherd work, but about being here in the first place. I can't fully blame myself for what happened; I was sick in the head and the kind of profoundly sad that I couldn't drink away."

"So, if you were to go back, you'd do it differently?"

PurgaTerry

"In a heartbeat."

"So, why can't we have that?"

"That's not the natural order of things. You throw out your meal before you're done with it, you can't root through the trash to fix the plate up like it was. At some point, you have to accept that you wasted food and move on." He then perked up, going "full Dean" again. "But hey, we're getting awfully existential about things here, aren't we? You'll figure things out in your own time. Remember, you've got a while yet in your time here."

There he went again, dodging the hard topics and her questions. But this time, Terry didn't find herself quite as frustrated with him. She sort of understood his side of it for once. It was a difficult subject to talk about, even as two dead people. But Terry didn't think that that should mean avoiding the subjects altogether. She had a feeling that was part of the problem and reason for why they did what they did in the first place.

"What if we made that question number six?"

"Are you saying you wanna cash in your next five questions?"

"I mean, as long as you're okay with it. You are the one with the answers and the one who proposed the whole question game."

Dean shrugged with a chuckle, holding out a hand for her to continue. "By all means, cash them in. It'll be a while before you get your next ones, though. Remember, you only get the twenty."

This way, at least Terry might get him to stay on the subject, and he wouldn't be able to brush her off. At least, not so easily. Terry had to think carefully about what to ask. How could she spin all of the questions she had into a simple yes or no format?

"So, 'did I really kill myself' is question six?" Dean clarified.

Terry nodded. It might seem obvious, but there was still that part of her that needed true, verbal confirmation.

Dean seemed all at once surprised and bemused by this. "You're here, aren't you? I mean, you're a resident of Purgatory and all. I feel like this might be a waste of a question."

"Just answer it, Dean," she said, her words coming out more amused than anything. She wanted to get some of the more obvious questions out of the way, now that she had the first burning ones about her brother sorted.

"Yes, as previously stated, you did," he answered. They grew silent as Terry let the answer sink in from its place hovering in the space between them. Terry watched Willow skating some more, to give her eyes somewhere to look before asking the next question.

"So, I'm really meant to be in Purgatory?"

Dean scoffed. "I don't think anybody really *means* to be there, but yes. You ended your life, you came here. Them's the rules."

"So, there were no external or extenuating factors in my case?" Terry asked, watching him intently for this question and trying to see any minute change in his expression that might give something away.

After a long (far too long in Terry's opinion) moment, Dean replied. "Yes."

"Yes there was, or yes there wasn't?"

"You're just gonna have to take that answer, all right? It's the best I can do," he said. "You only have two more left in this round. I'd think carefully."

"Would you tell me if there were… extenuating circumstances?"

"You're wasting another question, P-Terry."

"So, you can't tell me?"

"I didn't say that."

Terry was growing frustrated again, which tended to be a natural occurrence where Dean was concerned.

"I… I can tell you that I wouldn't keep something from you that you didn't absolutely need to know," he said, at last. "I'm bending the rules enough just playing twenty questions with you. There's things you're just not allowed to know."

"I get that—well, I don't really—but I get that you think I can't handle the answers."

"It isn't about being able to handle things, not all the way. It's about giving you a fresh start here on Level Eight so you can try and improve yourself and your situation without all the stuff

PurgaTerry

from your old life bogging you down. Whether or not there were any extra circumstances surrounding it, you did die by your own hand. We— I'm just trying to make things easier for you here than you had in life."

She couldn't help but smile a tiny bit at his revelation. So, he did care in some capacity—actually care about her and her well-being. That was certainly more than most of the other managers she had met. Cassiopeia seemed to care in her own way, but Dean was the only one, so far as Terry could tell, who actually appeared to want what was best for her. She wanted to believe him, to trust that she really didn't need to know everything. But it was difficult. "Okay, last question for this time around," Terry said. "If there was something that I needed to know about my death, would you tell me about it?"

Again, she analyzed his face to gauge his reaction. She thought he was going to avoid her gaze again, as he had done several times in the past. But he paused, looked directly at her, and answered.

"Yes."

Okay, Terry thought. She believed him, for now. She trusted that he sincerely believed that she didn't need to know any other factors around how she died. That didn't stop her from wanting to know more, because there was obviously still at least one thing that he wasn't telling her, but she could at least let that part go, for now. Time would tell if she would be able to circle back to learning about the day she died and just why Dean wanted so much to avoid the subject.

Maybe it had been her conversation with Dean that day or the group therapy session that had stirred up her subconscious, but for the very first time since coming to Purgatory, when Terry fell asleep, she dreamed.

Willow had told her that sleeping too much in Purgatory was

probably not the best idea, but Terry only chalked that up to Willow not wanting to know anything more about her past life. She didn't consider that these flashes of dreams she received were actually snippets of her own memories. Most of them were too short to really get a grasp of what they contained. A flash of a watering can, the view off a porch into a yard lined with trees, the feeling of cold clinging to clothes when someone came in from outside to give her a hug.

But soon came more substantial ones. Driving in the rain, then idling in her car in a parking lot, the rain pounding onto the roof of the car as a song played quietly on the radio. The song played as she wiped away hot tears, singing about ten million fireflies and the singer getting misty eyed as they said farewell.

Some—like that one—were so vivid that she could feel the tears running down her cheeks, feel the barrage of heat coming from the car's overworked heater, and hear the rain that continued to fall all around, making striped shadows in her headlights.

She could sense that it was significant, this memory, but she didn't know why. Like so many of the clues she had, Terry could sense their importance, but she just couldn't reach out to touch them.

Another dream came soon after—or memory—of hiding away in a bedroom, curled and cocooned in her blankets after an argument with—someone. And then hearing the distinct sounds of a disk being inserted into a DVD player, and the familiar first few notes of the score for a movie. Her favorite movie. She sat up from the bed, pulling the cover cocoon along with her, and eased herself up as she crept to the door to peek out into the living room beyond.

Her brother, Hatori, smiled from his recliner, remote in hand, ready to hit play on the film. He had paused right at the opening title. Terry could have cried if she didn't feel like she was all dried out from crying earlier. She made her way to the couch, and the two of them settled in for the movie, Terry feeling in that moment that—though she still wasn't all right and didn't

PurgaTerry

think things were going to get better—for the next hour and a half, she was okay. Because she had someone who cared enough to be there for her.

She woke to the drab sunlight of Purgatory streaming in through the window, Willow's bed empty and made, and tear stains on the pillow beneath her head.

9. Does Being Dead Make You More Attractive or Something?

There were no clocks in the resident areas. Indeed, the only ones Terry had seen were at the Main Hub and the bus station. And, since the activity room had no windows, it wasn't easy to tell what time it was supposed to be. But she was fairly certain it had been hours since they had started this game of Uno. All of their fellow residents had left the room for their quarters or to who knows where, leaving only Terry, Willow, Juliet, and Asher to complete their game. Their game which nobody seemed to be winning.

Willow had the most cards at seventeen, and Terry had the second most at twelve. The one with the least number was Juliet, but she was far too hesitant when it came to laying down one of hers.

The used card pile had become the regular stack so many times that Terry had lost count. She was getting immensely tired of seeing the same cards played over and over again.

"We've been at this for ages," she stated to the group as she lowered her cards. "I'm ready to call it if you are."

"Oh, but this is fun, Terry," Willow whined. She appeared to be the only one who still thought so.

"Um, I think Terry is right," Juliet piped up. "We could at least end this game and start a new one."

"Or better yet, just stop playing," Terry said. "It seems like every time one of us gets close to calling 'Uno,' we end up with a 'draw four' or something equally bad."

All three of the girls looked to Asher, who hadn't chimed in with his opinion. He actually hadn't said much in the last hour, and just like the other times Terry interacted with him, Asher was difficult to read unless he spoke.

"If Terry wants to admit defeat this easy, she can go right ahead," he said with a shrug. "It's not like she was gonna win this thing anyway."

Terry could feel Willow giving her the side-eye from her right and then a gentle nudge with her elbow. "Ooh, that sounds like a challenge, Ter."

"A challenge for a kid's game that I don't even care if I lose," Terry said. "I could just bow out now and take a break. This has been going on forever, and there are no stakes. There's nothing to keep me interested."

"What if we make it interesting?" Asher asked, which gave Terry pause. She looked across the table at him quizzically as he laid his cards face down in front of him.

"How so?"

"How about a bet? Whoever wins gets to take the person of their choosing to the Hall of Knowledge. One of us in the group, that is."

"The Hall of Knowledge?" she asked, then Willow answered.

"It's where all the information in the world is stored. That includes media, too. So, music, books, movies, and tv shows are all stored there. The Level Eight branch is pretty sparse and a decade or so behind on their selection, though."

"Even so, it's a great place to spend your downtime if you get permission from your manager," Asher continued. "And it ain't

PURGATERRY

hard to get permission if you've filled your quota for the day."

"That's also where a lot of people go to um... socialize," Juliet added. The way she was fidgeting with her sweater's sleeve made it seem like that wasn't all Juliet heard went on there.

"If by 'socialize' you mean 'hook up,'" Willow said. She must have noticed Terry's visible cringe at the prospect. "I mean, you don't have to hook up there, it's just that tends to happen a lot, and that's one of the reasons you need a manager's permission to go."

So, at best, this sounded to Terry like some sort of Purgatory dating activity or make out spot. Was there even dating in Purgatory? What would even be the point? This was a transient, liminal space; nobody who came here was going to stay put.

Willow had seemed to be an anomaly to her, in more ways than one, but her vested interest in getting some alone time with Juliet was a new—and big—one.

Still, she had become a friend, and Terry was only occasionally bothered by Willow's consistently sunny demeanor. She could play the game to try to help Willow win some time with Juliet.

She gave Willow a glance that she hoped conveyed she was going to be trying to help her win.

Terry thought she saw a hint of mischief in Willow's smile. Maybe she had the same idea as Terry about this wager.

They started the contest from where they had paused, with Juliet selecting a card from the top of the stack.

Terry had a handful of yellow number cards, a couple of blue ones, a "reverse" card, and one "draw four" wild card. She had been saving it for just the right moment.

Juliet added the card to her small collection. Evidently, she had no blue cards or cards with the number two on them, as a blue two had been what Asher had last laid onto the used pile.

Next, it was Terry's turn. Thankfully, one of her yellow cards was a two, and she hoped that meant a change in luck for her so that she could start getting rid of them.

Then came Willow's turn, and she pulled from her fan of cards a yellow "reverse" card. That meant that it was Terry's turn again.

There was no mistaking the sly grin Willow gave her as she put the card on top of the pile. She had a plan. Terry just hoped that they were indeed thinking the same thing, trying for the same outcome.

Terry went along with it and laid down another of her plethora of yellow cards, and then Juliet placed down yet another.

Asher laid another down in kind, this time utilizing the number and switching the color to green.

Terry saw Willow's eyes brighten.

"Reverse," she stated with a flourish, laying down a green color "reverse" card. It was back to Asher, who promptly placed onto the pile the black wild card with its display of each color used in the game.

"Red," he called the color change. *Shoot,* Terry thought. She didn't have any red cards, and she didn't want to have to use her own wild card unless she had to.

Once it was her turn, she decided that she might as well draw from the stack, and she had soon pulled out at least five cards before finally managing to pull out a red card. It was a red "skip" card, and as she laid it down for the others to see, she could see Willow's smile brighten even more.

Terry's card now meant that Willow would be skipped and that it was Asher's turn again. Willow did not look disappointed at all.

Asher put down another red number card, making his total down to five cards in his hand. Juliet had four, so if this game was ever going to end, they were the favorites to win.

Terry's goal was still to play in a way that would allow Willow to win and have her date with Juliet. But every time she tried some sort of strategic card move to give Willow an advantage, Willow would just drop it in favor of one of the other two.

She gave Willow a sidelong look, silently asking her what she thought she was doing. Surely her friend had caught on to what Terry was trying to do for her.

Willow avoided Terry's eyes, choosing instead to appear very fascinated with her own cards.

Juliet, too, looked like she wanted to ask Willow about her behavior, and Asher—unreadable as always—did not appear to have noticed anything.

Finally, the seemingly-endless Uno standoff was nearing its end. Whatever Willow was attempting seemed to get the game closer to being over. Terry and Juliet only had three cards each, while Willow and Asher had one apiece.

Willow had been the first to call "Uno," and it all came down to Juliet. Terry had accidentally seen her remaining cards when Juliet was distracted, and she saw that one of them was a "skip" and one was a "reverse." If Juliet played the skip, it would skip Terry, allowing Willow to lay down her final card and win the bet.

Terry saw Juliet stare down at her cards, then glance up to match gazes with the three of them in turn.

She might have imagined it, but from Willow's expression, it looked as if she and Juliet were having a silent discussion. She looked back and forth between the two, until Juliet hesitantly pulled out her "reverse" card and placed it on the table, face up.

Asher promptly slammed down his last card.

"Well, looks like Asher wins, darn," Willow said in a very poor imitation of defeat. Terry gave her an incredulous look and tugged Willow's elbow, pulling her up from her chair in one smooth movement.

"Excuse us for a moment, would you?" She smiled at the other two as she tugged Willow along to the other side of the room where the pictures from previous residents covered the walls.

"What were you doing?" she asked. "I thought you wanted to win to hang out with Juliet."

"I do wanna hang out with Juliet," Willow answered. "But it's not like we haven't been to the Hall of Knowledge before."

Terry raised an eyebrow at her, remembering what they had said happened in that particular hall. "What do you mean by 'been to the hall'? Like been there or *been* there?"

Willow scoffed at the accusation. "No, no, not like that. I mean, believe me, I want to. But no, I just meant we've seen it and experienced enough of what the hall has to offer. You've never been, and it's obvious that Asher wants to take you."

"What do you mean 'it's obvious'?" Terry whispered, trying to make sure they weren't overheard.

Willow rolled her eyes but matched her volume, leaning in conspiratorially.

"I mean, I think Asher really likes you, and you haven't seemed to notice one bit."

Terry sputtered. "What— I don't think— No, you're crazy."

"Am I? He doesn't seem to be able to keep his eyes off you, and, when he suggested the bet, I could so totally tell it was about trying to get a date with you."

"But— I mean— I didn't do anything to make him like me," Terry said. This whole business was triggering her anxiety. What had she said or done that made Asher think these things about her, if indeed Willow was right about this?

"You didn't have to," Willow answered. "Attraction is a weird thing, believe me."

"But do I have to do anything? What if I don't want to go on a date with him? I haven't thought of him that way. I don't think I've ever thought of somebody that way. At least as far as I can remember."

"If you want my opinion, I think you should give the guy a chance," Willow said in a way that clearly got the message across that she was going to give Terry her opinion whether she wanted it or not.

"I mean, we'll all be here for a while—some more than others—so we might as well enjoy what little there is to enjoy around here."

Terry looked over Willow's shoulder to see Juliet and Asher both watching them. And for the first time, she noticed that Asher's eyes were indeed trained on her and only her. His expression was, for once, clear. He was looking her over, contemplating something, and it made Terry wonder if there

PurgaTerry

really was any validity to Willow's claim.

Her stomach churned with uncertainty. She didn't want to lead him on if she ended up not reciprocating his assumed feelings. But on the other hand, he seemed like an okay person. If not attractive to her, at least attractive in the conventional sense that Terry could recognize. He hadn't said anything unkind or offensive that she could recall. Of course, he hadn't said much around her at all. But maybe that meant he was shy.

Willow appeared to notice Terry's mental quandary, for she tilted her head and lifted both her eyebrows in a gesture of "Well?".

"If you want, I can decide for you," she said. Then, after a few seconds of Terry making no moves to do anything but stand in the picture corner, Willow turned around and called over to Asher and Juliet.

"Okay, so what did the winner decide? Who's gonna be your choice?"

Terry followed, trailing behind Willow's determined steps back to their friends.

Asher looked from Willow to Terry, giving her a smile that was not dissimilar from the one he had when he'd won.

"If she'll agree to it, I think I'll take Terry."

She heard Willow give a tiny squeak of excitement as she looked between Asher and herself. Clearly, she was enjoying the show and was expecting only one outcome—a positive one.

Although it was still just the four of them in the room, Terry felt as if she were on display. How could she say no with other people watching? Willow's eager face pleaded silently with her to follow her advice and give this guy a chance.

Terry tried to avoid her gaze as well as Asher's, her anxiety at being put on the spot probably extremely evident. She grimaced as she waited one more moment before giving a soft sigh of resignation.

"Sure, Asher. I'd like that."

She heard Willow give the expected squeal of delight at her response, and it did sort of feel good to see Asher's face brighten up when she answered.

"But, if it's all right, I'd like Willow and Juliet to come, too," she said, tapping the surface of the table between them that was still littered with Uno cards. "I'd just— I'll feel more comfortable if I know they're there, too. They don't have to stay with us the whole time, though. If that's all right."

Asher shrugged, his smile fading a little, his unreadable shield being put back in place. "If that's what ya want. Get the okay from your manager, and we'll figure out a time."

Willow then began nudging Terry toward the exit to the hallway. "She will! She can't wait! Well, see you guys tomorrow!" she called as she continued leading Terry out of the rec room and down toward their own room.

"What was that?" Terry said as she wrenched herself free from her friend's grasp. Now that they were in the hall, Willow let her go and grinned like a Cheshire Cat as they neared their room.

"Brevity, my friend. Gotta leave him wanting more." She gave Terry a wink.

"But you didn't even say goodbye to Juliet."

"That would be my own activation of 'less is more.' You have so much to learn."

"From you?"

"Of course. I'm much more experienced in these things than you."

"How do you know? I'm older than you, you know. You don't know how experienced I am or not in... things."

Willow gave her another "Please" look.

"For one, nobody with any experience in dating or love or sex would call them 'things.' And two, I may look younger than you, but that's only because I died younger. I'm stuck being seventeen forever, but, technically, we're around the same age. Who knows? I could be older."

She overtook Terry as they entered their room, Willow sashaying around her and doing a little hop to land with a bounce on her bed.

PURGATERRY

"In any case, though, I've been here longer, so I'm more worldly about the ins and outs of Level Eight than you. So, just trust me, okay?"

Terry nodded with a sigh. "Sure, Willow."

With that, Willow bounced herself to the head of her bed and shimmied under the covers, leaving Terry to sit on her own bed, finding her reflection in the mirror to her other side. Looking herself over, she didn't think there was much to see or be interested in. Forget conventionally attractive, Terry thought she looked more like a slim cardboard box with limbs than a person. No curves to speak of. And her choice of wardrobe wasn't exactly alluring either. She had continued to keep the outfit she'd arrived in, only adding shoes and always her gray hoodie.

What exactly was it about her that made Asher interested in her in the first place? She still didn't know if this was a good idea or not. But she did suppose Willow was right about one thing. She was going to be here a while—at least according to Dean—so she might as well try to find some enjoyment in her time here while things got straightened out. Whether or not she was the one solely doing the straightening.

Who knew? Maybe something in the Hall of Knowledge might spark something in her memory. Silently, she held onto that hope as she prepared for bed. She had to. It was the only thing that made this whole mess just a little bit easier to bear.

10. Dean is the Corniest Man Not Alive

"Please, Terry?"

"No."

"Pretty please?"

"I don't care how pretty the please is, I don't want to go out with Asher." Terry was instantly regretting that card game, and especially accepting the bet. Now Willow wouldn't leave her alone about it.

"Come on, T. He likes you, I can tell," Willow said in a knowing, sing-song voice. "He always singles you out when we see him. Plus you already said you would."

"That doesn't mean anything," she said. Terry hoped that they could finish this conversation and that Willow might drop it before they reached the bus station. They had arranged to meet Dean there for once instead of him coming to them all of the time. She would never hear the end of it if Dean found out something like this.

"I don't like him that way," she said. "I don't even know if you can like someone that way here."

"I sure can," Willow replied, sounding mock-offended. "This is my big chance for a date with Juliet. Plus, Asher seems really cool, and he definitely likes you. Maybe if you give him a chance, you'll find you like him back?"

Terry tried not to look skeptical about that and failed.

"I don't think that's how it works, Wills. At least not for me."

"You don't think you had a boyfriend or girlfriend when you were alive?"

"Not that I can think of," said Terry, and before Willow could retort, she added, "And I know I can't remember much, but I think I'd know my own feelings and if I ever had them or not."

"So, you don't think you've ever had those feelings?"

Terry shrugged. "It doesn't sound right for me."

"Well, it sure does for me," Willow said, sighing and wistful. "I knew from when I was four and saw Elisa from that *Gargoyles* cartoon."

"Okay, we need to get you some new references, ones that aren't animated and/or owned by a mouse."

They were coming up on the bus station now, and Terry hurriedly shushed Willow as she saw Dean jogging toward them.

He met them less than a block from the building then stopped, hands on his knees, to catch his breath. This was yet another thing Terry found odd about Purgatory. How did one become winded in a place like this, *after* they'd died?

She knew better by now than to ask, though. At some point, Terry had just come to accept the weirdness of Level Eight. Although she didn't have much to compare it to. She had yet to visit the other seven floors of Purgatory, which were off-limits unless authorized. Not that that had stopped her before, but Terry now had a one-track mind when it came to doing her community service work: to get those answers to her twenty questions.

And that goal certainly did not involve going on a date.

"You okay, Dean?" Willow asked.

"Yeah, yeah," he said, standing back up straight. "Just had something to tell Terry before I forget."

PurgaTerry

Once he had caught his breath, the three of them started for their designated bus, but not before Dean caught her by the shoulder, a huge grin forming on his face.

"Hey, Terry, why can't you hear a pterodactyl go to the bathroom?"

Clearly he was setting her up for a joke, but she wasn't in the mood to play along. Stepping on the punch line would be more fun.

"Because they're extinct," she answered.

The speed at which his smirk turned to a frown made Terry grin mischievously.

"'Because they're extinct,'" he mimicked her in a high, tinny voice. "Ha ha ha, no. It's because the 'p' is silent."

Terry closed her eyes, shaking her head at the cheesy pun as Dean guffawed at his own dumb joke. It wasn't the worst pun imaginable, but she found the fact that Dean was the only one laughing funnier than the actual joke.

She rolled her eyes, trying to hide her smile as Willow joined in on the laughing with her own giggle.

"Oh, P-Terry, don't be a 'saur' loser," Dean added. "Get it?"

Terry nodded enthusiastically. "Oh, I get it. Can you take a breath and get us on the bus already?"

"You bet Jurassican," he said, giving her finger guns, as it appeared he couldn't help cracking just one more pun before they boarded the bus.

"Okay, it's time for the dinosaur jokes to go extinct," Terry said. "How about you save some of that verbal energy for my next five questions, which will be, when?"

"Don't you worry," Dean said. "They're coming up soon. Why, perhaps even after this very Shepherd assignment." He then added with a whisper, his hand close to Terry's ear, "And I've got a million of those jokes, so don't worry about that either."

"Oh, joy," she replied.

They neared the station, but not before Willow did the exact thing Terry was hoping she wouldn't do and spilled the beans to Dean.

"So, Dean, is it okay if we get clearance to go to the Library in the next few days?"

Terry blinked, and Willow explained, "Just another name for the HoK."

"I don't see why not." Dean shrugged. "It'll be just the two of you?"

Terry's eyes widened pointedly as her lips curled into a line, silently begging Willow to not explain any further.

Willow ignored her silent protest and grinned slyly. "Oh, we'll be meeting Juliet and Asher. I will be supervising Terry's first date."

They were finally in the large entryway, the buses were within sight, they were so close to their destination and yet so far. Dean halted, turned on his heel, and stared at her, visibly surprised.

"Her what now?"

Terry winced, the heat of embarrassment creeping onto her cheeks while Willow bounced beside her.

"Terry's got a date," she chirped, hugging Terry's arm while Terry herself wished she could melt into the floor.

"It's not— I don't— I lost a bet." She pulled her hoodie sleeves up over her hands for something to do while under Dean's shocked expression.

"Still, Ter, this is a positive development." He nodded, his smile from earlier returning. "At least you're out there socializing, making friends that aren't just me and Wills here."

"See?" Willow squealed. "Even Dean thinks it's a good idea."

"Dean isn't the boss of me," Terry grumbled.

"Actually, he kinda is."

Terry rolled her eyes. "You know what I mean. He isn't the boss of my love life, or my lack thereof."

"I wouldn't say I like Asher too much from what Cass has said, but who am I to stop you?" Dean interjected.

"You are absolutely in your right to stop me."

"And stunt your progress around here? Nah. Think about how

PURGATERRY

good this will look to Cass when she hears about it."

She didn't think it was entirely fair of Willow to pimp her out like this just so Juliet would feel more comfortable on her and Willow's date. They were supposed to be friends, but perhaps Willow would consider this 'what friends were for.'" On the other hand, Terry did kind of owe her, and she had been nothing but supportive of Terry's goals and hopes.

She squeezed her eyes shut and tilted her head toward the overcast sky, groaning in preparation for what she was about to agree to.

"Oh— Fine, I'll do it," she said, bracing herself for Willow's squeal and hug. She was not disappointed.

"Really?" Willow cried, jumping up to hug her exactly as Terry had envisioned her doing. "Oh, thank you, thank you, thank you!"

"I am already regretting this," she said through a crushed torso.

"No, you won't, I promise! You'll have such a good time. Plus, you'll be watching movies or shows, and you're supposed to be quiet during those anyway, so you won't have to do any awkward small talk or anything," Willow said as she finally released her.

"I'm not making any promises that I'll end up liking him," Terry added. "This is all for you, Wills."

"And I am so grateful, you have no idea!"

"Aww, this is sweet and all, ladies, but we need to catch our bus," Dean said, jerking his thumb toward the bus station they had gotten no farther into.

"Right, sorry, Dean," Willow said as she skipped past him, clearly too thrilled to even act like she was sorry.

"Hope you have fun on your date, P-Terry," Dean said as she passed him. "No coming home late, and make sure he is a gentleman."

"I thought you didn't like him," Terry said, not turning around as she followed Willow to the door of the bus station's office.

"Well, I'll give him the benefit of the doubt. Like I hope Cass gives you. You're a big girl, and you can handle yourself. I would say 'make sure to use protection' but given you're both dead—"

Terry covered her ears to block his words from activating her gag reflex. "Ew, Dean! I think I prefer the dumb dad jokes."

They disembarked at another park, this one much closer to a large city. Terry was so distracted by her surroundings, she forgot to ask Dean why they were so far from their intended destination.

But she was not nearly as distracted as Willow. Her friend had been dancing around behind them, lagging behind as she skipped and twirled, singing to herself about how life was better down where it's wetter, under the sea.

Terry was about to ask as she got back on her train of thought when Dean spoke up.

"Hold on a second, Ter—" He held up a finger for Terry to hold that thought and called out behind him, "Wills! That's enough! No more songs from the mouse today, okay? Switch it up."

"Can it still be a musical?" she called back, from further away than Terry thought she should be.

She turned to see Willow climbing up onto a fountain they had passed at least two minutes ago.

"Pick up the pace, and it can be," Dean said, walking halfway back to the fountain before Willow hopped down and sprinted to meet him.

Catching back up to Terry, Dean smiled as he caught his breath, shrugging animatedly as if to say "well, what can you do?"

Willow from that point on stayed close behind them, not wandering off but going through what sounded like her whole wheelhouse of songs. Terry tuned in and out as they walked, but she did enjoy Willow's rendition of "Pure Imagination."

"So, what was I saying?" Dean asked as they walked, nearly out of the park now.

"You were going to tell me why we were walking through a park when we have a schedule to keep."

He waved her words away with a hand. "Eh, we've actually

got plenty of time. We don't need to be there for at least an hour, and we're set to arrive at the scene well before then. I just decided to take the scenic route so Willow could get some energy out. She likes a good bit of sunshine every now and then. Refills the batteries."

"Okay," Terry said, guiding him back to the actual point he had drifted from.

"And I thought today would be a perfect day for your next five questions."

"Really?" she asked, surprised that he would offer up the next batch of questions so soon. "That makes fifteen. I thought you said I'd be here for a while. What's the rush?"

"Oh, look at you, actually wanting to turn down some answers for once? Are you starting to get used to things around here? Perhaps even enjoy your company?"

"*Some* of the company," she corrected. "That manager of mine gets on my nerves sometimes."

"And yet, you'd be lost without him."

"But really, you know I wouldn't turn them down, but is there a reason you're making this offer?"

Dean cleared his throat as if he was about to answer her question, straightening a bit and slowing ever so slightly.

"Are we there yet?" Willow whined as she lagged behind them again.

"A couple more blocks," Dean said, and Terry could tell that the moment he might have told her what was up had passed. They had exited the park and were now in a section of this city (whatever city it was) with brownstone buildings and tiny shops in neat rows all along the sidewalk they traveled.

Like the other times before, their fellow pedestrians' eyes simply looked past or even through them as they walked along with the flow of foot traffic. Terry supposed they had to really make their presence known to be able to interact with the living population properly. She assumed she might need as much practice with that as she did with Shepherding. She was getting bumped into with annoyingly regular frequency, but she noticed that Dean and Willow were as well, so at least there was that.

They passed through a Chinatown district, and they had to practically pry Willow away from one shop that had knockoff Pokémon figures. Terry had to admit, the oddly-shaped creatures were sort of cute in an ugly way, and she enjoyed laughing at their blatant off-brand quality with Willow.

The closer they came to their destination, however, the more all-business Dean became. Or at least, as "all-business" as he could ever be in Terry's opinion.

"Everything okay, boss?" Willow asked when she, too, noticed the change.

"Yeah, I'm fine, Wills," he said. "I just want to get this one done so we can get back to the station."

They came up onto a small music shop on their left, Dean checking the schedule again before nodding and gesturing for them to go in.

The shop had a hanging sign in the shape of a cello with the words "Cello Goodbye" and a sign on the window that read "Cello Good-buys for everyone, Minor to Major."

"Oh, you'll like this place, Dean," Terry quipped as the bell over the door jingled when she opened it.

"I already do." Dean chuckled. "We're looking for Damien Ewan Batey. Twenty-seven, six-foot even, sandy hair, green eyes."

"Is that him?" Willow pointed to a guy fitting that description a bit farther away, near the back of the store, talking to an older woman, both wearing vests with the Cello Goodbye logo on them.

"Ooh, he's cute."

"I thought you didn't like guys," Terry said as she leaned in so Willow could hear her in the small but fairly loud space.

"I don't, but objectively, that man is cute." She then brightened. "Let's let Terry do this one!"

"Let's not." Terry shook her head, holding up her hands to shield both Willow's and Dean's gazes as they landed on her.

"Why not?" Willow whined. "It'll give you Shepherd practice

and guy practice."

"One of those things is not necessary right now." She turned to Dean, hoping he'd side with her. "I mean, we're on a schedule, right?"

Dean shrugged. "It's not the worst idea. You need to get your feet wet. I'm for it."

Terry should have known. He didn't even allow her to protest, holding up a finger to silence her before snap-clapping his hands and pointing in the direction of Damien Batey.

"Make sure you numb him before anything happens," he added.

"Do you know what's gonna happen?" asked Terry. But Dean had already walked off. She wasn't sure how she was going to be able to touch this guy. It was one thing when they'd already dropped like James Hembree, but a perfectly lucid and healthy man was another.

The shop was crowded as well, but Terry noticed that a few of the customers were seated at small tables on stools, some testing out various instruments, plucking out tunes or tapping keys. He was assisting some of them and answering their questions; maybe she could take that route.

Choosing one of the ukuleles on display, she pulled it down and brought it to one of the stools.

She had no idea how to play an instrument of any kind, but Terry thought she at least knew how to hold one. Holding the long part in one hand, she took her right hand and gently gave the strings a strum like she had seen on TV. She apparently wasn't gentle enough—or not holding it tight enough—for the force of her strum sent the entire ukulele clattering to the floor. It might have just been her imagination, but whether or not the living actually paid them much attention, she could swear that every single eye was on her in that moment, staring and judging.

Thankfully, it did the trick. The man Damien came over immediately, looking apologetic and encouraging.

"Here, let me help," he said, holding out his hands for the ukulele. Terry handed it to him, settling back into her seat and wondering just how red she could get with embarrassment when she didn't have any blood flowing through her. She returned his helpful smile with a sheepish one of her own.

"Maybe string instruments just aren't my thing," she said with a nervous laugh.

"Don't give up on your island tunes just yet," he said, tweaking the little pegs on the neck of the ukulele to make sure it was in tune. "You're right handed?" Terry nodded.

"Ok, then you use your right arm to hold the ukulele in place so your left hand can move between chords and your right hand can strum. Try it again with a lighter touch as you strum," he said as he handed the ukulele back to her.

She took it with a hesitant look his way; she really didn't want to have to pay for a broken instrument. Or make Dean pay for one, since she was pretty sure she didn't have any money.

She tried to hold the ukulele the way he had shown her, holding it steady under her right arm. He hopped up and moved three fingers on her left hand to form a "v," each finger on a different string.

"Try that, that's a G chord. Just strum with the other hand, lightly." He emphasized the last word.

She did as he instructed, and the sound that came out wasn't that bad. And what was more, Terry was able to keep the ukulele in her hands the entire time.

"Now this one is one of the more high-end ukes," he began a sales pitch. "You could probably get the best quality sound from one of these, but just between you and me, the more mid-range-priced ones are just as good and like, thirty dollars cheaper."

"Are you sure you should be telling me this?" she asked. "Don't you get a bigger commission for selling more expensive things?"

He laughed. "Well, I also make it a point to give pretty ladies like you a deal."

Terry blinked at him. Pretty ladies like who, now? He couldn't possibly be talking about her. She wasn't used to compliments like that. Between him and Asher, she was beginning to wonder

PURGATERRY

if they did indeed see something she didn't.

"Uh... thanks," she said lamely. She had no idea how to return the compliment, or even how to answer. It had thrown her so much that she had nearly forgotten her mission and that this nice, not unattractive guy was about to get his ticket punched.

She assumed that she could use his flirtatious vibes to her advantage, if only she knew how to be flirty herself.

She gave him another smile, a bit broader this time, and tried to bat her eyelashes like she had seen women do in movies, hoping she didn't look like she was having some sort of episode. "Do you think you could show me another chord real quick?"

He obliged eagerly, hopping back over to her side and manipulating the posture of her fingers once more. Terry tried to focus and pull her proper emotions to the surface, for she wasn't sure how much time she would have nor how much skin to skin contact was required to make the emotional transfer.

She decided it wasn't quite enough physical contact, as she didn't feel much, if any, of the numbness she was trying to transfer. But she still allowed him to guide her fingers and show her how to form a couple more chords.

It was only when Dean reappeared hovering over them that Terry noticed how close the two of them had become. When Dean cleared his throat, she jumped away from Damien, hopping up from her stool and handing the ukulele back to him.

"Honey, did you find the one you want for your birthday?" Dean asked her pointedly. "Did you get the right feeling for one?"

"Uh, not yet—Dad," Terry stammered out her answer, hoping she was communicating what she thought she was, that she hadn't had enough time to numb him.

"Well, I guess just thank the nice man for giving you a complimentary lesson," he said, making her feel like an eight-year-old, but giving her an idea all the same.

"Yes, right. Thank you so much." She then tried not to giggle at his face as she pulled him into a hug, patting his back as she hurriedly tried to convey her emotional manipulation to him so he wouldn't feel what was coming.

When he finally pushed her away, Damien was still looking confused and a little weirded out but managed to say, "You're welcome," and "The Luna ukes are on that wall, if you want to keep looking."

They then watched him head off to help someone with a grand piano, opening the lid to where the strings and hammers were. As he was doing whatever he was doing inside the piano, he appeared to be caught on one of the strings by a shirt button. He didn't appear to start panicking until he began to choke, and Terry and Dean were out of the store before the lid fell on top of him.

His soul appeared in front of them right on the sidewalk. It was truly perfect timing, as the bus was pulling up right as they walked out.

"Sorry about this," Terry said to him as he stood in confusion, looking around as people began to walk through him. "At least we were able to numb you so you didn't feel anything."

Dean then took the ticket that had appeared in Damien's hand and punched it. "Now all you have to do is get on the bus behind you, and the nice driver will take you where you need to go."

Damien glanced at Terry and then Dean, utterly bemused. It was a look Terry was getting used to the souls having at the beginning stage of death. "So, what's going on? Why am I out here? Did you change your mind about the ukulele?" he asked.

"Sadly, no," she said, trying to be gentle about his predicament. "I mean, I don't know about the ukulele, I might go and pick one up; they seem fun. But you don't have to worry about it. You don't have to worry about anything anymore, actually."

When he still looked confused, she continued, "Just go ahead and show your ticket to the driver, and you'll get what I mean."

She smiled, trying to be encouraging without actually having to tell him the exact words "you are dead," and hoped that it was implied, and he might get it through context.

Terry assumed she had done a good enough job at hinting

PurgaTerry

about things without outright stating them, since he turned and began to climb the steps to the bus, only turning back when Dean called out to him.

"Hey, can I just ask? Did you really think she was pretty?"

"Dean," she blurted and whapped him lightly on the shoulder, scandalized that he would ask that.

"What?" he asked with a flinch at her hitting him (it wasn't even that hard). "You were looking mighty adorable and cozy before I came up. I just wanted to know if he really thought you were cute or if that was just a sales tactic."

"It shouldn't matter either way, as he is now no longer alive," she said, speaking low to try and keep Damien from hearing them.

"Ah, but neither are you," he replied with a wink.

Terry rolled her eyes. "Are you trying to pimp me out to every dead guy we Shepherd?"

"Not every guy, just ones who think you're pretty."

"Just drop it, Dean. It wasn't that big of a deal."

As they were bantering, Damien had boarded the bus, and it was beginning to drive off down the street. Neither Terry nor Dean paid it any mind as they continued down the sidewalk to find Willow.

"It's not like I'm going to be dating in Purgatory anyway," she said. "I don't think I want to, in any case."

"But what about your little date with Asher coming up?" Dean asked, causing Terry to groan.

"That is going to be a onetime thing to help a friend."

Dean nodded, his expression deadpan as he replied, "Sure, P-Terry."

11. Terry Gets Unintentionally Emotional

The bus stopped at a building across from a gas station. Apart from off roads that led to some residential streets, there weren't any other buildings around. It stood out among the fields on either side—semi-modern architecture against a pastoral backdrop.

"Liberty Senior Care" titled the building on the sign above the looped driveway. Terry figured that this was a much more typical place to be Shepherding a soul.

The sliding glass door was locked with a keypad, a round silver call button next to the numbers. Dean pressed the button, and the tiny speaker crackled to life.

"Yes?" answered a voice.

"We're here to see Ms. Phillipa Arnold," Dean stated, somehow able to remember the name from the file he had only been handed a few minutes ago.

"One moment," the voice answered. A few seconds later, a woman appeared wearing scrubs covered in a pink butterfly pattern. She must have punched the code in on her side, for the door slid open, and the three of them walked in.

"You'll need to sign in, but I'll show you to her room once you're done."

"Thank you," Dean said, a heaviness to his voice now that made Terry stop and turn to seek his face. He was putting on the act of a grieving loved one, and she wondered if she and Willow should be affecting that vibe in their faces as well.

She could tell Willow was trying very hard not to smile, and Terry decided her neutral expression looked sufficiently sad.

The nurse led them down a hall to another door that needed a code, and once inside the smaller wing, they were ushered to a tiny room in the very corner of a hall connected to a small, open activity room. Terry thought it looked a little bit like their residence in Purgatory. If this Phillipa Arnold was bound for Level Eight, at least she wouldn't be thrown by her surroundings.

"The rest of the family is in the main dining hall, if you want to go and meet with them," the nurse said.

Dean nodded. "We'll probably do that in a minute. I just—" Terry tried very hard not to raise her eyebrows at the hitch in his voice. "I just need a minute to say goodbye."

"Of course," the nurse said. Leaving the three of them alone, Terry saw her sit down and pull out her phone.

The woman in the hospice bed did not acknowledge them. Her limbs were twisted up close to her body, and her mouth was wide open, taking gasping breaths.

Only her eyes moved in the vague direction of Dean as he approached, that one slight movement the only thing revealing she was still conscious.

Dean shook his head as he took in Phillipa's form. He tutted. "Poor thing, she's trapped in this worn out husk. This lady is ready to be Shepherded."

Willow looked a bit more somber as Dean got to business, pulling out his pen and beginning to fill out some paperwork.

"These cases are always more sad for the families they leave behind," Willow said. "Once she's out of there, her soul won't feel so trapped."

"You say it like living is a prison," Terry said.

"No, that's not it at all," Willow answered. "What I meant was that—at this stage—it kind of is. She's stuck inside a body that won't work for her anymore. This is the kind of end the living should all hope for. Peaceful and prepared, after a long, happy life."

Dean looked up from his papers. "Willow, care to do the honors?"

Willow smiled, reaching her hand out to stroke Phillipa's hair, but Terry caught her by the wrist to halt her.

Something about this didn't sit right with Terry. Sure, she looked peaceful and ready, or however Willow had said it, but it made her ache inside that they were doing it when Phillipa's family wasn't in the room.

"Shouldn't... shouldn't we wait until her family comes back? Give them time to say goodbye?"

"She's ready now, Ter," Dean said. "And if we wait for the family, she might miss the bus."

"Plus, we don't want anyone asking questions," Willow said. "This is kind of a rare opportunity to Shepherd an elder without having to distract the loved ones."

Terry took in both Willow's and Dean's expressions; both of them seemed sure that this was the way to go. It still didn't feel right to her. She was alone, and her family would miss it. What if they hadn't had a chance to say goodbye? They should. People should always get a chance to say goodbye when someone they love leaves them.

Then she realized the irony of what she was thinking.

It wasn't the same though, not at all. Ms. Phillipa here would probably go directly Upstairs, to be greeted by other loved ones long since passed. Terry only wished that she could get just one last chance, though. One last minute for her final words.

Dean appeared to be reading her mind, for he gestured for her to come closer to where he stood beside the bed.

"Listen, I know what you're thinking right now. I thought the same things when I started doing this. You have to have some manner of separation though. This is about Ms. Phillipa here, P-Terry, not you."

He was right, of course. Somewhere inside her, Terry knew that she was being silly. Her death and this woman's were different. That didn't change the fact that neither of their deaths felt fair in the slightest.

Willow had wiggled her hand out of Terry's grip to gently hold her friend's hand. Terry found some solace in this simple gesture.

"Okay," she said. Letting go of Willow's hand, she lifted hers toward the woman's silver hair instead. "Can I do it, then?"

Dean stepped aside, surprised at Terry's request, but not unpleasantly so. "Be my guest."

They both backed away a few steps to give her some room. Terry found a chair and sat down at Phillipa's head, feeling uncomfortable just standing over her looming. Her fingers barely touched the woman's fine, wispy hair. She concentrated on exuding a feeling of calm, trying to picture in her mind what peaceful felt like.

Terry breathed in slowly, letting it out just as slow, and stroked Phillipa's head once, twice. She swept the stray hairs from her face and attempted a soothing stroking motion, all the while trying to transfer numb, soft vibes.

Phillipa's eyes and mouth began to slowly close, her muscles relaxing and her arms lowering to her sides. She stopped gasping, her breaths now shallow but even.

Terry barely noticed when Dean punched her ticket, for she was so focused on the woman's face, making sure to gently lull her into the afterlife, and making certain that Phillipa knew that she wasn't alone.

She nearly jumped when Dean placed his hand on her shoulder. Terry blinked and turned to look up at him, as if coming out of a daze.

"Look who's here," he said. There, beside Willow, stood

PURGATERRY

Phillipa, or rather, her soul. She beamed at Terry, mouthing a *thank you* before Willow led her toward the bus that now sat outside her window.

Terry and Dean made the silent decision to discreetly exit Phillipa's room before her family returned. They stood in the hallway that connected the open space to the residents' wing, Dean nodding his approval.

"Nice job, kid. I'm impressed."

She smiled, then thought she should seize this opportunity. "Impressed enough for five more questions?"

He chuckled. "Right to the point, huh? Well, I suppose so, but again, we'll have to go somewhere outside Level Eight."

"We're outside of it now," she said.

"Outside but not on official business," he added.

When Willow returned, they took a moment to get their bearings before Dean led them back outside. The nurses had already been inside the room and found the empty shell that was once Phillipa Arnold. Terry heard one of them radio to call the family in.

"Wait," she said, grabbing Dean by the elbow. "Can we wait until her family gets here?"

He looked skeptically at her. "We don't want to draw attention."

"I know, but— I just want to see them."

Dean sighed through his nose, head tilting. "Fine. But just a couple minutes, then we gotta go."

He turned to Willow. "Go ahead and call for our bus. That'll give Ter a couple minutes."

"Sure thing," Willow said and walked back toward the sliding glass doors.

"Thank you," Terry said.

"I'm only doing it for you this time because I know it was your first real one—not counting the one Willow and I forced on you—so it's a little more personal," he said. "But we can't be hanging around and chatting with the loved ones of every soul we Shepherd, got it?"

CELIA CLEAVELAND

"Absolutely," she answered, smiling more than she probably should be when about to go and try to comfort people in bereavement.

The family didn't rush into the room demanding to see her, like in the movies. Most of the adults somberly eased inside, a couple halting at the doorway before joining the rest. There were five in all, a woman probably in her sixties, a man about the same age, two men looking about their forties, and one girl who couldn't have been older than twelve holding the older woman's hand.

The little girl let go of her hand and backed away before entering the room. She looked like she had been woken up from bed, her matching pink pajama top and bottom contrasting with everyone else's normal-looking clothes. Her shoes were the only thing that didn't match her Pj's, and the laces weren't tied, so she must've been in a hurry.

Halting just shy of the door, the girl backed away a little more, even when Terry heard the girl's family quietly call for her.

Terry bit her bottom lip, uncertain if what she was thinking would be the right move. She couldn't blame the girl for not wanting to approach. At that age, Terry didn't think she even gave death a second thought. This might have been her very first interaction with the reality of the concept, and that caused something inside of her to call out to the girl.

Although she was removed from the grief, Terry knew what she was going through, and perhaps that was why she approached her. "Hey," she tried, getting the girl's attention. Terry thought to put her hand on her shoulder, but thought better of it. This girl was a stranger, after all.

She turned to look at Terry, her eyes skimming over her clothes.

"Are you a nurse?" she asked.

Terry shook her head. "No, I'm just visiting."

"Oh," the girl responded. "Who are you visiting?"

Her question was natural, but her tone had an edge, as if she were trying to figure out why this complete stranger approached her.

It made Terry feel even more awkward.

"Uh," she said for a loss of words. "Let's um— Do you want to sit down over here?" Terry gestured toward a gray couch not far from Phillipa's room, close enough that the girl's family could peek out and tell Terry to get lost if they wanted. With one more quick, guilty-looking glance to the room, the girl nodded and followed Terry.

They sat on either end, the girl bouncing slightly as she settled onto the seat, her feet not quite touching the floor. "So, who are you visiting?"

"My, uh... my grandpa, Floyd," Terry said. "But we're getting ready to go in a bit. The girl didn't respond; she looked down at her hands. Her pink cell phone rested in them, but the screen was dark.

"Is this, um, your first time losing someone in your family?" Terry asked.

No response again, only her fingers running over the edges of the phone.

"What's your name?"

She thought the girl might not answer, or tell her to leave her alone, but after a few seconds, she heard her soft voice answer, "Audena."

"Hi, Audena, I'm Terry." Terry attempted a smile that she wasn't sure Audena saw.

"Listen, I... I just saw you over here and noticed that you didn't seem to want to go in there with your family. Who was she to you?"

Audena met her eyes, looking even more guilty than she had earlier.

"Meemaw, my great-grandmother," she said. "But I didn't know her really well."

"Ah," Terry said, automatically understanding where the guilt was coming from. Audena probably felt about as removed from her family's loss as Terry did.

"So, you weren't that close to her?"

Audena shook her head. "Grams took care of her for a little bit when I was a baby, but she's been in places like this for as long as I can remember."

Taking a risk, she went ahead and placed a comforting hand on Audena's shoulder. "You know that's okay, right?" she asked. "To not feel as sad as everyone else?"

She looked uncertain, her fingers fumbling and turning on the phone's lock screen for a moment.

"But Grams, Gramps, Dad, and Papa are all so sad. They used to bring me here sometimes, but it was just... weird and kinda scary seeing her in her bed."

"And you're more sad for them? Or you feel like you should be sadder?"

"Yeah, am I a bad person?"

"Of course not," Terry said. "Just because you aren't as sad as they are doesn't mean you didn't love her, too, in your own way."

She thought for a moment, wondering if this girl was old enough to get things spoiled for her and for it not to matter.

"Do you believe in Santa Claus?"

Audena blinked at her. "What?"

"I'm just asking if you still believe in him."

Now Audena definitely thought Terry was crazy, but at least she gave her an answer. She shook her head, a tad sheepish.

"Okay, so you don't. But just because you don't doesn't mean you can't enjoy seeing younger kids who still believe in him. It's a little different from you, but it might make you feel better to play along for them."

"I don't get what you're talking about."

Terry hmmed, unsure if she was being clear. "Maybe it's not the best analogy, but what I mean is that your family in there right now is grieving. They probably don't expect you to be as sad as they are right now, but you can pretend to be as sad, to help them cope. Be there for them and match their vibes, I guess, but don't ruin the illusion."

"You're right, it's not the best analagy thing," Audena said.

PURGATERRY

"Look, I'm trying to make you feel better about this. You don't need to feel guilty is what I mean. All you can do is just be there for your family."

"Okay," she said. Terry didn't think she had helped much at all, but at least this girl knew now that she wasn't alone, and that she didn't need to feel guilty. She just wished that she had better material than some weird Santa Claus metaphor. Even if that's kinda what she thought Dean would come up with.

Remembering Dean, she looked up from the couch to find him, spotting him on the opposite side of the room, watching her. He looked approving, or at least he didn't look *disapproving*, so maybe Terry was doing some good in his eyes. She wondered, though, if this girl really wanted to be sad, or if Terry had the power to do that.

She placed her hand on Audena's shoulder again, concentrating as she had done over Phillipa, this time pulling from within herself the grief that she felt at her own losses. The grief from losing her life, her memories, all that might help her figure out who she used to be. There were other random flashes of emotions too, a sense of loss similar to Audena's—a grandparent—and something for a pet, and—Hatori. Something had happened to Hatori.

This realization caught her off guard, and before she knew what was happening, her eyes had teared up, her throat felt tight, and she lost her grip on the feelings, allowing them to cascade over her, leaving tears running down her face.

Through the haze of her own sudden onset of grief, she could see that Audena's face mirrored her own. Her face was splotchy and tears left streaks down her face. Her breath came out in hiccups, and she sniffed as she leaped from the couch and ran into the room, her grandmother swiftly coming to comfort her and close the door.

Terry tried to wipe her face but was yanked sharply by the elbow. Dean pulled her up to a standing position and marched her toward the glass doors, his face stony but this time far from pretend-sad. His eyes were burning, and Terry felt like crying even more as her heart sank into a pit in her stomach.

It wasn't until they were on the bus back to Level Eight that Dean even looked at her, much less spoke.

He took in a long breath, letting it out slowly through his nose, before turning to Willow. "Wills, can you go up a couple of seats? I need to talk to Terry."

Willow looked nervously from him to Terry, evidently unnerved by his tone as well. She did as Dean asked and left them alone, Terry feeling more and more as if she were about to receive a stern reprimand.

She wasn't wrong.

"I'm trying to see things from your perspective here, Ter," he said, the disapproval bubbling below the surface of his words. "I didn't hear what you were saying to that girl, but I saw what you did."

"What I—" Terry began, then remembered the feelings she had passed over to Audena.

"Yes, and I know you're still new at this, and you did do a good job today, so I'm not going to report this to Cass, but Terry, we *never* use our emotional manipulation on someone who is not our target. That is a big deal. You could be at risk of going straight Downstairs if you do that again, you got it?"

The timbre in his voice went from the low growl of disappointment to a hitched high tone of concern. Terry had never seen Dean so upset, and it didn't help her already guilt-stricken conscience.

"Okay," she reassured him. "I didn't know. I won't do it again, I promise."

He sighed, apparently accepting her apology and promise. "Okay, good. Just keep that in mind. I may not always act like it, Ter, but I'm looking out for you."

"I know," she said, and she meant it. Terry tried to convey that in her tiny smile, but it was hard to meet his gaze when there was still so much vexation there.

PurgaTerry

So, she'd done a good job and then spoiled it all in the span of about an hour, probably less. Terry didn't know if that was some kind of record, but she wouldn't doubt it.

It wasn't until they'd returned to their room that Terry spoke up. Now far from the angry, deeply disappointed eyes of Dean, she hoped that Willow might give her some clarity on just what exactly she had done wrong, and why it was such a big deal.

"I mean, I get that I made a little girl cry, but I don't understand why Dean reacted like that," she said once she and Willow had settled back into their room.

Willow hugged her pillow, sitting cross-legged on her bed and watching Terry pace in the space between their beds.

"It's not the crying thing," she answered. "It's more about manipulating a living person's emotions."

"What do you mean?" she asked, slowing her pacing a bit and walking to the other side of her bed toward the mirror on the far wall.

"I mean there's other things you could do with that power than just numbing a soul or making somebody cry. If you used it on the wrong person, it could hurt their whole mental state. Especially if they're in a bad mental state in the first place."

Terry came back around her bed to sit closer to Willow. She felt like she sort of understood what Willow meant but that her friend was still avoiding mentioning the real reasons for Dean's reaction earlier.

"Like, if a living person is depressed, or had depression, what's to stop somebody like us from emotionally manipulating them into feeling worse?"

"Why would somebody do that?"

Willow gave a nose sigh and loosened her grip on the pillow some.

"It's called 'cheating.' When... when somebody here in

Purgatory uses that power to make a living person want to kill themselves. It's one of the worst things you could possibly do here, and it's something Dean... something he really didn't want you to know about."

"What, did he think I'd actually do something like that?" Terry felt offended that their manager would think so little of her.

"No, no, no," Willow corrected. "It's just it's a really big deal, like I mentioned. But now I've told you, so at least you know why he flipped out like that. Just make sure you don't do it again, and everything will be fine, okay?"

"Okay," Terry said, repeating her promise she had made to Dean. Now when she considered her actions from earlier, she guessed it was sort of a big deal. She still thought it absurd that Dean would think she'd do something like that. Of course, she had died by suicide, but that didn't mean she wanted to put someone else through that. She didn't understand why that was even something someone would think to do.

But the way Dean had reacted, Terry felt small at the memory, mentally cowering away from the thought of such a disapproving, disappointed look from her manager. She'd keep her promise to them both. Even if she still didn't understand it fully.

She pulled down her covers and slipped underneath them, watching as Willow crawled to the head of her own bed to do the same.

Terry didn't want to bring it up again, but her mind wouldn't let it go quite yet. It chewed on the concept as she drifted off to sleep. What would make someone want to do such a thing? Terry supposed people could ask the same thing about what she'd done, about her suicide. Perhaps she should consider Orion's advice and look inward to understand what she could recall about that. Maybe then she'd understand some more. If only she had more memories to go on.

12. Have a Magical Day

Terry awoke the next day to a distinct lack of sound. Ever since she'd arrived in Level Eight, things had been deficient in the way of ambient noise, but she had at least come to expect the occasional hums or snippets of singing from Willow as she began her day. More than expecting it, Terry had come to rely on it. It was the only real way to tell when it was morning and time to get up. That or whenever Dean came in with the air horn.

For once, though, her questions were answered immediately and without actually having to voice them. A note was stuck to the mirror on what was designated "her side," and from where Terry was sitting up in bed, she could clearly make out the name "Willow" at the very bottom of the paper.

Rolling out of bed with an involuntary grunt, Terry rubbed her eyes free of any sleep remaining before standing to retrieve the note. It was short and more to the point than she would have expected from Willow, and the words themselves gave her pause.

"Went out with Dean, we'll be gone all day. He says you have the day off. Have fun with it!" then merely a drawing of a heart and Willow's signature. Nothing on what they were doing, where they were going, or what Terry should do in the meantime. It did raise more questions, but the ever-curious part of her was for once drowned out by the side of her that relished in the idea of free time. Of course, she didn't know what she might do with it, but it was time she had unsupervised by her manager. That could mean searching for more ways to find out more about her life. But the second that idea rose up in her mind, Terry shoved it back down. There was no way that Dean didn't enlist Cassiopeia or someone to watch her while they were gone, and, what was more, she did promise to do better and stop actively trying to snoop around.

If she really wanted her next five questions answered—the only sure way to learn anything about her past—she figured she should follow the rules Dean had laid out. Which did unfortunately mean following the rules of Purgatory, which still felt unfair and archaic. But they were what she'd been given.

The day dragged on slowly without Willow and her chipperness, and Terry wasn't all that sure about what she should do with this unexpected downtime. Finding Juliet in the rec room, Terry plopped down next to her just for something to do.

Juliet was quietly sketching a dog, some sort of small terrier, and she didn't look up from her paper to acknowledge Terry.

After a while of this, Terry began tapping absentmindedly on the table, which appeared to have finally gotten Juliet's attention. She looked up in a daze, as if wondering how she even got into the rec room.

"Oh, hi, Terry," she said, still appearing to be coming out of her artist's zone fog. "Sorry, I was really focused."

"I can see that," she answered then looked back down at Juliet's drawing. "That looks good."

"Thanks," she said. "It's not the best since I don't have a reference, but I think I remember a dog like this."

"That's a handy talent to have if you aren't allowed to remember things," Terry said. She was a tad envious that she, too, didn't have some form of artistic ability to help her with her search.

"So, I couldn't find Willow when I woke up this morning, and then I found this note she left me," Terry then showed the note to Juliet. "You don't know anything about this, do you? Have you seen Willow today?"

Juliet shook her head. "I've been the only one here for about an hour. I don't think I've seen her at all today." Juliet took out her notebook and began to flip pages thoughtfully. "What day is it, do you know?" she asked.

"Is that the kind of question you can ask here?" Terry asked, genuinely confused. Time did seem to work differently here than on Earth, but that didn't stop their superiors from knowing just how many days had passed in the living world, or how much time she still had to work off.

Juliet only appeared to be half-listening. Evidently unsuccessful in her search, she closed the notebook.

"Well, it must be today, or I don't think both Willow and Dean would be gone."

"What must be today?" Terry asked.

Juliet blinked at her, looking back down at her notebook hesitantly before answering. "Every year—or at least I think it's the same time each year—Dean and Willow go off somewhere together. It seems personal, so I've never tried to ask about it, but they're usually gone for a whole cycle. I just know that when she gets back, Willow is always so happy. So, it must not be anything bad."

"Then what are you doing today?" Terry asked.

Juliet shrugged. "I don't have to be at my post until my manager comes to retrieve me. He's leading a group session happening soon, so I guess I'm waiting around for that."

"Seems like there is a lot of waiting around that happens here," Terry said.

Juliet let out a sigh. "You don't know the half of it yet." Terry then watched as Juliet's gaze froze at the entrance to the rec room. She quickly turned, her blonde hair forming a curtain to shield her from seeing whoever it was as she fumbled for her pencil again.

Looking up to the entrance herself, Terry spotted Asher coming in—alone, as appeared to be his preference—hands in his jacket pockets and looking just as lost for what to do today as she did. When he caught sight of them, he wove through the tables with a growing smile.

"If it isn't Pj's, hanging out with Willow's girl behind her back, huh?" He pulled out a chair to sit backward on it beside them. Terry hadn't yet sat, so she decided to pull out the chair closest to Juliet and join her properly.

The relief she saw in Juliet's eyes was short-lived. Whatever Terry could sense between her and Asher, it set her blonde friend ill at ease.

Juliet pushed her chair back forcefully, scraping it against the floor loudly as she stood. "I-I need to go sharpen my pencil," she said as she tried not to trip over her chair on her way.

"What was that about?" Terry asked in a lowered voice, pointing with her thumb toward the shelf where Juliet was taking as long as possible to sharpen her pencil.

"Hmm?" Asher made a questioning sound before catching her meaning. "Oh, it's not a big deal. I know you hate being told stuff like this, but it's private between me and her."

Terry couldn't help but roll her eyes. "You're right, I don't like hearing that. But I guess I'll accept it for now, as long as she's okay."

"Oh, I'm sure she's fine, girl's just jumpy," he said. "If you wanna keep talking to me, though, we could go out into the hall. She's looking like she's about to lose her pencil in that thing."

Terry looked back over to Juliet, who was indeed grinding her pencil down further and further. It concerned her how anxious Juliet was acting, but if she could take Asher out of the room for her and alleviate that, she supposed she should. But as she nodded and stood to follow him back out into the hallway, Terry

PurgaTerry

looked back for a second at her friend-of-a-friend, wondering exactly what it was that was making her so "jumpy."

"So, did you want to talk about anything specific?" she asked when they had rounded a corner and were making their way aimlessly through the identical halls of the building. "I have the day off, apparently, so I've got nothing to do."

"How'd you swing that?" he asked.

Terry shrugged in answer. "Beats me. Honestly, that should pretty well describe my whole experience here so far. No answers, no forward movement in my opinion, just one enormous shrug."

"So, I take it you didn't have any luck at the Welcome Building?"

Terry blew air out of her mouth. "Nope, I guess once the memories are extracted or blocked or whatever, they're immediately stored in the Hall of Records. It wasn't a total loss though, because—"

She hesitated, not sure if she should divulge what Dean had shown her, nor if she should mention her arrangement with him. Even if Asher didn't seem like the strict, rule-following type, his manager was Cassiopeia, and she was definitely as rigid about rules as they came. At least as far as Terry was concerned.

And also, that afternoon with Dean had been sort of special, something that he had trusted her enough to show her, and Terry felt like it might be an infringement of that trust to tell someone else about it.

"Because I got to see it for myself," she backpedaled lamely. "It was a good tip all the same, so thanks for that."

"No prob, it was the best I could do at the time, with the managers watching and all. I didn't even get to tell you about my post in the HoR."

She halted in place, frozen from the shock. He had to be kidding.

"HoR? You work in the Hall of Records?" Terry asked, astounded. "I wouldn't think that any of us residents would be allowed. That place is 'off-limits,' as I have been repeatedly told."

Asher cocked his head and turned to stop in front of her.

"True, you do need special clearance to be able to get in, but if your manager or supervisor assigns it to you, your ID can let you in." He peered over her shoulder for a second, then leaned in and lowered his voice. "And once you're in there, security is a joke. They don't monitor you or what you're doing. That's how I was able to find out as much as I did about my life. The files are all in this weird code I couldn't crack at first, but with some help, I was able to find my file and decipher a few things."

"What kinds of things?" she asked, not daring to hope this might be the answer she was looking for.

"I already knew how I died, but in my file, I found out the circumstances. I had a girlfriend; her name was Serena. I guess when she died, I couldn't take it, and then I died to try and be with her."

"And do you know if she's here?"

Asher shook his head. "Nah, it said something about her getting an 'immediate pass' like most folks get. She's probably Upstairs, but there's no way for me to be sure."

That must have been why Asher was so adamant on getting his service done as soon as possible. This girlfriend of his was the only piece of his past that he had, someone he knew cared about him and could give him answers. It was natural that he'd want to speed up the process.

"Do you... do you think you could find my file for me and help me decode it?" she asked.

"I can't just take it out of the building; my supervisor would catch me. She's already on my case as it is. Plus, I don't know what happens to the files if they get taken out anyway."

"What do you mean?"

"You take something out of the Library, it'll disappear and reappear back where you got it from. I haven't tried, but I guess it's the same thing if you take a file from the HoR."

"Well, maybe you could write it down for me or something?" she asked. "Make a copy somehow?"

"They'd search me on my way out for that exact reason. I guess people have tried to do that in the past."

"Well, then, how can I get in there to see my file?"

"You could ask me nicely," he said. "I can lend you my ID card, and it'll let you in and let you get to your stuff. You'd need someone who knows how to decipher the code, though."

"How did you manage it?"

"I had somebody teach me what they knew. A lot of the residents will trade favors for each other, help them out if they happen to work in different departments and have certain skills."

"So, you had someone help you?"

"I couldn't risk writing it down, so I memorized as much as I could. You could probably do that. Or have someone who knows it go with you. Mine chickened out."

"Who was yours?" she asked.

"Juliet," he said. "She wimped out, but I wasn't that shocked; she's not the most courageous of folks around here. I'd ask your friend Willow, too. She's been here a while, and she and Juliet are pretty close, if you know what I mean."

Terry thought she did, and she definitely did like the idea of getting Willow to come along if she was okay with it. She trusted Willow probably the most out of anyone she'd met in Purgatory. If anyone could help her and keep it a secret from Dean, it'd be her.

Of course, she had held secrets for Dean from her before, but that was before Willow knew how much finding the answers meant to her. Surely her friend would be able to keep things from their manager if the opposite was true.

"So, all I need is your ID card. How does that work?"

Asher flipped his card out of his pocket and held it between two fingers, almost as if offering it to her then and there.

"It's registered to me, so whoever holds it has access to all the stuff I do. The places, the information, the powers, all of it. You trade IDs for one night, and trust me, we can both get what we want."

It was more than tempting, that was for sure. Terry didn't

even mind the danger of repercussions that getting caught might yield. It was strange that he wanted her card in exchange for his, though. She didn't know what he could need it for. Terry didn't have any special access that she knew of.

"What's in this for you? Why do you want my card?"

Asher smiled. "So, it's like that, huh? I see you, you gotta know all the answers. I guess I don't blame you. Your card can get me back to Earth, and let's just say I've got some unfinished business I need to take care of and leave it at that. I don't need to know what you find out when you use mine, so you don't need to know what I do with yours. I told you we could help each other out," Asher said. "So, you in?" He held out the hand that contained his card.

Terry eyed his hand for a second, eyes flicking up to his face momentarily. She wasn't sure how much she trusted Asher, but that might have been just the fact that Dean wasn't sure about him. As much as he annoyed her with his lack of helpful information, she had grown to like Dean, and she usually trusted his decisions, even if she didn't like them. She should probably trust his sense of character as well.

But at the same time, Asher was offering her the chance to get answers where Dean wasn't. Asher knew what it was like to be left wanting, to feel like a part of you was missing, and to have an urge to find someone connected to the past you weren't allowed to recall.

Asher was able to learn where his girlfriend was, and with his help, she might be able to find out her brother's whereabouts, too. If there was a chance that Hatori was Upstairs, or even still alive, she had to know.

It wasn't until another body slammed into her that Terry brought herself back to the world around her. She'd been so caught up in Asher's proposal that she hadn't even noticed as Puck had tripped right into her, knocking her to the floor.

"Oh, Terry, sorry," he said as he helped her up. When he was sure she was standing, he patted himself down and then started scanning the floor looking for something. "Crap, crap-crap-crap, did you see where it went?"

Terry was about to ask what he was talking about when she felt her foot slide on something. She moved it and bent down to pick up Puck's ID. He sighed with relief, snatching it from her without asking.

"Oh, thank God—or whoever—I am not losing this today," he said with a kiss to the laminated card he now held. Tucking it back into a pocket of his jacket, Puck began to make his way down the hallway once more. Terry was curious what that was all about, but she was going to mind her own business—she really was—until Puck called out to her from over his shoulder.

"Hey!" she heard him say and turned around to see him pause a few feet away. "Have either of you seen Jules? Is she in the rec room with Willow?"

Asher nodded. "She should still be there, but Willow's not with her."

"Apparently, she and Dean are doing some private thing today," Terry added.

Puck's brow furrowed for a second, but realization appeared to dawn on him. "Oh, it's that day. Wow, is it that day already? Aw, she's going to miss it. I'd like for her to come, the same as Juliet."

"Miss what?" Terry asked, for the moment ignoring that Puck evidently knew what mysterious activities her roommate and manager were up to, in favor of this new development.

"My farewell party," Puck said enthusiastically. He took out his ID again and brandished it in front of her face as Terry stepped closer. "Bam, I'm all out of P's, and I'm leaving today."

So it seemed. Puck's ID number—which was a similarly random jumble of letters and numbers as Terry's—now ended with a Px0, where Terry's ended with Px7.

"Wow," Terry marveled, legitimately impressed by this feat. Besides Willow, she hadn't known anyone who had even one P erased, let alone all of them. She almost thought it was a myth if she hadn't been assured of its existence by Dean. Seeing it, though, right in front of her, it filled her with something resembling hope. So, there really was a way out.

"I know, right?" Puck said proudly. "And I'll be on my way to the elevator in the Main Hub soon to go to the top floor. Buuut not without my little sister."

Terry nodded. "Yeah, of course. Juliet will be thrilled for you. Oh, and congrats," she said, probably a little too late to be polite, but Puck appeared not to notice or care.

"I'm sure she will be, partly," he said, stowing the ID away again. "The thing is, I was kinda hoping that Willow would be around on my last day to sorta... be a shoulder for Juliet to cry on, ya know?"

"I guess I can understand that," Terry said, not knowing just how long Puck and Juliet had been friends. "But how many people are allowed to come with you?"

"Oh, nobody can actually 'come with me,'" Puck laughed. "But I can bring a few people to the top level to see me off."

"What's at the top level?" Terry asked, knowing that it was probably top secret information that she wasn't privy to.

Puck considered her for a moment before answering, stroking his chin before pointing to her. "Why not find out for yourself? You said you've got nothing to do today, wanna hold Juliet's hand through this and see me off?"

"Sure," she answered, realizing a bit too late that she might have sounded more enthusiastic than the occasion called for. "I mean, I'd be happy to help."

Puck aimed a smirk her way, "I know what you really wanna do. You want to get a look at what happens when all of this is behind you. Well, Terry, I can't say for sure, honestly. But if you help Juliet through my departure, I'll let you go as far as they'll allow. You can bring your little boyfriend here, too, if you want. I'm sure Juliet won't mind."

Terry mentally cringed at the word "boyfriend," but she tried not to let it show on her face. She barely even knew Asher enough to even call him a friend, let alone that. She hadn't even gone on that date they were supposed to have yet.

"Sounds good to me," Asher said.

"Let's go let Juliet know, and I'll meet you up on the top level." Puck gestured for them both to follow him back to the rec room.

The Main Hub had eight floors, one for every level of Purgatory. Each one dealt with a different department of the various community services. Terry—as a Shepherd—didn't need access to the other floors, so she had never been allowed clearance to ride the elevator until this special occasion. Since they were with Juliet, they were allowed as long as they stayed with her, per Juliet's manager.

"I'm usually on Level Three for the Predetermination department," Juliet explained, indicating the number on the elevator's list of buttons. "But today, since we're seeing Puck off, we can go all the way up to Level One."

"They go backward?" Terry asked, wondering why Level Eight was at the bottom and One at the top.

"Yeah, I guess that's because Level One is directly in between Upstairs and Downstairs."

Terry took another look at the buttons while they waited for the elevator in the lobby. There were no buttons indicating what Juliet referred to as Upstairs or Downstairs, but it was fairly clear what she meant by them.

The sign on the wall next to the elevator doors listed each of the departments in a column. "Level One - Top Floor," "Level Two - Judgment Consultation," "Level Three - Predetermination and New Soul Integration," "Level Four - Hall of Knowledge Branch Keepers," "Level Five - Hall of Records Security," "Level Six - Scanning Machine Tech," "Level Seven - Transportation," and Level Eight, where they were. There was no specific department for Level Eight; it was only labeled "Welcome Center and Residences." Purgatory was bigger and more complex than Terry realized. She supposed that since Shepherds appeared to be the only ones who had clearance to board buses and travel to the living world, it would make sense that others also had specific clearance levels that limited what floors they visited.

What didn't make sense were the odd and fairly dirty looks that she got from some of the people they passed by.

"They do their community service on the other levels. A lot of them think they're better than the ones serving on Level Eight," Juliet said. "I don't think that way, but it's a weird kind of pecking order, and I guess somebody had to be at the bottom."

"Which makes us the bottom of the bottom," Terry mumbled, remembering Dean's words. "The managers around here don't seem to care that much about us, either."

"Technically, I think that'd be more the bottom of the middle," Asher mused. He was watching the lights above the elevator doors indicating which level it was on. It had stopped on Level Five for the longest time. Juliet had hit the button to call it at least five or six minutes ago.

"And this is the only elevator in the whole building?" Terry wondered aloud, mostly to Juliet.

"Sadly, yes," Juliet said. "You'd think with the number of people using them to travel between floors they'd have conjured up another one."

"Conjured?" Terry asked, thrown off a bit by the word choice.

"I don't exactly know what to call it when they add things," Juliet said. "Things just kind of... appear when they're needed or at least when the managers decide to add them."

"But, then, why don't they just do that?"

"It takes a whole committee to get anything done. That's what Orion says, anyway."

Finally, the lights began to change, and the elevator appeared to be descending down to the bottom floor.

The elevator dinged and the doors opened, letting off a few people Terry thought might be residents and their manager. She wondered just how many souls were in Purgatory; she had only been acquainted with this small part of it. It felt like every time she had one question answered, two more popped up to replace them, like the heads of the mythological Hydra.

They followed Juliet into the elevator, Juliet showing her ID badge to a small window next to the buttons, giving her clearance to the upper floors. She pushed the button with a number one on it, and the elevator doors closed. The semi-reflective surfaces of the walls were almost enough for Terry to clearly see herself, but only just. The lights around the buttons lit up white to match the several round inset lights above them. Oddly enough, she didn't feel any jostling of the elevator starting or stopping as she would have expected. The ride was a gentle glide upward, and before she knew it, they were at Level One.

"So, how are you able to get access to the top floor?" Terry asked.

"Well, Level One is where we send off souls for their judgment, but it's also where we send off the final blueprints of a new soul or a reincarnated one," Juliet said. "That's what my department deals with."

"You deal with new souls?" she asked. "Like, babies?"

Juliet nodded. "It's a lot more tedious than it sounds. You have to help design every aspect of the new soul's makeup, and it's much harder to make a person up here than you'd think down on Earth."

When the metallic doors of the elevator opened again, Terry stood in awe. She had no idea what she was expecting the top floor of Purgatory to look like, but she would not have guessed it to be the Garden of Eden.

Lush, green foliage surrounded them in every direction, gorgeously blooming trees with white and pink blossoms were scattered among the greenery, and a wide expanse of meadow was bursting with all kinds of wildflowers in every color and variety, some Terry had never seen before. Butterflies and hummingbirds flitted about between the flowers to the trees, and a three-tiered fountain sat close by, shooting and trickling water that left little rainbows of light as the drops fell.

Juliet led them in their exit, not seeming fazed at all by the botanical wonderland that surrounded them. There was a stone walkway past the fountain leading through the meadow, lined with trees that definitely would never be seen in the same place at the same time. At least Asher appeared to mirror her interest in their surroundings, even if he wasn't acting as astonished.

"Been a minute since I've been somewhere this nice," he said. "Really makes you miss being on Earth, huh?"

"This feels way more like I'd imagined the afterlife. You know, before I got here," Terry replied. "Too bad we don't get to come here more often."

"Honestly, this might be one of the only times before it's your turn to go," Juliet added, a bit more confident it seemed now that she was in her element. She didn't even seem shaken by Asher's presence anymore.

"So, Puck is going to be leaving from here?" Terry asked, trailing a bit behind the others because she just had to stop and admire the natural beauty of this place. She followed Juliet through the dappled light from the trees and along the walkway, having a very odd vague sense of déjà vu. This forest was lush, green, sunny, and hopeful, though. The memory that flashed in her mind was different. For one, clouds hung low over the sky above the trees in her mind, and there was no walkway to lead her. She recalled walking with purpose, no shoes to protect her bare feet from the sticks and rocks, but also no shoes to keep her from experiencing the grass and undergrowth beneath her feet. It was a sensation that she wanted to savor... to remember. Before she knew it, Terry had used one foot to take off the other foot's shoe, and then she used her now bare foot to remove the other one. She picked them up and carried on walking behind her friends, wanting to feel the stones underneath her and the grass that had begun to grow between them. There was a memory there—an important one—hiding just out of reach in the corners of her mind, and Terry had managed to coax it out from its hiding

PURGATERRY

place just for a second. She hoped that walking barefoot might entice it to come out into the light again.

After nearly ten minutes of walking, she hadn't been able to glean anything new from the memory, but she was beginning to feel like this was a hiking trip. Not that she minded the view surrounding her, but Terry didn't recall liking to hike all that much. At least she hadn't encountered anything that might hurt her feet, which Terry noted as odd but not unlikely, given the perfection of this place.

They finally reached their destination. Puck stood in the middle of the pathway facing a new elevator doorway that looked as if it was woven and braided out of tree branches. Indeed, it appeared that there was no pathway past it, so this must have been the end of the road. Literally.

A soft breeze blew through the clearing, and a few blossoms fell from the blooming trees. Puck looked calmer, more at peace than Terry had seen him before. He smiled, his eyes bright as he caught sight of Juliet, who Terry noticed was already tearing up.

"Jules and Co., thanks for coming," he said. "The paperwork is all done, and Orion has already said his goodbye, but I wanted to wait for my 'little sister' before I walked through."

Juliet didn't speak; she sniffed as her tears now spilled over, and she leaped into Puck's arms and hugged him tight, which Puck returned without hesitation.

"You take care, Juliet," he said when they finally pulled apart, and he wiped a tear from her cheek. "Stick with your friends and get your years in, and I'll see you on the other side, huh?"

To Terry and Asher, he gave a grateful nod. "Take care of this little baby, guys," he said. "And feel free to take anything in my room that you want. I'm not leaving behind much, but I can't take it with me."

Despite not really knowing Puck that well, Terry was feeling a tad emotional herself. However, she settled for only a handshake for Puck. As sorry as he was that Juliet was losing him, she was finding this whole experience more fascinating than anything.

"So, you're going to—what—walk through the archway? Then what?"

Puck shrugged. "I don't know, go on to my judgment meeting, I suppose. That's where they'll determine where I go from here."

"You've gotten all your Ps removed," said Juliet with a squeak and a sniff. "You've done all your service. You're definitely going Upstairs."

Puck sighed, looked from one of them to the other in turn, and held out his arms for one last hug from Juliet. When he'd let her go, he turned to face the archway, where it stood benignly, patiently waiting for him to walk through. Terry wasn't sure how to feel about the entrance to the afterlife proper. It wasn't menacing, and it wasn't quite inviting, either. It just simply... was. She wasn't sure how she would feel when, one day—who knew how long from now—it would be her turn to walk through and face her own judgment.

The three of them watched as Puck took five confident steps toward the archway, paused, and then took one large step through. The millisecond he had placed a foot on the other side, he vanished. There was no ceremony or pomp and circumstance, he was just gone. Gone from this plane forever.

"So... that's it?" Terry asked, hoping she didn't sound disappointed, because she wasn't. She wasn't entirely sure what she was expecting.

"Why don't we get to board the buses like the souls we Shepherd?" she asked.

"I don't think they go exactly where we do, or at least, not where we go first," Juliet answered. "They get a free bypass of this place; this is just Purgatory's exit to whatever is next."

"And what is next?"

Juliet shrugged. "Everybody has different ideas. We say Upstairs or Downstairs like we're sure, but who really knows once we walk through there? That's the exciting part, I'll bet. No matter what, I'll bet it's an adventure."

She sounded so hopeful about it, even though one of the

options might be what everyone referred to as Downstairs... a place so often spoken of with fear and trepidation.

But she sort of understood Juliet's meaning. For them, at least, there really was no way to know where one might end up after they walked through to their judgment. There might be a secret third option Terry didn't even know about.

This was a lot to process philosophically for Terry, and Juliet appeared to notice this, so as they walked back toward where the main elevator doors stood unconnected to any other building structure, she and Asher allowed Terry to walk in silence, giving her space to contemplate the nature of her own being, and how even as a dead, bodiless soul, she still didn't have all of the answers.

She knew that, of course, she still wanted *her* answers, but concerning the archway and whatever waited on the other side of it, Terry concluded that, for now at least, it was best not to know.

Puck and Juliet's manager must have been more accommodating than others to let them share a room. That, or he just wanted to keep them together to keep an eye on them both. From the little she'd known of Puck, he seemed like the type Orion might want to be extra vigilant about watching. The room looked very much like hers with Willow, and Terry assumed that they were basically uniform throughout the residences. There was a mirrored wall on the left that extended to the tiny, nearly a bathroom directly across from the door. The headboards of the beds went up against the far wall with shelves opposite them, and the one floor-to-ceiling window was on the far right, closest to—in their room, anyway—Willow's bed.

Asher hadn't joined them to poke through Puck's belongings, and he'd been fairly silent on their way back to Level Eight. He merely reminded Terry that they still hadn't set a date for their "date" to the HoK, and she had tried to be vague about just when they might actually do it.

There wasn't much that Puck had left behind, and evidently, most of it would either be donated to the Library or tossed, so Juliet was determined to save at least something of her Purgatory roommate. Terry didn't remember ever being in the room of someone who had "died" before. She knew of course that Puck had already been dead when he set foot here, but the fact that he had moved on from this place... it almost felt like a death in her opinion.

There was an eeriness to the room. Terry chalked some of it up to the fact that it looked so much like their room, but it was also the fact that she was surrounded by the detritus of someone who was gone from here and would never return. This was Puck's legacy left to Juliet and Level Eight. All that remained of his time here.

The bulk of his things could all fit into one box, but still, Juliet needed to go through them and decide what went and what stayed. A battered diary with a red cover, a couple pulpy mass market paperback novels, cassette tapes, half-full containers of Tic Tacs, and a plush toy of Snoopy from the *Charlie Brown* cartoons.

There were most likely a few more things scattered about the room that hadn't yet been collected, but Terry found it so odd that a person's entire being could be summed up in this eclectic garage sale fodder. The Snoopy was cute, at least.

"I think I'd like to keep the diary," Juliet said, opening it and thumbing through some of the pages. A picture slipped out from between a couple of them, and she pulled it out and smiled at it wistfully.

Terry leaned in over Juliet's shoulder to see, hoping that she wasn't being rude by looking. It was a picture from what looked like one of those cameras that instantly prints the picture—Polaroids? It was of Juliet and Puck, clearly somewhere in the garden of Level One. They each wore a crown of flowers on their heads, Juliet smiling shyly as she usually did, Puck with his tongue out and giving the camera the peace sign.

"Was this a special occasion?" was really all that Terry could think to ask, admiring the flower crowns in the picture. One looked to be made of orange lilies and one of yellow and white daisies.

Juliet shook her head. "No, just a random day. That's how Puck was. I think he had had a bad day, so we went up to the garden and had a little tea party—without the tea, because neither of us liked it." She smiled again, her expression growing sadder the longer she talked. "We chatted, and he told me about things he remembered from when he was alive, and I told him what I remembered, and he called me baby girl. He did that a lot..."

Terry's eyes landed on the other side of the room on a pastel-pink camera that sat on what she assumed was Juliet's side.

"Do you do a lot of photography?" Terry asked, feeling comfortable enough in the room now to begin to wander from Juliet's bed to the wall opposite where the shelves were.

It was probably a dumb question, seeing as she had the camera, but there weren't that many pictures on the walls that matched the type in the diary. Most of them looked like they had been cut or torn out of magazines or books.

"I do," Juliet said, brightening up at the question. "It was kind of expensive, and Puck shouldn't have gotten it for me, but nevertheless, that camera is my favorite thing." She made for the shelves, where two fat photo albums sat. "I don't have these all filled yet, but most of what I've taken pictures of are in this one." She handed Terry one of the albums.

Terry sat back down onto Juliet's bed with Juliet on the other side of her opening the album to begin looking through it. There were some fine, and quite artsy, shots of some of the items in the rec room, pictures of the main buildings on Level Eight, more shots of the garden on Level One, and a few at a place Terry didn't recognize but assumed to be where Juliet did her community service.

Turning each page, though, Terry noticed something that they all had in common.

"They're taken in Purgatory," she said, more thinking out loud than actually saying something to her.

Juliet sighed. "Yeah, I don't have clearance like you do to go back to Earth, so I just have to make do with what I have."

That was when Terry noticed the subjects of the pictures torn from the books on the wall. They weren't just people, but animals, places, cars, buildings, all sorts of things Terry figured that Juliet didn't get to see in reality anymore since coming to Level Eight.

"I really miss being there, but I guess we all do sometimes," Juliet said. "I wish that I could go back down there to visit like you guys get to do."

It's fine, really," Juliet added when she noticed the concern that must've bled through onto Terry's face. "I get to see it through screens when I'm doing my work in New Soul Integration. We have to keep tabs on the newborn souls for the first year or so."

Terry's gaze fell back down onto the pages of the album. She took it from Juliet's gentle grasp and turned a couple pages, noting a few pictures of Willow among them when she paused on a candid shot taken at one of the tables in the rec room. Another young woman sat at the table with them, eyes downcast as she scribbled in one of the composition notebooks. Her short, wavy hair had streaks of bright cyan, and part of a tattoo on her left forearm peeked through her sleeve. Her face was neutral, concentrating in the shot, but as Terry turned another page, she noticed a couple more photos including her, one with her smiling next to Willow with Dean slightly behind them. He was not completely in focus, but it was clearly him.

"Who's this?" She pointed to the woman, and Juliet frowned when she looked where Terry indicated.

"Oh, that's Dels— Uh, Delilah. I would've thought Willow would have told you about her."

Terry blinked. "Why?"

"Because she was one of Dean's residents before you got here. I don't think they were as close as you and Willow, but she was

PurgaTerry

here for a while, and Dean trained her, same as Willow."

"What do you mean 'was'?" Terry asked. Something about what Juliet had called her—Dels—sparked something in her memory. "Did she lose all her Ps or something?"

Juliet scratched at a peeling edge of the album page they were on, avoiding Terry's eyes.

"Not exactly," she eventually answered, softer than before. "I don't think we should talk about her though. You should ask Willow or Dean."

"But, I mean, did you know her very well?" Terry prodded, hoping that Juliet might give her something since clearly both Dean and Willow had failed to mention her. But then it hit her. Dean. Dean had mentioned this Dels in that conversation she'd overheard with Cassiopeia. He'd mentioned something about what Dels did, and Cassiopeia had brought up similarities between her and Terry.

"I'm not really comfortable with talking about it, or her." Juliet had abandoned the peeling corner and closed the album on Terry's hand.

Terry pulled it out without comment. She was sorry she'd made her friend uncomfortable, but now her mind was reeling with the indignation of yet another thing her manager and supposed friend were hiding from her. Or at the very least had failed to mention to her. Of course there would be no point confronting Dean about her, but perhaps she could get something out of Willow. Who knew, maybe Willow could explain things, and it was just an oversight on Dean's part. Still, Terry didn't think that would be the case if things had ended smoothly and correctly for this Delilah.

"You know," Terry said, getting an idea, "since we do get to go back down to Earth, Willow and I could always take pictures for you with your camera and bring them back to you."

Juliet gasped, her grin wider than Terry had ever seen. "Really, do you mean it?"

"Of course. Make a list of what you wanna see, and Willow

and I will do our best to take pictures with it," she said. Also, I promise to make sure Willow doesn't break your camera."

"Wow, that's so nice of you," she said. "I don't know how to thank you."

"If it's okay, can I have those pictures of Delilah?" she asked.

Juliet hesitated for a moment, spreading her fingers over the cover of the album, before she gave a small nod and turned back to the photos, pulling them from their places and handing them to Terry.

"Just... don't tell Willow I told you anything about her, okay?"

"Sure," Terry agreed as she took the photos from her. She placed them carefully into her pocket with the Hatori wrapper. Just more clues to add to her collection.

Terry skipped the group session this one time. If Dean and Willow were going off to do who knew what, then she could take time off to visit the Library on her own.

Apparently, Asher had been only partially right about taking things from the building. Books and other materials could be checked out, but only for a short time. They would appear back in the hall when they were due back whether or not they were returned.

Terry had found a couple old paperbacks she thought looked interesting—one about ghosts, which she found ironic. So, she lay on her bed, waiting for Willow to return and reading the exploits of a teenage girl medium who fell in love with a ghost.

The sun had set by the time she heard the door click open. Naturally, there wouldn't be anything to do until the sun came up again. Whenever that would be. Terry still hadn't gotten a handle on how time worked in Purgatory just yet.

The book was actually getting sort of interesting, so, at first, she didn't acknowledge Willow as she entered. When she did look up from it, she saw that her friend looked absolutely exhausted but had the brightest grin she'd ever seen.

Willow flopped down onto her own bed, letting the blue plastic bag she held fall to the floor.

Terry finally put her book down on the nightstand between their beds, sitting up to get a better look at her. Willow was face down on the bed but had slowly turned toward her, holding up a finger at Terry.

"Gimme a minute," she said. "I'm soaking it all in. We did a *lot* of walking today."

Scooting closer to the edge of her own bed, Terry peered down at the bag Willow had dropped. There was a castle with fireworks on it, and a logo Terry didn't need her memories to recognize.

Her eyebrows raised as she put it together. "Did you guys go to Disney World?"

"Disneyland, the one in California," Willow corrected her, slightly muffled as her face was now in her pillow. She propped herself up on her elbows to speak more clearly, still looking tired but happy.

"Dean takes me there every year for our... *my* birthday," she said. "It's one of the things he lets me remember. That's what my parents did for us on my and my brother's birthday."

Springing to life again, Willow scrambled for her bag.

"Oh, I got you something!" she said as she crinkled the bag in search of Terry's gift. She waved Terry closer with her other hand, and she obliged by sitting on the edge of Willow's bed with her.

"You actually got to go to a theme park, buy stuff, and bring it back to Purgatory?"

"I know what you're thinking. Everybody says 'you can't take it with you.' Which—I mean—is sort of true, but Dean says it doesn't count if we're already dead."

"And the other managers just let Dean do this?"

Willow took a second from her search to glance up at her, her bright smile turning awkward. "Well, it's a secret. But I figured I could tell you since he's bending the rules for you, too."

Turning her attention back to the bag, she pulled something

out with a triumphant "ha."

"Hold out your hands," she said, her own hand closed around the item.

Terry did so, and Willow placed a shiny pin into her hands. It was gold tinted on one side with a pattern of Mickey Mouse heads, and on the other side was a familiar character.

"I wanted to find you a dinosaur or dragon or something since you have your pterodactyl shirt, but I saw Eeyore here and just thought of you," she said.

Eeyore, the perpetually depressed donkey who was constantly falling apart. That was flattering. But still, Willow had been thinking of her, and that was sweet in its own way.

"Thanks," she said, meaning it. "You didn't have to get me anything."

Willow shrugged. "I know, but that's what friends do. Wanna see mine?"

Terry nodded, watching Willow pull out two more pins. One was Tinkerbell, and the other was Daisy Duck in a teal dress and sunglasses.

"Tink is for me," she said, taking the backing off the fairy pin and putting it on her shirt. "And... I got one for Juliet, but it's whatever."

"Uh huh," Terry said with a pointed look to Willow, not hiding her skepticism that it truly was "whatever."

"So, Dean does this for you every year?" she asked.

"Yeah, but just Disneyland, not the other park, California Adventure. He just knows it was important to me, and it just... makes me feel more connected to my old self, you know?"

"But you could get in a lot of trouble if the higher-ups knew."

"Dean always just tells me not to worry about it," she said. "It's my own special day. I'm sure you'll get one, too."

Terry wasn't so sure about that. "But he let you remember that about your birthday. What about my past is there to experience?"

"Dean will find something, I'm sure."

Terry remembered Willow's comment about the fireflies,

and it didn't skip her notice that she'd chosen that particular pin for herself.

"What's so great about Peter Pan for you?" she wondered aloud.

Terry almost wished she hadn't, for Willow's eyes grew bright, and she bounced over to Terry's side of her bed.

"Oh, it's one of my strongest memories that I have. Playing Neverland with my brother. I always wanted to be Wendy because she was smart and kind, and she didn't want to grow up either. But my brother—he wanted me to be Peter or a lost boy. Now, don't get me wrong, I'd love to really be a lost boy—or girl—but I just connected more with Wendy, you know?"

"If that's so, then why didn't Dean name you Wendy when you got here?"

Willow let in a sharp breath, then let it out slowly, and Terry only noticed then that Willow was tearing up.

"I'm sorry, I didn't mean to upset you."

"It's fine," Willow answered, wiping her eyes. "And Dean didn't know about that at the time. You know him, he picks the first thing he thinks of."

Terry leaned in closer, brow creasing. "So, what made him think of 'Willow'?"

Willow sniffed and gave a small, sad laugh. "For this exact reason," she said, indicating her tears. "When I woke up from the Lethe Machine—the thing that takes your memories in the Welcome Center—the first thing I did was look for a mirror. I don't know why, but when Dean showed me what I looked like, I just started weeping. Full on weeping. I don't know how to describe it, but seeing myself—how I am here—it felt so right that I couldn't stop crying. So... Weeping Willow became my name."

Terry was relieved that Willow seemed to be recovering from her emotional response. It was difficult enough to figure out her own emotions without having to handle other people's.

"Sorry," Willow said. "There's me being overly dramatic." She gave a breathy laugh, wiping her eyes one more time for good measure.

"It's fine," she replied. "I guess it's just that kind of day. I mean, how does it feel to have a birthday here?"

"Oh, we're not normally supposed to remember them, but Dean likes to commemorate birthdays and death-days in some way or another."

"You mean he's done this before for other residents?" she asked. Terry was probing, she knew. She'd decided that it couldn't hurt since they were now in each other's confidence.

"Not... really," came Willow's answer, just as hesitant as Terry would have thought. "He disappears on another day by himself, but he won't even tell me what that's about."

Blinking and then grabbing for her bag again, Willow dove back into it, excitedly telling Terry about her day at "the happiest place on Earth." Very much changing the subject, in Terry's opinion. But for now, she didn't mind.

After hearing about the teacups, the Peter Pan ride, Pirates, and how Dean stood in line for twenty minutes to get Willow something called Dole Whip while she watched singing birds, Terry could tell the temporary burst of energy she'd gotten from recounting had ebbed away from Willow. After asking her for the twelfth time if she liked her pin—and Terry assuring her every time that she did—Willow grew quiet as she took off her own pin, the fairy's wings glinting in the light from the nightstand between them.

"Maybe next time, I might like Jiminy Cricket," Terry said, recalling their conversation about missing things again. Crickets made a soothing sound that made Terry sleepy but comforted at the same time.

"Hmm?" Willow said, not paying attention. Terry recognized the faraway look in her eyes. Willow was lost in memories of her own, memories and perhaps just as many questions as she had.

"Do you remember much more about your family, your brother?"

Willow's eyes slid from her pin to focus on Terry, and she shook her head.

PURGATERRY

"What if I told you I have a way we could both learn everything about our lives?"

Willow lowered the pin and sat up on her elbow again. "How'd you manage that?"

"Promise you'll help, and I'll tell you all about it."

She didn't ask a follow-up question or say anything about Dean or getting his permission. This time, Willow held out her hand, extending her pinkie finger. Terry smiled and hooked her own pinkie in hers. A bit childish and silly, in Terry's opinion, but coming from Willow, it meant the world.

"Okay, now I don't mean to spoil your good mood, but before I tell you my idea, I need to know about this girl." Terry pulled out the photos Juliet had given her and handed them to Willow.

Visible recognition dawned on her face, and Terry knew now that there was no doubt that not only did Willow know this Delilah, but they really had to be keeping something from her.

Willow gave a tiny grumble as she grimaced, clearly not expecting Terry to ask and uncertain that she should spill the beans.

"You know I'm not going to let it go," Terry said. "Now, who is she, or who was she?"

Willow sighed, rolling her eyes as she placed her Tinker Bell pin down again and grasped the photos with both hands. "She was a trainee Shepherd, same as us. She got here a little bit after me, and she was from New York City. That one song was on the radio a lot then, so I guess that's why Dean named her Delilah."

"Why haven't you or Dean mentioned her before?"

Willow bit her bottom lip then made a popping sound with it. "Because I don't know how much I'm allowed to say. We don't really talk about her anymore since she kind of... got sent away."

"You might be able to say more than that," Terry coaxed.

"Remember that whole 'cheating' thing I told you about when Dean got upset that day?"

"Yeah."

"Well, Dels got sent straight Downstairs because of that."

"Straight to Downstairs?"

Willow nodded. "I told you, they are serious about it. Because if the living person you manipulate with the emotion power does kill themselves, that almost doubles their time they'll have to spend here."

"Why would that happen? Why would someone even attempt that, the cheating?"

"It's in the name, it's a way to cheat the system. If you get a living person to die by suicide, they automatically go to Purgatory in your place and take on all the years you had left on top of their own."

Terry's eyes widened. This seemed like a big gamble. "So, you'd go straight Downstairs afterward? So, why risk it?"

"Honestly, we're not fully sure where they go, the ones who choose to cheat," Willow explained. "I only know Dels went Downstairs because Dean made a point to find out."

"But again, why do it? Why manipulate someone like that?"

Willow gave a sad shrug. "I guess for some people here in Purgatory, they get tired of waiting. They want to get out of here as fast as they can, and they don't care if they hurt someone else in trying."

Terry took the photos from Willow's hands and looked back on them with new eyes. This woman had done that. She'd used her powers to get someone to take her place here in Purgatory. She got someone to kill themselves all so she wouldn't have to be here anymore.

"But there has to be something else to it," she said. "Was she just tired of waiting? I guess I just don't understand what could drive somebody to do this."

"Well, they say once you leave here, you get your memories back in full, no matter where you end up. Maybe Delilah was after those."

Guilt began to twist in Terry's stomach at that thought, because that was honestly something she could understand. She'd never even consider going to such extremes, of course.

PurgaTerry

But if this Delilah was so desperate for answers, and Dean had been just as secretive with her as he was with Terry, then Terry could at least see a bit of where she was coming from. But then another thought came to her, and she voiced it, watching closely to gauge Willow's response.

"So, that's why Dean didn't want me to know about her, because of what she did? He didn't want me to find out and think that cheating was an option for me?"

Willow bit her lip again, looking down at the photos Terry now held before glancing back up to her. "Yeah, that's part of it."

"Part?"

Now Willow looked about as uncomfortable as Juliet had. "Look, Ter, I really can't talk about this anymore with you. I'm sorry. If you want to know any more about Delilah, you'll have to try asking Dean."

Terry was afraid she'd say that. As much as it frustrated her, Terry decided to let this one go for now. But there would be no mistake that she'd be getting this information out of Dean one way or another.

"Okay, that's fine. I'm sorry to bring it up and spoil your birthday," she said.

Willow seemed relieved that Terry had dropped the subject so fast.

"Thanks, Ter, and it's okay. You didn't spoil anything. Can I tell you more about my day at the park? Did I tell you about the Mickey waffles?"

Terry gave a small laugh through her nose, smiling at her friend's backtracking. She knew this was an attempt to deflect, but for now, she'd let it slide.

13. The Land Behind the Times

The Hall of Knowledge—or the Library, as the residents called it—certainly looked like a library from the outside, but its proper name implied it held all the knowledge of mankind, more so than any one library. This turned out to be false. While the "main branch," as their managers called it, indeed housed every piece of creative expression known to humans, the Purgatory branch on Level Eight could not boast the same numbers.

This library was stocked about as well as any one Terry could remember on Earth, but with the added drawback of every piece of media being at least ten years out of date.

"Let me explain it to you this way," Willow said as they handed their ID cards and permission slips from Dean to the attendant. "The latest Disney animated movie they have is *Chicken Little*. That came out right around when I died."

Seeing her puzzled expression, Willow added, "Or how about the last Pixar movie? They only have up to *The Incredibles*."

She supposed that was a bit more memorable, but she was having trouble following Willow's logic.

"Do you always measure spans of time in cartoons?"

Willow shrugged. "Once you've been here for a while, time just kinda stops meaning much. So, I try to keep track as best as I can. This seems to work for me."

Juliet met them just inside the entrance, looking quite cute in a cap sleeve white dress patterned with small red roses. Terry felt underdressed next to her and Willow in her own teal skirt and cardigan combo, but she had adamantly refused to let Willow dress her up for the occasion. She wanted to feel as comfortable as possible in this very uncomfortable situation.

Terry listened as Willow and Juliet made small talk about their favorite movies, noting how many animated films were mentioned (at least five). It made her wonder what film might be in store for them this evening. Terry had let Willow choose, and she was keeping it a surprise. This kind of surprise Terry didn't mind, but she was wary of what other surprises might be in store once Asher joined them.

They made their way past shelf after shelf of movies, books, and CDs, with Terry noticing the large empty spaces between them. The center of the one cathedral-sized room had at least thirty small square oak tables arranged in a patterned square of its own on a green carpet that stretched the entire floor.

At the end of the one giant room was a tall dark curtain, which is where Willow appeared to be leading her and Juliet.

She parted the curtain and beckoned them to follow her inside, where Terry saw what looked like a home movie theater. The type ultra-rich people had in their mansions. A few rows of theater-style seats sat in front of a moderately-sized screen. It looked more like a large television than a movie screen, but it was still not something Terry had been expecting.

A figure in the back row turned to look toward them, disrupted by the sound of their entrance. He stood once he noticed Terry. Asher put his hands in his pockets, shifting from surprise to the cool, casual demeanor Terry was so familiar with.

She was relieved that he apparently hadn't thought to dress

PurgaTerry

any differently than normal. His outfit was casual, matching hers.

"Well, see you after the movie." Willow took Juliet by the hand and scampered off down the rows to sit closer to the screen, Juliet giving a soft giggle. Terry assumed that meant she wouldn't be hearing from them for the next two hours or however long the movie Willow had chosen was.

This left her alone with Asher. Alone with Asher and the cloud of awkwardness that had begun to form around them. It wasn't so bad when they were with other people or in a more casual setting, but this was officially a date. Now Terry had no choice but to face what Willow kept hammering into Terry's mind—that Asher was interested in more than just friendship.

"Sooo." Terry nodded and dragged out the word just for something to say. "You're a back-of-the-theater type of person?"

Asher shrugged, not betraying any nervous energy if he had any. "Always seemed like the better spot. Everybody's focused on the screen; they wouldn't look back to see what you're doing."

"Oh, I guess like if you snuck in snacks or something."

Asher laughed. "Yeah, or something."

She took the seat to Asher's left, the aisle seat, so she could get up if she felt like she needed to. Now that they were sitting, at least Terry had an excuse not to look at him and be focused on the screen.

"What do you think Willow's picked for us to watch?" Asher asked her.

"Something in the cartoon family, I'm sure," Terry answered automatically. "She's almost like a cartoon character herself."

"You could get a sunburn from how much sunshine that girl shoots out," he joked, but his tone seemed like he considered that more of a negative trait.

"Hey, there's not much to be sun-shiny about around here," she replied. "I kind of admire her for keeping all happy and optimistic, considering our circumstances."

"Not making fun of her or anything, Pj's. I just think that much optimism might get tiring after a while."

Terry wasn't sure who he thought Willow's attitude might get tiring for, Willow or Terry. Either way, she felt like he was wrong. She might not always be in the mood for Willow's demeanor, but Willow was her friend, and Terry wanted to defend her, even if just from Asher's criticism.

"She's actually a good person, and I mean it when I say I admire her spirit. It takes a strong person to keep hopeful when things have gone so badly for them."

"Okay, okay." Terry caught Asher holding up a hand to shield himself from her words. "You don't need to be like that. I was just making a comment. No judgment."

This coaxed a smile out of her, which he returned, seeming glad that she was at last offering up some eye contact.

"We get enough of that for how we died and stuff around here; I don't wanna be somebody who does that shit to other people."

"I understand that," Terry replied. "I mean, I guess I can. I've experienced some of that kind of judgment, but probably not as much as some."

"I might have said it before, but you're lucky, then. I get it all the time, especially from my manager."

Terry raised an eyebrow. "From Cassiopeia?"

"Don't look so surprised, Pj's. You know she gets after you, too," Asher said. "Woman's got a big-time stick up her butt."

As much as she wanted to agree with him, Terry couldn't completely when it came to Cassiopeia. Sure, she was strict about the rules and making sure Terry wasn't going to break them, but she'd also found out that the very same Cassiopeia had bent some of those rules for Dean. There was some amount of caring behind the all-business facade, and Terry wasn't sure if Asher had looked hard enough to see that.

"She just wants you to do your best, I'll bet."

"Pfft, you've been hanging with your manager and Willow too much," he said. "You drinking the Kool-Aid and gonna start doing mindfulness exercises or something next?"

"I just think I've found my own reasons for wanting to do

better here."

Asher shrugged. "Oh, so I guess you don't wanna go ahead with that whole 'helping you find your file in the Hall of Records' anymore?"

Terry's head snapped toward him, eyes wide.

"Yeah, I thought so."

"Don't kid about that; of course I'm still interested. Can we talk about it now? Wait, are we making the switch now?"

"Easy, easy." He put a hand on her shoulder to set her back down, which was when Terry noticed that she had physically begun to stand from her seat. "After the movie, sure. We can talk about it. Glad you're still willing and able."

A part of Terry still had reservations. She didn't know what was in it for Asher to switch IDs so he could go down to Earth, but maybe it was personal, maybe it had something to do with that girlfriend he mentioned. She'd died at the same time or around there—an accident? She didn't quite remember what he'd said about it, but she wasn't sure it was polite to ask. She supposed she could wait until after the movie. That would at least help her have time to think of a way to bring it up without seeming indelicate.

The movie began, the lights dimmed, and once the first notes of the score had started to play, Terry knew immediately what they were about to watch. She didn't know how she knew, but it was so clear and distinct a memory that it couldn't possibly be anything else. *The Land Before Time.* The first one, a classic. It was something that lingered in the back of her mind, and somehow, both a sense of excitement and a presence of calm washed over her as she took in the first scene of the film.

She looked past where she sat with Asher to the backs of Juliet's and Willow's heads. Willow turned around momentarily to grin widely at her. She must have chosen this movie specifically for her. Terry didn't think Willow knew she had a connection with the movie. How could she when even Terry didn't realize until just now? She must have chosen it based on Terry's shirt. But in any case, Terry was thrilled. Even if she couldn't recall the specifics, she knew in her heart that this film was special to her, and that she must have watched it many, many times, because she could anticipate every action and recite each character's lines in her head right before they said them.

The only thing that marred the experience was Asher's oddly forward advances. He had tried to hold her hand when Littlefoot's mother told him about the tree stars, tried to put his arm around her in comfort when Littlefoot's mother died, and he kept trying to get her to put her head on his shoulder even though Littlefoot was now meeting his new friends, which was crucial to understanding the plot and Asher should be paying attention. This movie was important to her, and if Asher was truly interested in her like Willow said he was, then Terry thought he should be interested in learning more about her. She had given off plenty of signals by this point that she wanted to watch the movie, and that she wanted him to watch the movie.

"You're not really into this, are you?" he asked after another failed attempt to get her attention and do Terry had no idea what.

On the contrary, she was very interested in watching the adventures of the dinosaur children on their way to the Great Valley. What she *wasn't* interested in was all of this touching he wanted to do.

"I'm just... not into touching, I guess," she replied, unsure of what she could say that would get her point across but not hurt his feelings.

"Got it, no touching," Asher said, sounding only a tad put out. "But lemme know if that changes, okay?"

Even though she still didn't really want his hands all over her, Terry felt that he might deserve an explanation at the very least. "Sorry, I'm just— It's just that I don't think I'm used to a lot of that physical stuff, you know? Plus, this actually turns out to be one of my favorite movies."

Asher nodded, looking back to the screen for a moment. "A'ight. I get it. It's just not what I'm used to doing in a movie with girls."

"You're not used to watching a movie?" she asked. "Well, then what are you used to doing?"

He casually pointed toward where Willow and Juliet were sitting, and Terry blinked several times to make sure she saw what she thought she saw. The two silhouettes that had been her friends were now one big black mass of arms reaching for hair and faces mashed together. Willow was turning more toward Juliet in her seat, moving her lips down Juliet's neck and causing the other girl to squeak with laughter.

"Oh..." Terry said finally. Honestly, doing something like that hadn't even crossed her mind. She didn't think she had much experience in that stuff, nor much interest in trying it out.

"So, you did that in movies with your girlfriend? When you were alive?" Terry asked. She had hoped that bringing up Asher's girlfriend from his former life was all right. It might have been a painful subject, and she thought perhaps she might have tried to be a bit more tactful. "Oh, no, sorry. Is that all right to ask about?" She winced but noticed that Asher seemed unfazed.

"Nah, it's cool. Yeah, I seem to remember we took as many opportunities as we could to make out and stuff. That's just how we were, I guess. Honestly, I don't think I've ever gone out with a girl who didn't want to jump me right from the get-go."

"Well, I'm happy to be the first, just as long as you don't take it as an insult," she said. She contemplated the why of her feelings, or lack of feelings. It seemed like she probably should have them, if she were actually interested in Asher, even a bit romantically if not sexually. "I don't think it's you, I sincerely think it's me."

"What, not into dudes?" he asked. "If you don't remember that, I get it. I won't hold that against you."

She processed his statement and thought about it a little longer. Did she like girls? Maybe... but it didn't feel like it. "Honestly, I don't know if I like anyone."

"Now that I don't really get. But you do you, I guess, Pj's," he said. "Again, just lemme know if that ever changes."

"If it does, I will," she answered then smiled uneasily. "Do you think we can just be friends in the meantime?"

It took him a moment of his own contemplation, but then he bobbed his head in a nod and shrugged one shoulder. "Yeah, I guess that could still work."

"Still work?" she asked.

"Yeah, I could always use more friends, I guess."

"Well, then great," Terry said. "I'm glad you took this so well."

"I don't tend to take rejection well," Asher said. "But, yeah, at the end of the day—or life, I guess—what can I do? You gotta do you, and I gotta do me, and I guess we won't be doing each other any time soon. And that's okay by me."

"Nice rhyme," she said. She thought he deserved that compliment for being such a good sport.

"I heard something like it somewhere before. I can't remember where." He then leaned in to whisper to her, making an effort not to touch her as he did so. "So, these little dinosaurs are all orphans or...?"

Terry spent most of the movie's run half watching and half answering Asher's questions, explaining the characters' perilous journey. They had almost reached the Great Valley for the happy reunions when Asher spoke up again, this time talking about something other than Littlefoot and his friends.

"So, I heard about your first day on Shepherd duty. You and Willow had a hard time?"

Terry exhaled through her nose, nodding at the memory. "You could say that. The guy started seizing up, and it was like his soul wasn't prepared to leave, and he was stuck."

"Sounds freaky," he said.

"It was. I mean, it wasn't like he was a great person, from what

PURGATERRY

I saw, but he didn't deserve an end like that."

"I coulda told you that Hembree dude was no good. Sounds like he got what was coming to him."

Terry eyed him skeptically. It was an awfully harsh thing to say about someone he didn't know, and besides that—

"Wait, how did you know his name? I didn't mention it."

"Oh, got it from good ol' Cassiopeia. It's also not a big secret that you had a rough start. Word gets around here fast."

Terry still wasn't completely certain about that answer, or maybe she was just surprised that Asher knew as much as he did about the incident.

"Well, in any case, I don't think we would have had as hard a time if Dean hadn't left us to give Willow some solo time."

Terry instantly regretted mentioning that bit of information. It was probably not something Dean would want her sharing if it could get back to Cassiopeia.

"But I mean, we weren't in any real trouble, and he didn't know that thing with Hembree was going to happen. I'm sure, if he did, he wouldn't have left us."

"He still left you by yourselves when it was your first day," Asher said. "Sounds pretty sketchy to me."

"It wasn't that bad, really," she tried to correct herself. "I mean, he didn't even understand what could have happened with the man's soul. He said something about looking into it, though."

"That sounds bogus, too. Who's to say he wasn't lying about the whole thing, since he lied about having to leave you?"

"Dean wouldn't do that," Terry replied.

"But Dean did," he shot back. "Like I told you, they're all the same."

"Dean's not like that," she fired back defensively. "I trust him."

Asher rolled his eyes. "Right, I forgot he's the one manager to top them all. You guys aren't—you know?"

"No!" she exclaimed, loud enough to cause Juliet to glance their way before Willow regained her attention. "No, it's definitely not like that."

Terry wasn't sure how to explain it so that Asher would understand. He seemed just too set on believing that the managers were either uncaring or out to get him for some reason. She calmed herself and tried to articulate her feelings a bit more clearly.

"He's just—I don't know—I just feel like he gets it. Like he understands me and how we all feel. I think I'm beginning to understand why he does what he does."

Asher looked skeptical, rolling his eyes and looking toward the screen again.

"Believe what you want, but I don't think I've ever seen a manager who's really invested in us. One who really cares."

"Dean's different," she said.

"So, he's not keeping your file from you, then?" Asher asked, accusatory. "You look at me right now and tell me you one hundred percent trust that he isn't keeping secrets from you."

Terry frowned, sighing through her nose. She couldn't. Even after what they'd shared with each other, Terry still couldn't be certain that there wasn't something that Dean was hiding. And Asher knew that. He only nodded and didn't seem to feel the need to say "I told you so."

"They're all the same, Pj's," he said when he spoke again. "At the end of the day, if we really wanna get what we want around here, we can't trust them."

Terry still didn't know if Asher was right about that, but a part of her still thought that he couldn't be entirely wrong. There was still stuff that Dean was keeping from her and she assumed things that Cassiopeia was keeping from Asher. Her mind went back to Dean, who she could tell had his reasons, and she wanted to try and explain to Asher that maybe Cassiopeia had hers as well. He didn't seem as receptive to that kind of thinking, though.

So, they watched the movie for a little longer, and as it was close to the finale, Asher spoke up again.

"Look, I get if you're scared of getting in trouble, but what I have planned can get us both what we want. If you trade IDs with me just a couple of times, I think you can get your answers, and I can get me some closure."

"What do you mean 'closure'?"

"Just the stuff I learned about what happened when I died. It's gotta be part of my 'unfinished business' or whatever, but I haven't been allowed to do anything about it because I'm not allowed to go to Earth. I need somebody's ID who has access to the buses."

Terry put a hand on her notebook where her ID was pressed along with her clues. She had been using it as a kind of shield between them to keep Asher from touching her further, but she pulled it down from its place dividing them and laid it flat on her lap.

"I did have a deal with somebody to use theirs, but then they up and moved on from this place, and I never got to," Asher continued.

"You mean they finished up here without telling you?"

"Pretty much," he answered. "I just figure if I can get to Serena's family, I can make amends for what happened, I don't know. It might help me get outta this place."

"What exactly happened, if you remember?" she asked, then added, "And if it's all right to ask."

"It's fine. I don't remember it, naturally, but from what I was able to get from my file, Serena made a case for me. We died within hours of each other, and it was my fault that she died, but it was an accident. My death, though? Not an accident."

"But she convinced whoever is in charge to let you come here?"

Asher nodded. "I guess they take things like that into account sometimes. I owe her a whole lot because of that. She could've let me go straight Downstairs, but she didn't. And even if I don't remember her now, I sure want to, and I sure want to do something for her family if I can."

"So, that's why you want my ID?"

"Yeah," he said. "Not every day, just a few times for me to track them down. Then you can use mine to get into the HoR."

"I guess that doesn't sound too bad," Terry said. "Do you think we'll get in trouble?"

"Only if we get caught, and we won't."

"Okay," she said, uncertain still if this was her only option. If they were caught then it could mean being sentenced to more time here or even a ticket straight Downstairs. She didn't know how severe an infraction this would be.

Then there was Dean. Even if she weren't caught, it nagged at her that this was most definitely a violation of his trust. She remembered that look he'd given her when she'd messed up back with Phillipa Arnold's great-granddaughter, a look blown way beyond disappointed and closer to downright disgusted. Her actions had hurt him in that moment, and she didn't know if she could handle seeing him look at her that way again.

"So, you're in?" Asher asked, bringing her back to the present.

She nodded before she could give herself time to think and possibly talk herself out of it.

"Sweet. Are you up for swapping now?"

Terry's head snapped up to Asher's face, a jolt running through her. Right now? Already? "Uh, maybe tomorrow, or sometime later?"

"You're right, we should swap on a day we don't have anything going on. And at the start of the day so nobody will suspect anything."

Terry relaxed, noticing only now how tense she had become.

"I've got something I'll need to take care of before we do this anyway."

Before Terry could ask when a better time would be, Willow glomped her from behind, almost making Terry lose her balance.

When she'd let Terry go, Willow smiled a Cheshire Cat smile at them. "You two were looking awfully chummy. What were you talking about?"

"Nothing much," Terry answered, trying to sound nonchalant. But that only appeared to make Willow's interest grow.

"Okay," Willow said, dragging out the word in an unconvinc-

PURGATERRY

ing manner. "Well, we have to be going now, so she'll see you later, Asher!"

She then looped her arm through Terry's and dragged her away back toward their resident building.

14. Not Seeing the Whole Picture

In Terry's and Willow's room across from their beds was a single dresser with four drawers, two of which were assigned to Terry. She had yet to put anything in them, mostly because she didn't have anything. That was, until the notebook.

She hardly wanted to admit it, but the notebook she'd gotten in group had actually been coming in handy. Besides keeping track of the questions she'd asked Dean, she was also able to hide her small clutch of clues within its pages. Thankfully, the wrapper and the photos were flat enough that sticking them in the notebook didn't draw any attention to it. The photos may have passed for something innocuous, but the wrapper—Terry worried if someone like Cassiopeia discovered it, it might get her and Dean in trouble. She wasn't supposed to even know about her brother, after all.

She had also been jotting down the faint memory-laden dreams she had been having. The harder she concentrated on each of them, the more she could recollect, like letting her eyes adjust to a darkened room.

CELIA CLEAVELAND

There was the movie, Hatori putting it on for her after a hard day, the car in the rain, and flashes of other things, mostly just feelings with nothing fully visual to attach them to. But the more she tried to remember, the stronger this sense of dread became. It radiated from inside her at the thought of her still-living brother, causing an ache of grief that she didn't think was possible toward someone who wasn't dead. She couldn't shake the thought that if not death, something happened to him, something that wrapped guilt around her dread and tucked the ends in.

Terry hardly noticed when Willow tried to get her attention, saying something about meeting Dean, to which Terry only nodded.

Willow whistled and waved a hand in front of Terry's face. "Yoo-hoo, Terry. I said *we* need to get going to meet up with Dean."

Terry blinked, slamming the notebook closed to protect her accumulated secrets. She did trust Willow, but there were just some things she wanted to keep to herself, and the contents of her notebook were some of those things.

"Yeah, all right, I'm coming," she said distractedly as she pulled out the top drawer and tossed the notebook inside. "Are we doing the usual, meeting him at the station?"

"Mm-hmm," Willow answered, making sure her Tinkerbell pin was well secured on the olive-green cardigan she wore. "He said it's one of the more standard ones, so we're probably going to a hospital."

"Nice of him to switch things up for us." Terry pulled on her dark-gray shoes over purple socks. "Something resembling a normal place for a Shepherd to go, or at least, normal for this job."

Willow giggled. "He does like to pester Angie for the more interesting cases. Come on, we're gonna be late."

Despite it being a normal place for a Shepherd to find souls, Terry found the hospital uncomfortable the longer they were there.

PURGATERRY

This place was too crowded, and there were too many sounds and smells that caused Terry's stomach to churn. There was just something about simply being there that set her ill at ease, and, thankfully, Dean had noticed and allowed her to stay in the waiting room while he went to find their target soul for the day.

It was probably normal, Terry thought. There were plenty of people who got anxious in hospitals, but she couldn't help but sense that something intrinsically important to her life, or her death, was somehow connected to being in a hospital, or rather, *this* hospital.

Willow opted to sit with her, even though Terry figured that at least one of them should go with Dean to get credit for the hours of service. But her friend sat alongside her, kicking her feet and humming what sounded like a song from *The Phantom of the Opera*.

Terry half smiled at Willow's inability to keep still, even for just this short time. There weren't as many people in this waiting room as there had been on the ground floor, which Terry was pleased with. The nurses' desk or station or whatever it was called wasn't too far away, and every so often, she would hear snippets of conversation as the doctors, nurses, and other staff passed her. She had mostly tuned them out, choosing to focus on the small child in the center of the room playing with one of those twisty bar puzzle tables doctor's offices always seemed to have. That was, until a familiar name sprang up to her ear.

"Did you check 203's activity? Dr. Rojas wanted to see if there were any changes."

The other nurse shook her head, looking guilty. "Sorry, I'm new, is that the coma patient?" She fumbled for a file on her cart before continuing. "Sutton, Hatori H?"

The older nurse nodded tiredly. "Yes, but you should know we don't use their names around here, room numbers only."

Terry's eyes widened, and if she had a pulse, she knew it would be speeding up. She almost couldn't believe what she had just heard. But it had to be her Hatori. How many Hatoris could be around here? She tried to act casual as she shot a peripheral glance toward Dean.

"Willow," she whispered as her friend slowed her leg kicking to lean in toward her. "I'll be right back. Can you just... not tell Dean where I'm going?"

"I can't tell him if you don't tell me where you're going," she replied with a wink.

Terry flashed her a grateful smile and headed down the hallway to find Room 203. She carefully noted each room number as she drew closer to the right one, only to be halted by a locked door with a keypad. A pair of small windows on the doors allowed her to see that Hatori's room was just on the other side, if she could only get past this barrier.

As if someone were listening, the doors slid open, and a couple white-coated people came through, leaving Terry a few precious seconds to sneak past them and enter the restricted hallway.

She pumped her fist with enthusiasm. If it wasn't adrenaline coursing through her, at least something was causing her excitement. She could see Room 203 just ahead, and she nearly sprinted toward it before a large hand landed on her shoulder.

The hand held her in place, spinning her around to reveal a large male nurse staring disapprovingly at her.

"Who let you in here?" he asked. "I'm sorry, but there's no visitors in this wing right now."

"Yes, but you see..." Terry tried to make up an excuse for why she was there. "I'll just be in and out real quick, I promise."

The man shook his head. "Sorry, but you need to go back to the other part of the hallway." He indicated the doors as he began herding her toward them.

Her stomach dropped as he saw Dean peering at her through the circular door window.

"Looks like someone is waiting for you," the nurse said. "Go on now."

He scanned his hospital ID card, and the doors opened again,

PurgaTerry

Dean having backed up for them to let her through, and the nurse then practically shoved her to the other side.

Dean motioned for Terry to come with her. "Thank you, sir. I was looking for her."

"Just make sure she stays with you next time," the nurse grumbled before walking back through the doors.

The second they opened again, Terry made a break for the other side, Dean moving to block her way, but she faked right and went left, only for Dean to grab her arm and pull her back. He was physically holding her now, arm across her chest as she struggled to get free.

"Dean, you don't understand—"

"Oh I understand, Ter," he answered, face stern, but his tone kind. "But you can't go and see him. Not yet, all right?"

"But he's right there." She continued to struggle against Dean's grip, feeling hysterical now. Hot, embarrassing tears began to form and threatened to overflow. "Hatori—"

"This isn't the time." Dean's voice was all calm and soothing, which only made Terry struggle harder.

When the doors were fully closed and locked and there was no chance that she could get back in, he let her go. She rounded on him with a feral growl.

"Why didn't you tell me he was here?" She shoved him for good measure, willing him to strike back. She wanted a good reason to hit him properly. But Dean didn't rise to the bait. His voice remained even, his expression neutral.

"Let's go get some air; you don't want to cause a scene."

"Oh, I think I do, and I think I'm justified."

"Take a few deep breaths, and clear your head. We'll head outside, and then once you've calmed down, we'll talk about this."

"Why, so you can keep more secrets from me? So you can lie and hide more stuff? I don't want to listen to what you have to say right now. I just want to see my brother."

He tried to put his arm around her and steer her toward the elevator and back to the ground floor, but Terry jerked out of his comforting hold.

"Dean—" she pleaded, the tears streaking her face now much to her surprise and mortification. She lowered her voice, but she couldn't keep the audible hitch from it. "Please, he's right there on the other side of those doors."

Dean grew somber, nodding but refusing to look at her, only downward.

"I know, but you can't. Not right now, at least. Give me time to pull some strings and arrange something for you. You're right, I should have warned you that he was here, but I was afraid of exactly this happening. Just trust me, all right? We'll come back, I promise."

Terry took a shaky breath through her nose, letting it out through her mouth. She took her hoodie sleeve and wiped the tears from her face, finally allowing Dean to lead her away from the doors. Away from the one piece of her past that had been just within reach.

They passed Willow in the waiting room on the way to the elevator, and upon spotting them, she hopped out of her seat and followed. Dean made a gesture for her to keep her distance, which she did, and Terry was reluctantly grateful. She couldn't handle Willow's sun-shiny attitude at the moment; her own dark clouds were far too thick.

The hospital had a small courtyard outside, and as Willow made herself comfortable on a bench to wait out for their bus, Dean guided Terry out toward the one spot of green among the gray buildings.

The courtyard was quite small, but it brought forth a strange yearning to be surrounded on all sides by green, by the density of a wood. She felt the pull to head to where the trees grew so close together that they blocked out most of the sunlight. Where only streams of dappled light came through, and where the undergrowth would be soft beneath her bare feet.

Terry blinked, looking back down at her shoes, returning to reality and the heartache of being barred from seeing her brother.

PurgaTerry

She felt Dean's presence beside her and took another deep breath as he instructed, as she had instructed Willow to do on her first Shepherding.

"Dean, is it time for another round of questions?" she asked. "You offered before."

"And you turned them down, if I recall."

"Well, I want to cash them in now," she said. "And asking for them shouldn't count as a question, so don't be cute about it. I'm not in the mood."

"Wasn't planning on it." He shook his head, still maintaining that irritatingly calm tone. "But go ahead, if this'll help you, shoot."

"I was barefoot when I arrived in the Welcome Building," she said. "Or at least when I woke up there."

"That's true, but not exactly a question. Any chance you could reword that?"

"Was there a reason why I had no shoes or socks on when I arrived?"

Dean didn't look over at her as they stood side by side, facing a small birdbath, but Terry again watched for any expressions that might betray something he didn't want to reveal.

"Yes," he said. "There's a reason."

"When I died, did I... did I walk through some woods?"

She saw Dean flick a glance her way, and Terry noted that he made sure not to make direct eye contact. "Yes, you did."

"And you were there, right? You were the one who found me?"

Dean's mouth pulled tight for a second, still avoiding her gaze. "Yes. I was the one who found you."

"So, you were the one who gave me the choice after I died to come to Purgatory?"

"Not exactly."

"What does that mean?"

"Is that your last question for this round?"

Terry chewed on her lower lip, considering. Dean might let her take that one back since it was her fifth question, but another part of her truly did want to know. Her curiosity was nearly the winner in this inner argument of her mind. She wasn't sure he would answer that one honestly, but he had surprised her before...

"Yes, it is," she said, finally. "And no 'classified' stuff this time."

"That's not part of the established rules," Dean said.

"Well, tough. I'm getting tired of that excuse, and you're wearing it out."

"It's not an excuse," he said a tad defensively. "There really are things about you—about your memories and what happened specifically—you're just not allowed to know. That you're not ready for."

"Well, still. As much as you can tell me, what does that mean?"

It took several seconds before Dean finally answered. Terry turned to face a couple of hospital staff on the far side of the courtyard having a smoke break.

"It means—" he started, leaning onto a low stone wall separating the courtyard's walkway from the plants, looking upward toward the sky. "It means that we—I—was too late to keep you from doing what you did, and I was too late to actually give you the choice."

"So... I didn't have one, or did somebody else give me the choice?"

"That's another question; you'll have to wait for the next round," he said, smiling again.

"That's bull, and you know it." She rounded on him, looking straight at him. "Come on, you can't give me that answer and not expect me to want to know more."

"I don't control the questions. That's on you," he said. "I just answer them to the best of my abilities."

"But you control the whole thing. You could change the rules." Even though Terry knew that he wouldn't, she thought it was at least worth bringing it up. Up until now, Terry had tried to understand Dean's side of things, to try and find a reason that he wouldn't be allowed to give an answer to her questions. But this time, she really didn't understand. If she couldn't see Hatori, then he could at least explain what he meant. If he wasn't the

PURGATERRY

one to give her the option, then who was? She couldn't have just not been given the choice.

"How about the other girl—she was the one who Edie mentioned—the one you don't appear to want to talk about. Did she give me the choice? Did she know anything about me? Was she even there?"

"That would be Dels, Delilah," he answered. "But that's all I can say about your case. She was one of my trainees and worked under me, like I told Edie. She... she left about the same time you arrived."

"And I had to learn about her secondhand, by chance." She flung the sentence at him as an accusation. "You trusted Delilah enough to bring her to Angel's, to see your family," Terry said. She hadn't really put the pieces together, hadn't realized that Dean had been so close to her.

"Yeah," Dean answered, a tad wearily, turning around and facing the walkway while still leaning on the low wall. "That was my mistake. But I brought you there, too. What does that tell you?"

"You only brought me there to explain yourself," she said. "I wouldn't think it was because you thought anything particular about me."

"It was a bit of a bribe, sure. However, I was taking a chance on you, too. Those things that Cass said about you, they were true. You and Dels have a lot in common, or at least you did. I didn't want to see you go down the same path as her. Not because it would make me look bad—well, not only that—but because I like you. You seemed like a good kid, Ter. You just needed the right push to do what you needed to do."

"Do you still think that?" she asked.

"Well..." He stretched out the word playfully, and she shoved him just as playfully, actually managing a laugh. "Of course. And I'm glad I wasn't wrong this time around. I thought that Dels. Well, I guess it doesn't matter now what I thought. But I am glad I was right about you."

Terry didn't want to press him about his relationship with

Delilah. She didn't really have much experience with such things, but the way he danced around things concerning her was different from when he avoided her usual questions about herself. There was a kind of relationship—connection—there that Terry thought she shouldn't remark upon. It seemed a little bit too personal, no matter how close she had grown to feel toward him.

"So, Cassiopeia would be on your case if you'd let me see Hatori?"

"That's part of the reason why I couldn't allow you to see him. It's not like me and my family. Cass and I have an understanding about it. He might be part of your unfinished business, but there's a right way of going about things."

"Why does she dislike me so much, though?" she asked.

"She doesn't. On the contrary, I think she can see what I see in you. Potential. Whether that's potential for good or bad, I don't know. She wants to be certain of the same things I do. That you make the right choices. You've already got your past decisions stacked against you, you know."

"Oh, I know," Terry said, rolling her eyes. "You guys won't let me forget it, or anyone else for that matter. It seems like all I'm ever doing here is trying to prove myself."

"I suppose that's part of the whole process of the place," Dean said. "You're proving you can make up for the things you did before and that you're capable of moving on from them."

"What's the alternative, though?" she asked. "To stagnate? To just stay in Purgatory forever?"

"It's not unheard of. Eventually, you will have to transition one way or another, though."

Terry thought about what Willow said of Purgatory being like a giant waiting room... a liminal space. Somewhere she wasn't meant to be in forever. That lined up with what Dean was getting at.

Although it had been a warm day when they arrived, the sun was beginning to set, and the air was growing cooler. Terry smiled when she spotted a couple flickers of fireflies, a little

PURGATERRY

bummed that Willow wasn't there to see them. The frogs and crickets had begun to sing their songs, and she savored their sound, closing her eyes as if to reach out with her mind and touch the memories that were clicked on by the sound but still just out of reach.

"You'll let me know when—if—we get Hatori's schedule, right?"

Dean tapped out a rhythm on the wall, licking his lip before responding. "We don't know if he'll be getting his ticket punched just yet, P-Terry."

"But if we do, you will tell me?"

He nodded. "Of course. But you don't think I've had Angie looking out for him just the same as for my April?"

Terry couldn't help but let a smile form. She was honestly touched that he'd even think to do that for her.

A siren grew louder, and Terry watched as an ambulance pulled up to the circular drive at the front of the hospital, EMTs rushing a gurney through the sliding doors. Dean had been watching, too, and when he spoke again, Terry wasn't sure he was really talking to her.

"You'd think we would remember when we were first told that everything dies, including us."

"I don't think that we can actually comprehend the concept until we're older, though," Terry replied. Even though it seemed like he had only been voicing a thought, not asking for feedback.

"Still, it's a fact of life that people just seem to accept on the surface but don't ever want to mention."

Dean gave a sigh, still leaning onto the short wall. "And suicide even more so, it's more taboo than many other ways to go. That might be why we—well, you all—are seen as such second-class residents in Purgatory."

"But if we all have things to repent for in Purgatory, why is our cause of death so much worse?"

"Because it's cutting your nose to spite your face, maybe?"

"What does that mean?"

Dean smirked. "Old-timey phrase, I suppose. Now, I know the

platitude 'it gets better' gets thrown around too much these days, but even if it doesn't get completely better, how will you know if you decide to end the race early?"

Terry contemplated that, remembering Dean's metaphor about dropping her full plate. Before she made that choice to die that way—even if she couldn't remember the specifics—she would have thought that it was a selfish act. Leaving your life and forcing one's loved ones to deal with the fallout. But that wasn't all that true, not completely. Forcing yourself to stay alive only for your loved ones might be just as bad. Finding somewhere in the middle, finding a reason to live for yourself and finding hope so that you can continue, despite the reasons your brain tries to bully you into believing.

"I guess you just have to find reasons, even if they aren't just for your loved ones. Why do you think you decided to do it?"

"Isn't that what I've been trying to get you to tell me since the beginning?"

"Yes... but I want to know what you think the reason was."

Now he sounded like a teacher who knew she knew the answer to a question but just wanted to hear her say it. The problem was that Terry hadn't fully dug that deep into her feelings of 'why.' Wasn't that what Orion had wanted them to do at some point? In any case, she tried to bring up what she could remember feeling in that one memory, with the rain falling on the car's roof, and the radio, and her sobs.

"I... I think I legitimately felt like a burden? Like no one actually cared. I was just an obligation."

It was strange, the more she thought about it, the more she could remember how it felt. The way it collapsed time made her forget her memories even before the Lethe Machine. It was an endless, suffocating loop of nothing that weighed her down and drowned her until she couldn't even think of calling for help.

Her mother—something about her mother and her brother. They were upstanding citizens, they were contributing to life and the world, and what was she? Who was she compared to her

PURGATERRY

brilliant brother and her altruistic mother? Why couldn't she remember her mother's name, her face, but she could recall all the ways that she made her feel inadequate?

She figured she mustn't go down that road, not right now. She'd save that for her notebook when she was safely back in her room.

Now that she was pulling herself back into a better headspace, she remembered her promise to Juliet to take pictures while they were there. She fumbled for the bag Willow had lent her, lifting the flap and pulling out the camera. The courtyard was a nice enough spot. She wasn't entirely sure what Juliet would prefer pictures of, but she began pointing and shooting anyway. A bee had been buzzing around a few flowers, and Terry caught a shot of it just as it was landing on a bloom. She found Dean in the viewfinder and attempted to take a candid snapshot until he spotted her and made a face at the camera.

She smiled and laughed a short, breathy laugh before searching for other things she could photograph—a few more shots of the hospital building and parking structure and the parked ambulance at the front.

"Didn't know you were taking up photography," Dean said. "You may want to stow that away when we head out to get Willow."

"It's Juliet's." She lowered the viewfinder from her eye and made one last look around for subjects. "She wants some pictures of Earth while we're here, and I said I'd take some."

"Surprisingly kind of you," Dean said then backtracked when Terry looked offended. "No, no, not surprising that you're being kind, I'm just glad to see you taking more initiative, P-Terry."

"How is this helping me with my community service?" She held the camera up to emphasize.

"Every little bit of participation helps. You trust me, right?"

"A few weeks ago, I would have said no." She held the camera back up and looked through at some of the people exiting the front hospital doors. "But now—"

Terry paused, momentarily stunned and uncertain she had

actually seen what she had seen. For a split second she could have sworn she saw Asher exiting the sliding doors and going toward the corner of the building. She lowered the camera for a second and then brought it back up to check, wishing she knew if this thing had a zoom in feature. Once she was homed in on the spot she thought she saw him, she snapped another picture, but by the time she had, whoever it was that might have been Asher was already gone.

It couldn't have been him, though, she reasoned. He didn't have the right form of ID to be able to get access to Earth. And even if it was him, and he had somehow gotten that access, why would he even be down here? Of course, the answer came to her immediately. The same reason why she had been so desperate to get to Hatori. Asher, too, had unfinished business, living people to get in contact with. She couldn't blame him even if it really had been him.

Even if she was wrong about it, a part of her knew she should probably bring this up to Dean. If it had been Asher—well, she didn't think it could be, anyway. Terry didn't want to get Asher in trouble for something that she thought she saw. If she told Dean, he would tell Cassiopeia, and it would be a whole thing that could have been avoided. Not to mention if she did indeed take Asher up on his offer to trade for answers, getting him in trouble would absolutely jeopardize that.

So, Terry stayed silent, the words dissolving on her tongue upon finding Dean's gaze again. He seemed to be appraising her, perhaps making sure she was well and truly okay now.

"I'm good now, Dean. You don't have to worry."

"Maybe I'm not worried, hmm? Maybe I just want to make sure you're not going to sneak off once we get back in there."

She rolled her eyes. "I won't, *Dad.*"

She led the way back to the inside this time, but before she turned from him, she could see a pleased, bordering on smug expression on Dean's face.

15. The Whole Picture

Terry didn't exactly try to listen in on people's private conversations, really, she didn't. It just so happened that this time she had rounded a corner and found herself witnessing another one happening right out in the open, this time between Asher and Orion.

"You're lucky it was me who found you with this and not your manager," she heard Orion as she'd approached the rec room. Noticing both him and an uncharacteristically emotional Asher, Terry backed up silently to hide behind the doorframe.

"No, please don't," Asher begged, his voice hitching and sounding like he was fighting back tears. "I didn't think any of you would understand, especially Cassiopeia. But I just— I just wanted to go home. Or as close as I could get to it."

"You should really give us managers more credit," Orion replied. "This needs to be disposed of; it should have been destroyed the moment Delilah left here. But to ease your fears, I won't tell Cassiopeia."

"Oh, thank you, thank you, Mr. Orion," Terry heard Asher

sniffling through his words, and it put her a little out of sorts. She hardly thought that Asher would be one to expose his emotions like this, but she had been wrong about people here on Level Eight before.

"You're welcome, Asher. But this is a serious matter. I don't want to hear about you being found with any other items that might get you in jeopardy. And perhaps this might help open you up to trusting the people around you a bit more."

"I'll definitely think about that," Asher said, the thickness of his emotion still evident in his speech. "Thank you so much."

A chair scraped against the floor, and Terry could hear footsteps, so she figured she might emerge from her hiding place and enter the room proper. Orion passed her without comment but appeared to be mildly surprised to see her. She approached Asher cautiously, as he was still sniffling, his back to the doorway.

"Um, Asher?" she inquired, uncertain how she should handle him or if he needed some space.

"Is he gone?" he whispered, lowering his hands from his face.

Terry turned around to check and saw no sign of him.

"Yes, he's gone," she said. "Are you okay, though?"

At the mention that Orion was gone, Asher immediately straightened his posture, sniffed one final time, and turned to face Terry with a sideways grin, not a tear evident on his face.

"Oh, I'm fine, Pj's, it's all good."

"Then what was that?" She jerked her thumb behind her in the direction Orion had gone. He waved her gesture away and made a sound of dismissal.

"That was just to make sure Orion didn't rat me out about using that old ID to get to Earth."

"Wait, you had another person's ID to get to Earth? If you had one this whole time, what did you need with mine?"

"Insurance," he said. "I wanted to find a different way just in case you backed out. An opportunity presented itself, so I took it," Asher said. "That ID was supposed to be destroyed, but I picked it up before they could find it. I've been using it for a little while, but I knew something like this would happen eventually."

"So... you still want to use mine?"

"If you're offering. It's not like that old one would've stayed active if its owner isn't in Purgatory anymore anyway. But that was all I had until you."

"But you knew you'd get caught with it, so why even take the risk?"

"Why not? I think you know the answer. You'd do crazy shit to get your closure, right?"

Terry had to agree. She was still entertaining the idea of trading with him to gain access to the Hall of Records.

"Look, was the Delilah ID plan doomed from the start? Probably. But it was the only one I had until this whole 'swap' thing presented itself. If you're still down, we might wanna do it somewhere we won't draw attention."

Her hesitation appeared to annoy him slightly, but she couldn't help it. And he couldn't exactly blame her, could he?

"Can I have a little more time to think about it?"

He paused before answering, "Sure, we can meet up at that party-mixer thing they're doing tonight. And, Pj's, don't think too hard about it. This is what'll get you what you want. They want you to move on, so this is just another way of doing that."

It was hard not to think hard about it, but she supposed Asher had a point. On the other hand, Willow also had made a valid point that she should consider the possible consequences. The uncertainty churned inside her and didn't put her in a very party-like mood. But she did want to show she was participating, so she began to prepare herself mentally for the night as it unfolded.

The party was supposed to have karaoke, and it was all but mandatory, according to Willow. Terry hadn't sung since she came to Purgatory, so she didn't know if she even could. But Willow said it was a nice bonding social activity. And if Terry was going to be more active and social to earn her five more questions, then this was the best type of thing to show Dean she meant what she'd promised.

The other residents were gathered in a large gymnasium-looking room off to the side of the residents' wing. The DJ and karaoke equipment were still being set up, and Terry began to notice that there were other faces there that she didn't know, ones that looked older than her.

"Are they combining different departments?" she asked.

"Yeah," said Willow. "These are about three or four other groups that all fall under the same district as us, the North American branch, and we're the YA group for just the US and sometimes Canada if they need."

"The whole country is our district?"

"Well, there are more subcategories, but that's our main title, I guess."

They found Juliet milling about the crowd, looking like she was lost without her 'big brother' to guide her.

"Oh, hi, guys," Juliet said with much more energy than Terry had seen her have before. The moment she spotted them, she looked relieved. "I'm so glad I finally found someone I know."

"Jules, that's the whole point of this mixer, though. To make new friends," Willow said. "Why don't we go and find some new people to talk to?"

She turned to Terry. "Will you be okay by yourself for a little bit?" she asked.

Terry nodded. "Sure, of course. Go on ahead. I'll be around."

Willow hugged her and then whispered close to her ear, "Thanks, T. I've been trying to hang out with Juliet alone again since the Library date."

"No problem," she responded.

After Juliet and Willow had gone off somewhere, Terry guessed that she could start to mingle as well. She, too, didn't see anybody she recognized.

She approached an olive-skinned girl with long black hair and introduced herself.

"So, what district are you from?"

"*Qué? Lo siento, no hablo inglés,*" the girl said.

"Okay... sorry, my bad," she said. She hadn't realized there would be people speaking other languages here, but perhaps that was her privileged United States way of thinking coming to rear its ugly head. It was common sense now that she actually gave it a thought. There were people dying all over the world, after all. Not all of them would speak her language.

Something about that encounter, though, sparked a memory in her mind, a faint déjà vu kind of feeling, that she had heard—and even spoken—another language before. It wasn't Spanish, with its musical lilts and dips, but a sharper, more clipped dialect that reminded her of summers, and ice cream, and... grandparents?

It wasn't a fully tangible thing, but Terry was ecstatic all the same. She could remember her grandparents, or at least that they spoke another language, and she'd had to learn it to communicate with them. If she could only remember what language...

"Hey, it's Pj's," a familiar voice called to her, and Terry came out of her reverie to see Asher smiling slyly as ever. Willow continued to say that he looked like that because he liked her, but Terry couldn't be sure. He might just look like that with everyone. In any case, she didn't really think she was interested in him that way. She didn't feel like she was interested in anyone that way, if she was honest with herself.

"Hey, Asher," Terry greeted him, hoping that—if he did like-like her—she wasn't putting off any signals other than friendly ones. "Are you going to be taking part in the whole karaoke thing?"

"Nah, that ain't my thing," he said. "You go on ahead, though, if it's yours. I'm good with just watching."

"Honestly, I don't know if it's my thing, either," she said. "I might just stick with dancing."

"Well, then be sure to save me a dance, won't you?" he said. He then tried to take her hand, but she moved it away, trying to pretend that she hadn't noticed.

"Sure, you can dance with me and Willow and Juliet, all of us."

Asher laughed, somewhat nervously in Terry's opinion, but he didn't look too rattled at her words. She dearly hoped that she hadn't insulted him. At the same time, though, she really didn't feel comfortable leading him on.

"So, you got an answer for me?" he asked through the din. The music was a high-energy techno number, and Terry thought that it would have been easier if they hadn't chosen this party as the meeting place. At the same time, she didn't want to string him along any more than she had been. He had been nice enough to offer her something risky, and she should be nice enough to give a response as promised.

"I don't think I should," she admitted, talking over the music close to his ear. "It's just that Dean—"

"Dean, Dean, Dean," he criticized loudly. "Pj's, I keep telling you, not a single one of those managers gives a shit about us. If Dean is so great and different and whatever, why has he been keeping secrets from you?"

"How do you know they're secrets? Dean's told me a lot—or as much as he can. I don't want to betray his trust and risk getting him in trouble, too."

Asher groaned, rolling his head back dramatically. "Oh, come on! Don't be so naive. You don't think he's been keeping the real secrets from you? The whole reason you're even in Purgatory to begin with?"

"What do you mean?"

"I mean, I got curious and found your file when I was on duty earlier today. It was password protected, but it linked up to Delilah's old file, the one whose ID I'd been using. You know that Ticket Repository they got? Your ticket was a backup copy, meaning somebody took the original."

"I have no idea what any of that means, Asher."

PURGATERRY

"It means that you may have died by suicide, but someone put you up to it. Someone cheated you. That girl Delilah, actually. Dean's former recruit. So, it was all his fault you're here, and he's trying to cover it up."

The music halted suddenly, fading away from Terry's ears and being replaced with a ringing sound. A numbness overcame her, a dread that what Asher was saying might have been right. Because it would make sense; it would explain so much.

"You're lying," were the words that came out of her mouth, though she didn't recall forming them.

"I'm sorry to say, I'm not," he responded. "Delilah influenced you to kill yourself right under Dean's nose, and he's been trying to bury the evidence ever since you got here."

The ringing sound and the numbness were getting stronger. Terry's mind was reeling, and she started feeling off-kilter, as if the news were sinking in so rapidly that it was affecting her balance.

Not knowing exactly how she died, she could remember feeling the presence of a person who left her before Dean showed up. Dean's extreme reaction to her use of the emotion manipulation on a living person... it all started to come together in her mind. He always skirted any talks about her death, and he seemed even less inclined to discuss Delilah.

Terry had to be sure, though, and there was only one person at this party who could give her the truth.

She pushed past Asher and through the crowd to the last place she could recall Willow being. She found her friend on a circular sectional couch with Juliet, apparently taking a break from dancing.

"Hey, Ter," Willow greeted her with her usual chipper tone, but upon reading the panic in her expression, Willow stood and guided her closer to the far wall where there were fewer people.

"What's wrong?" she asked, and Terry didn't beat around the bush.

She watched Willow's eyes carefully as she asked, "Did Delilah cheat me? Did she manipulate me into killing myself?"

Willow's eyes grew and her face paled, the sunshine gone from her expression.

"Terry... I'm sorry."

"So, you knew? You knew, and both of you kept it from me!"

"I'm so, so, so sorry, Terry!" Willow pleaded. "But Dean made me promise. He said it was for your own good that you didn't know."

"So... so I don't just have my years to work off here, but hers, too?"

"I'm sure Dean would've told you eventually," Willow tried to reason, but reason was becoming a faint memory for Terry. Her numbness had subsided and been replaced with the growing heat of a righteous anger.

"Dean could have told me from the start!" she shouted, thankfully still not loud enough to be heard by everyone over the music. She yanked Willow by the elbow and dragged her out into the much quieter hallway.

"Let me see if I understand this," Terry said once they were out of the cacophony. "Dean's former Shepherd trainee—whom you also knew—manipulated me into killing myself, forcing me to take on the years she had left here, so she could move on from Purgatory. So, instead of, like, sixty years here, I might have double that?"

"Like I said, Dean thought you didn't need to know about that yet. He thought that it might discourage you."

"Oh, he thought I didn't 'need' to know the entire reason I'm here was because someone manipulated me?"

"It's not all Delilah's fault," Willow said. "You were someone who was already high risk, but—"

"So, you're blaming me, the victim?"

"No, no!" Willow said, backpedaling. "I'm not blaming you, not really. I'm just saying that even if you were cheated, you still had a choice just like all of us. Every one of us here had the choice to take our own lives, and you were already at a risk of doing it.

PURGATERRY

Delilah kind of... pushed you over the edge."

"It sounds to me like I didn't have a choice," Terry spat. "It sounds more like I got my choice taken away from me. Wasn't I supposed to be able to decide for myself if I wanted to be stuck here? It's freaking convenient then that I don't remember that or anything before I woke up in the room with the Lethe Machine isn't it?"

"Dean thought—"

"I don't care what Dean thought. Dean was wrong. He was wrong to keep this from me, and you were wrong to help him." In the distance, Terry caught sight of Asher as he scanned the crowd for her, and she marched past Willow to meet him.

"I'll be right back. You're going to help me find out what else Dean's been keeping from me."

Leaving a stunned and severely ashamed Willow, Terry moved back through the crowd to Asher, who appeared to have been waiting for her to return. She whipped out her ID and shoved it into his chest, to his surprise and amusement.

"So, I take it you got confirmation I was telling the truth?"

"Yeah, and here's my ID. Go nuts. Do whatever you want with it. Now give me yours. I'm going into the Hall of Records tonight."

As far as Terry figured, the party was a good distraction to keep everyone away from the other buildings while she and Willow broke into the HoR. Well, not truly 'breaking,' since they had Asher's ID, but Terry certainly felt like breaking something at the moment.

Willow had convinced her to head back to their room, which was as good a place as any for Terry to figure out her plan from there.

"Ter, I know you're really upset about what Dean didn't tell you," Willow began, "but I don't want you to do anything rash, okay? Just think really, super hard about what breaking into the records hall might do, how it might go."

"I know how it'll go, Willow," Terry said, already forming the plan in her head. "I'll finally get the answers before I have to hear secrets about myself from somebody else."

She flung open the empty drawers just to slam them shut. Terry knew perfectly well that she hadn't put anything in them; she just wanted something to slam.

"I get it, T, I really do, and Dean understands as well. He must, or he wouldn't have made such an effort to keep it from you."

Willow watched her as Terry paced through the entire length of their room full of emotions that she still couldn't contain. Not finding the pacing any better at clearing her head, she flopped down on the bed to scream into a pillow. She'd seen people do it on TV, and it looked cathartic.

She heard Willow slightly muffled through the pillow.

"All I'm saying is that you should take a day or so to calm down, maybe just a night. If you still want to do it tomorrow, we'll go. I still don't think it's a good idea, but I'll go with you to support you. But I really think that once you've had time to think, you'll reconsider.

"No, I'm not reconsidering anything. I'm doing this now, with or without you. But I could really use someone with me. Face it, you owe me, Willow."

Willow couldn't argue with that, and her sheepish avoidance of Terry's fierce gaze told her that she wouldn't.

"Okay," she said quietly, nodding but looking down at the floor.

"All right," Terry said. "We leave in five minutes. If you need to get something or do something, do it now. We only have until the party is over."

16. Flashback to Reality

The Hall of Records, at first glance, looked just the same as the Library. From the outside, it had the same brick exterior with matching arches and the same gray brick pathway leading up to the door. This door, however, was not an open window sliding glass door, but a big heavy metal door. Not being able to see inside only added to the unease that Terry felt.

She swallowed it down, though. Still riding high off the rage from the revelation at the party, she let that internal anger fuel her as she pulled Willow up to the menacing metal door. Willow followed behind her with surprising meekness as she let Terry literally drag her along.

"Are you really sure about this?" she asked, speaking for the first time since it became clear that Terry was not in a talking mood. "I mean, I completely understand why you're angry, but this might not be the best idea. If you just take a second to clear your head—"

"Oh, my head is plenty clear," Terry said. "I know exactly what I'm doing. And if we get caught, it'll be Dean's fault for not giving me the whole truth when he had the chance."

She took her eyes off the door for a moment to notice Willow's eyebrows creasing. She bit her lip as if to hold back all of the things she wanted to say, as well as any emotional outburst. This was the first time since she came back from Disneyland that Terry had seen Willow upset. It was unnerving and made her pause to remember that Willow didn't want to be a part of this.

"Hey, if you want to just stay out here and keep a lookout, that's fine," Terry offered.

Willow hesitated, but she shook her head.

"No, it's okay. You're set on breaking the rules, I might as well go down with you."

"Seriously, if you're not comfortable, you can stay outside."

Another moment of consideration from Willow. She steeled her gaze as she looked at Terry.

"I do think Dean was just looking out for you, and that he thought he was doing what was best. But I don't agree with how he's gone about doing things... so if this place can help you find answers then I want to help."

Terry smiled. She'd only known this girl for the couple of months she'd been in Purgatory. It warmed her heart to see Willow so ride-or-die for her like this. It almost made her forget about her anger toward Dean. Almost.

Terry fished Asher's ID from her hoodie pocket, her mind flicking back momentarily to Hatori's name tucked inside her notebook. Soon. Soon, she would know everything, and maybe she could see him again. For the first time since she died, at least.

The door had a number lock and a place to swipe the card, and it took her a couple of tries to get the right combination of steps, but eventually, the little light above glowed green, and the locks tumbled into place with a satisfying thunk to let them inside.

Terry took a deep breath, half expecting there to be an alarm or some type of extra security measure, but she pulled the door open with both hands, hearing no alarms and seeing no sign of a maze of lasers or anything. It was almost too easy. But then again,

PURGATERRY

the hard part was getting access to the ID clearance she needed.

The door made a loud, unpleasant metallic sound behind them as they stepped into the darkness. Terry took a few tentative steps through the complete blackness before pausing to test that the floor kept going ahead of them. As if at the detection of her footsteps, a trail of lights began to stretch out before them, illuminating the walkway. The sounds of large light switches being flipped on echoed through the enormous chamber Terry now saw themselves in. Every few feet or so, a new overhead light would burst to life, one by one, until the entire structure was fully lit with bright-white light.

"Wow," she heard Willow exclaim from behind her. "It looks like the inside of the EPCOT ball."

Terry chuckled. "You would think that."

The walkway stretched out another two or three yards ahead of them before stopping in the very center of the globe. Terry spotted at the end of the walkway what looked like some form of computer console and possibly a microphone attached to it. She eased her way closer, taking care even though they could now see. The walkway was narrow, with only a skinny handrail separating them from falling to the bottom. Although she knew she was dead, Terry wondered if the height would be enough to kill someone if they fell off.

They made it to the end after a slow walk with Willow clinging to her side. She hadn't realized Willow was afraid of heights, which was ironic, since she, too, was also dead. But she didn't voice these thoughts to Willow as she didn't think they would help.

The console at the end did indeed have a small microphone sticking out of the center. It was black and all curves with the oddest assortment of buttons and switches that Terry couldn't even begin to decipher how to use.

A red button near the microphone blinked on and off, winking at her along with the near Christmas-tree levels of multicolored lights. This red one was different, however. It blinked in a rhythm out of sequence with the others. This might have been what drew Terry's eyes to it, and what compelled her to choose it to push first.

Willow had finally relaxed her grip and pried her fingers away when it was clear that the center and end of the walkway weren't going to collapse under them. She hung back as Terry pressed the button.

The button changed to green when pressed, and a computerized tone echoed through the vast expanse. A projection then cast itself in front of them, giant words hovering above them on an invisible screen.

The words that appeared read "Hall of Records: Level Eight clearance required" followed by blank spaces where Terry assumed she needed to input some form of passcode. Asher hadn't said anything about this part, although he might have thought it was obvious or not worth mentioning.

But it was worth mentioning. If she needed to have some form of password that only the managers knew, she'd have no way of knowing what the code could be. What was more, there was no keyboard for her to enter a code in a way she understood. She assumed the tiny switches did something, but she didn't want to risk flipping one and causing some form of error.

"Maybe the different colors do different things?" Willow offered, pointing at some of the lights on the console.

"Worth a shot," she said. Terry tried pushing a green light, which turned red, then a red light, which turned blue, then a green light, which turned purple. With each different color, a new color would crop up. Terry couldn't make any sense of it. She must have gotten lucky with the first button, and that had used up most of her luck for the night.

"Maybe you need to hit the lights in a certain order?" Willow tried.

Terry frowned at the blinking buttons, not sure if there was a pattern to follow. It all seemed so random to her. That was, until Willow tapped a yellow button at the same time she hit a blue one, and they both lit up green and stayed that way.

PURGATERRY

She looked up at the hovering words and noticed that two of the blank spaces had been filled in with asterisks. So, they had at least done something.

With each failed try, the lights that had turned green would blink off, and Terry would have to start again, this time trying to remember the correct sequence. She had done this at least five tries, and she hoped that there wasn't a finite number of tries before something would happen.

"If you keep getting it wrong, an alarm might go off," Willow said, unhelpfully.

"I know, I know," Terry grumbled, frustrated with herself for continuing to get the last two spots wrong. She was so close to finding it that every failed attempt was like a personal insult smacking her in the face.

"Wait, did you notice that the first one goes in backward rainbow order?" she asked. "Leaving out green, of course."

Terry blinked, turning fully toward Willow, one eyebrow raised. "You think you found a pattern, and you didn't think to tell me this, like, ten tries ago?"

"I wasn't sure about it at first," Willow said with a shrug. "It looks like it goes purple, blue, yellow, orange, and red. But you start with yellow and skip green because they all turn green."

Terry supposed that was a kind of logic, sort of. So, she tried the pattern Willow laid out, starting with the yellow and going from there. Immediately, she got through six colors in a row, all lighting up green and staying that way. She then punched in the remaining two, bracing herself for something to happen.

And something did happen; the lights all lit up green for a second, the words and spaces dissipated from the space above them, and the words 'Access Granted' flashed in their place.

Terry breathed a sigh of relief, now suddenly energized by anticipation and excitement instead of her earlier anger and rage.

Willow bounced and squealed next to her. "Yay, we did it!" Then, noticing that her cheers echoed in the globe, she changed to a whisper. "Yay, we did it. Now what?"

"I guess we test it out," she said. "But I'm still not sure how to—" Then a thought occurred to her. "Wait, maybe I speak into the mic."

Not sure what sort of command to give the console, she settled for just speaking her name, or the name that she knew, anyway.

She cleared her throat and leaned toward the mic. "Files on resident Terry, of Level Eight."

The words cleared themselves and were replaced by new ones that read "Resident Inquiry, last four digits of resident number required."

Crap, she didn't know her last four digits. They were on her ID, but that was with Asher. Maybe there was another way to bypass the requirement.

Willow—now growing bored, it seemed—patted Terry on the shoulder and took a few steps away down the walkway. "It looks like you've got this handled, right? I think I'd like to get off this tiny walkway, just for my own peace of mind."

"Okay, fine," Terry answered, distracted. "Have a look around, and if you see anything that might help, let me know."

"Okie-dokie," Willow said, and Terry heard her shoes clacking down the metal walkway.

Terry inspected the lights, which were back to blinking their rainbow of colors, and the various silver switches. What had Asher mentioned before about some sort of "scanning machine"?

She couldn't see anything that might call this "scanning machine" forth, but then she thought that perhaps the microphone might work again if she tried it.

"Um... scanning machine?"

Immediately, the words "Calling: Scanning Machine PT-0165519" appeared, and a long, snake-like metal tube uncoiled itself from one of the panels in the globe's enormous side.

Once it was straightened out, it shook itself as if it had just woken up and blinked a large camera resembling an eye at the end of the long, articulated body. It looked around the cavernous room, finally spotting the console and zooming down toward it.

PURGATERRY

It blinked again as it caught sight of Terry, and she did indeed have the feeling that it was scanning her. It moved its large eye up, down, and across her form.

Then, a computerized voice spoke from the eye stalk. "Resident DCR-129. Finding file matches."

One second later, the invisible screen floating there was filled with images popping up like windows one right after the other. They kept popping up, stacking on top of each other, each resembling a small video screen window, and each showing a first-person view of a life... her life.

They were still stacking on top of each other until the screen was a blur of jumbled colors. Terry was overwhelmed by the choices. Taking a chance, she flipped a switch near the left side of the console, and immediately, the chamber echoed with a thousand sounds as each video memory played at full volume. In the cacophony, Terry could make out voices, sirens, cars honking, music, every sound that accompanied her life all crashing down on her in one sonic wave.

Willow had found a side walkway and followed it to one of the seams of the globe. Terry watched as she covered her ears and shouted something that Terry could—of course—not hear over the din.

She frantically scrambled to flip that switch off, dousing the noise and dropping the room into silence again. Both she and Willow let out sighs of relief.

"I'm going to try and find a way to isolate one memory," she said across the way to Willow, who raised a thumbs up toward her but otherwise still covered her ears as best she could.

As Terry fiddled with the switches, she observed out of the corner of her eye Willow's progress around the dome, pausing every so often to feel for something or make some exclamation that Terry wasn't paying any attention to.

She still didn't have a handle on how time worked in Purgatory, but she knew that it was most likely not long until the sun rose. Eventually, she would have to take what information she could and get out of there. She ceased her switch flipping and spoke again into the microphone. The scanning machine who had been watching her leaned in toward her, as if waiting for an instruction.

"Uh, DCR-129 files on Hatori."

The scanning machine blinked at her, and then new video windows popped up in front of the old ones as over half of them went away. An image of a boy no older than ten speaking to her and covering her skinned knee with a bandage, one of the same boy, but older, holding a video game controller as her past self's gaze went from him to the screen where images of the game flashed. One of the boy, now a young man, sitting at a table in a kitchen, poring over books, a laptop screen illuminating his increasingly tired face. She saw her own hands nudge a coffee cup full of hot liquid toward him, and him take it with a sleepy smile, one hand coming up toward her head.

This was Hatori. This was Terry's brother. She still hadn't found a way to hear the individual clips, but she could see him plain as day. She wondered if they looked alike, if her form here in Purgatory was a good mirror of what she looked like in life. He was fair-skinned; even a couple freckles stood out across his face. Dark eyes and hair, and a smile that warmed some indistinct part of her, something that made it feel like home.

The videos kept coming, though, showing more moments with Hatori that weren't so pleasant. They were arguing, and Terry was unable to understand his words, but the look on his face and the speed at which his mouth was moving indicated he was shouting. She could make out a word or two, but only ones like "so stupid" and "how could you?" She saw him look away to the right, and the camera (that was her past self) whipped in that direction as well to reveal a small but older woman, with similar features and hair color to Hatori and—she assumed—herself.

The older woman—their mother?—spoke slowly, holding out her hands to the both of them, apparently trying to ease the situation. Like with Hatori, the sound was muted, but from her expression, it didn't seem like she was happy about whatever

PURGATERRY

situation they were in, but at least she wasn't shouting about it at Terry.

Another video popped up with this woman, a close-up of her crying as Terry apparently had just finished hugging her, and her past self looking across the room to reveal Hatori—now looking close to thirty—in a hospital bed, various wires and tubes attached to him, but he showed no acknowledgment of them or his mother's cries.

Past Terry's vision blurred, and she stepped out of the doorway and into the hospital's hallway, evidently unable to control her tears either. A nurse looked at her from a desk, and Terry could make out that they were asking if she was okay, but Past Terry waved her hand away.

Noticing that the latest window had a white outline around it, unlike the others, Terry hoped that meant that the memory was isolated. She flipped the volume switch again, to hear the sounds of a hospital, and only a hospital. Her mother's cries bounced off the walls, and Past Terry seemed to steel herself enough to go back into Hatori's room. She was beginning to approach the bed and her now-kneeling mother who prayed and cried for her son.

She had almost made it to her mother's side when she heard her say, "Don't leave me. Don't leave me all alone."

She remembered that. Terry could actually recall that moment. She knew exactly what she was feeling in that moment. The swift, hard kick in the stomach her mother's words caused. If Hatori died, she'd be all alone? The pain of those words—that realization—radiated through her, causing a throbbing static in her head and the back of her neck.

She backed out of the room, her mother not noticing or acknowledging that she was there.

Terry stood on the platform, staring at her past self hiding in a bathroom stall, overwhelmed by the gravity of her anxious, racing thoughts. The memory clip couldn't show how she felt in that moment, but Terry could remember all too well.

She remembered hearing the voice before, feeling the

hopelessness and uselessness that voice brought forth whenever something would go wrong or when she felt she was the cause.

But she never heard it as loud as in this moment. This was the first time she heard it clear enough to start to believe it.

She was alone, her mother didn't care, she was worthless and undeserving of what she had. Unworthy of any of the love and kindness and any good things she received. She was a failure, and nobody would notice if she were to disappear.

She felt the tears falling down her face before she realized she was crying.

"Hey, are you okay?" Terry heard Willow's voice from far away, even though she knew logically that she must be right beside her.

She sniffed, wiped her nose, and turned away from the images.

"Yeah, just fine," she said, knowing that Willow would see through that since she wasn't even attempting to hide her tears.

"I'm not gonna say 'I told you so,' but just that I figured there would be things you might not wanna see."

She couldn't tell if Willow was watching the memories as they started disappearing from the space above them, but she at least had seen the reaction they had caused. She held herself, trying to quell this crashing wave of grief that swept over her. Grief directed toward whom, though? Hatori? Herself? She wasn't sure.

It wasn't until Willow spoke again that she remembered where they even were.

"Hey, what's that thing?" she asked, and Terry looked to see her pointing at the scanning machine, its huge eye now trained on Willow. It leaned in close and blinked again, as it had done with Terry.

Again, the voice spoke, "Resident AGT-821. Finding file matches."

"Wait, what?" Willow said, an unpleasant surprise coloring her exclamation.

Soon, new memory windows opened up, this time showing a family with a dark-skinned mother, a lighter-skinned father, and another boy who looked almost exactly like Willow.

PurgaTerry

In the same way as Terry's memories did, each popped up with its volume blasting, but here, there was more shouting, more angry, loud voices, and Terry thought she heard a name through the din, a name that caused Willow's face to fall.

"No, no I don't want to see this," she said, panicked. She turned from the windows, covering her ears against the noise. "No, no, no, no, I don't want this!"

Terry flipped the switch to shut the sound off, but the windows kept popping up. There were plenty of good memories mixed in with the bad, Terry noticed. But she also noticed that the older it appeared Willow became, the more angry the expression on her father's face became.

She caught a brief glimpse of Willow's living self in a mirror— hair short, chest flat, light stubble along a squarer jaw—before her past self whipped around to see her father standing in the doorway to her room. He ripped the dress she wore off her and spoke very fast. Terry couldn't make out any of his words, but she could sense their meaning, especially when she could decipher two final words: "get out."

"Willow... I—" she started, but her words died on her lips when she saw her friend trembling beside her, tears now flowing down her cheeks as well. She still covered her ears, and her eyes were shut tight against all stimuli.

"I didn't want to know this, I told you, Terry!" she whispered harshly. "I told you I didn't want to see or know anything about my life. I knew it would be bad, I just knew it."

"Wills, I didn't mean for it to lock on to you. Here, I'll fix it," Terry said as she tried frantically to delete the clips that still played silently before them. But all she managed to do was isolate specific ones and make them bigger. The last few popped up in a barrage of frantic short files. Terry could tell she was reaching the end of Willow's life, and she agreed with her that she didn't want to see the ending.

She took a shot, and spoke again to the machine. "Stop, um— Halt file sharing. Cancel search request." She tried several combinations of commands before it finally ceased, the offending memories blinking out of existence, although the aftermath still lingered.

They stood silently for a few minutes, both attempting to compose themselves to varying degrees of success. Terry was the first to speak again after they both had dried their tears.

"I'm sorry, Willow. I didn't know that would happen."

"But you didn't stop it once it did," she snapped. "The second it zeroed in on me, the moment that you realized the images and memories coming up weren't yours, you should have stopped it immediately." She stared hard at Terry, harder than she ever thought sweet cinnamon roll Willow could be capable. "But you didn't, because you were nosy. You wanted to see what was so bad about my life, didn't you? You didn't think about how seeing all of that would affect me. You saw what your memories did to you!"

"I didn't think—" she started, but Willow cut her off.

"That's right, you didn't think. I've been trying to be your friend since you got here, Terry. But you have such a one-track mind that it doesn't seem to matter what happens around you or who you might hurt in the process of getting what you want. You just can't understand that the rest of us *don't* want our memories back. They're hard, and painful, and sad. The whole point of agreeing to come here was that the trade-off was we didn't have to be burdened with those memories anymore."

"I know," she said, trying to find something better to say. "But remember, you *had* a choice to come here. I didn't."

Willow scoffed, but in a way that also betrayed that she was close to tears again. "Yeah, I know. Dean hid it from you, and I know you're upset about it, but this whole thing is so stupid. He should have told you from the start, and you shouldn't be going behind his back to stick your nose in places you shouldn't and definitely probably don't really want to see."

Her words burned Terry's heart, but she couldn't dispute them. She had been on a mission to obtain as much information as she could about her life, her past. She *hadn't* been thinking about the

PURGATERRY

people around her, or really paying attention to what they said they wanted, or when they warned her not to go poking around.

"I couldn't have said it better myself," came a woman's voice from the other side of the walkway platform.

They both saw Cassiopeia at the far wall, arms crossed tightly across her chest and wearing the most pronounced frown Terry assumed she could muster.

"So, Ms. Terry, you decided to drag your friend into your little criminal operation," Cassiopeia said. "So, both of Dean's charges were in on this break-in. I'll have to have some very strong words with him. This could lead to a demotion for him and an exceedingly stern punishment for you two."

Terry stepped forward, slowly coming to meet her on the other side. "No, Ms. Cass. Please don't punish Willow. You're right, I did drag her into this. She didn't want anything to do with it, but I made her."

Her words were met with silence, but Cassiopeia's eyebrows were raised.

"But as for me, I didn't even break in. I had Asher's ID." She pulled it out of her pocket to show her. "We traded, and I don't know what he was going to do with mine, but I used his to get in here."

Now Cassiopeia's brows creased, and her frown became more pronounced, if that was possible.

She snatched the ID out of Terry's hand and stowed it in her own pocket. "So, you freely admit to stealing Asher's ID. My charge reported his ID missing an hour ago. It only took me this long to find that it was used to access this hall."

Terry did an actual double take. "No, Ms. Cass. Asher and I traded. I didn't steal anything."

"That's not what Asher told me."

"Then check him to see if he has my ID. He must still have it," she said.

Cassiopeia pulled out a tablet and tapped something into the screen, flipping it around to show her what it said.

"This tracker indicates that your ID is in your room."

"But how can you see it if you can only track when it's been used?"

Cassiopeia pushed a button to make the tablet screen go dark. "As you will no doubt be aware, you are a special case for this level. So, I have been using my privileges as your upper manager to check in on you periodically."

"So, you're spying on me? But you didn't even know that Asher and I traded IDs?"

"I'm of the mind to believe my charge, Ms. Terry. Especially as it isn't he who I caught accessing private files."

"But... but that's not fair. I'm not lying, I swear, it was even his idea."

"I'll check with him again, if you like," Cassiopeia said dryly, clearly still not believing her. "In the meantime, Ms. Willow is free to go, but I am contacting Dean, and we're going to decide what to do with you."

Terry bristled. This was profoundly unfair. And why would Asher lie like that? He knew what they had done; he had to have her ID still.

Willow, her fury now subsided, gave Terry a sympathetic look as she walked past her. Terry couldn't blame her for wanting to get out of there as fast as possible. Between what she had been forced to relive (in a sense) and getting caught by Cassiopeia, Terry would have taken any out she could if she were Wills.

Cassiopeia escorted her out of the Hall of Records, and they stood in the pool of light from a streetlamp outside its gates and watched as the weird Purgatory sun rose, waiting for Dean to arrive and for the other shoe to drop.

It was nearly twenty minutes—or at least Terry thought so from the movement of the sun in the overcast, gray sky—before Dean arrived. He barely looked at Terry, focusing his attention on Cassiopeia.

"Okay, Cass, I'm here. You can leave her with me. I'll handle this."

PURGATERRY

"Oh no you won't," she said. "This matter goes over your head. I'm going to have to file a report, and she'll be lucky if she isn't immediately sent for judgment."

"She still has decades of CS to do here. She can improve."

"I'm sorry, Dean. This system is only as flawed as its users—both of you should know that better than anyone—but it is the system we have, and as upper management, I have to see that the processes are carried out."

"Terry, go back to your room, okay? I'm going to have a talk with Cass."

Terry looked warily from him to Cassiopeia, feeling like the kid being sent to bed so Mommy and Daddy could argue without her around. She obeyed, however mad she still was at him for hiding things from her.

They made sure to only begin speaking when she was out of earshot. Terry knew her way around at this point, so she couldn't even use getting lost in the fog as an excuse to loop around and eavesdrop anymore.

She didn't know what was going to happen to her, but she could sense that things might have fractured between all of them and that it wouldn't be the same on Level Eight for her ever again. And it was all her fault.

17. Breaking the Cycle

Terry and Willow lay in their room, Willow scrunched up on her bed with her back toward Terry in defiance and Terry flipping through her notebook, sulking, while the weight of their fate pressed down on them.

The first thing she'd done the moment they arrived back to their room was search for her ID. Cassiopeia had to be mistaken, and Terry wanted to prove her wrong. But the longer she searched, the more she believed her efforts were futile. Cass had already made up her mind about Terry.

She'd screwed up. She knew she'd screwed up. Terry knew there was a chance they'd be caught, but she assumed (or hoped) that it would be Dean who found them, and she could throw his lies and secrets back in his face as a valid reason for disobeying. Willow had been right, though, she'd gotten cocky, or nosy. She hadn't needed to look at the information the scanning machine gave her on Willow, especially when she knew Willow didn't want to know about the events leading up to her death. She knew that she'd dampened her friend's sun-shiny demeanor, and for that, she really was sorry.

Leafing through the notebook gave her something to do, and if she was going to be punished for accessing her HoR files, she might as well look through the records *she* had been keeping. It wasn't much, but she had something. She'd documented her feelings, her thoughts on what she could remember, things she wasn't as comfortable sharing in group. She also had copied down her questions to Dean and his answers. They didn't provide any new information, but at least she could take her mind off their imminent punishment.

She found the entry she'd made about her first Shepherding excursion, and how it had started going wrong, and she'd helped Willow figure out what to do. Dean had said that he'd look into it, and she wondered if he'd found anything new about it. Terry only vaguely recalled writing this entry, but she noticed that she had made a note of describing how things had felt "off" there in that park.

It was a distant feeling, like something she could hear only faintly but sense strongly. She remembered more clearly another time she had felt that same thing. It was an oppressive weight, a feeling of intense shame and hopelessness. Though she remembered the feeling, she was having trouble recalling when the memory took place. Why shame, though? That was a color that her feelings did not normally wear. Was it residual shame coming off their mark, Mr. Hembree? She didn't want to admit it, but if it had been, he deserved to feel that way. What had Asher said about him, that he got what was coming to him?

A pang of guilt stabbed her at that thought. She had the realization that she was thinking in a way that Delilah might have done to rationalize her actions.

Delilah, the one who had cheated her and manipulated her into ending up here. It wasn't Dean's fault, she realized, it was hers. As much as it was Terry's own fault that they were in the predicament they were now. She doubted Willow would want to talk to her about anything at the moment, much less about

PURGATERRY

Delilah, but as she looked back through her notebook, she felt that was a missing piece she needed to hear about.

"Willow, I know you're angry at me—and you have every right to be—but can I ask you some things about the girl—woman—who cheated me?"

Willow gave a heavy sigh and a sniff, wiping her eyes as she eased herself up on her bed, only glancing over her shoulder at Terry. "What do you want to know?"

Terry scooted to the right side of her bed closer to Willow's, leaning forward so as to possibly encourage her to continue speaking. "You knew her, right?"

It took her a moment, but Willow did turn around to face her, her eyes mostly dry. She swung her legs over the edge of her own bed and crossed her ankles.

"Yeah, I did, but I swear, I didn't know what she was up to, or I would have stopped it if I could have. And you know Dean had no idea either, or he definitely would have done something. Dels kept it really close to the vest, I guess." Willow slowly stood, making her way over to Terry's side. Willow's weight as she sat on the side of the bed made Terry dip slightly.

"What was Dels like?"

"Quiet, for the most part," Willow answered. "She kept to herself and didn't make many friends here. She refused to participate in anything. She was kinda like you when you first got here." Willow seemed to have noticed that Terry might have been offended by this, and she corrected herself.

"But she was nothing like the real you, T. Nothing like the you I've gotten to know. Looking back, she did seem like the type to do something drastic to get out of here ASAP, but you're not. You've proven you're not. You've proven that when things get tough, you can really buckle down and get your work done. You're also way nicer than she was."

"How do you think she—how did she do it?"

Willow popped her lip, sucking air through her teeth uncomfortably.

"Like I said, I didn't know she was doing it, but I figured that it wasn't all at once. She would disappear sometimes, but Dean didn't mention anything about that, so I assumed he knew what she was doing. You've seen for yourself how the emotional manipulation can affect the living. If you do it all at once, they get overwhelmed, but you can't compel them to do something like kill themself in one go. You'd have to do it gradually, and it would probably only really work on someone who already had some mental health issues. You probably had depression already, and that's likely why she chose you."

So, she must have been targeted because of the depression she was already facing. This Delilah had made it worse and worse, making it grow and fester inside of her until she got what she wanted.

"And once we—once I—made the decision to end my life, was that what did it? Was that what made the deal to take on her years, too?"

Willow pulled her lips into a line, shrugging with one shoulder as she stroked Terry's comforter.

"I don't know, but that sounds like how I've heard cheating goes. They don't exactly discuss it in group sessions. Guess they don't want us getting any crazy bad ideas."

That was understandable, but if cheating was such a well-known secret, why hadn't they cracked down harder on it? And it was odd for suicide to be so taboo in a place where so many people had died that way. Maybe Cassiopeia was right when she said it was a flawed system, especially if it allowed for people like Delilah to take advantage of living people who were already suffering. "What kind of a system is this?" she asked, mostly to herself, "if something like this can happen?"

"You can't measure the whole thing from the actions of one person," Willow said.

"I guess not, but I wish that I could do something to fix this place. Make them care more like you and Dean do."

"I'm glad to hear you remember that Dean really does care.

PURGATERRY

About this place and about you."

"Of course I know he cares, I just wish that he'd told me all of this from the start, then I wouldn't have had to go behind his back like I did."

Then she realized, that in some way, that was another thing that Delilah must have thought.

"But what do you suppose made her do it?" she asked, more to herself than to Willow. "Even if I can understand how she must have been feeling, what could bring someone to push another person over the edge to suicide like that?"

Willow shrugged again. "Maybe she thought she was doing the right thing for herself, and she didn't care who she hurt."

"But why me?"

"That, I don't know. Maybe she had a reason, or maybe you were just there. Either way, what's the point in dwelling on it now?"

Terry supposed there wasn't any, but something inside nagged at her to ponder it more. Her mind hovered back to her notebook, to the feelings she had experienced on that day with James Hembree—that weight and forceful feelings pressing down on her, she recognized that. It was linked somehow to her walk through the woods, her finding her old playhouse—their father had built it, she suddenly recalled—and then the feeling that someone was with her, but as she slipped away, they left her all alone.

Why had she felt that on that day and on the day she'd died? Had she been unintentionally manipulating him? No, that couldn't be it, but then she remembered somebody else might have.

Her head snapped up, a new and feverish resolve to find her ID coming over her. Now she hoped that she really was wrong, because if it wasn't there, there was only one other place it could be. As she tore open all of the drawers, looked under both beds, and scanned over every corner of their small room, she couldn't find any trace of it. She turned toward Willow and thrust out her hand.

"Willow, I need to borrow your phone."

Willow blinked at her, startled by her sudden movement and request. "Uh, sure." She fished her phone out of the purse she had beside her bed and handed it to Terry.

Terry unlocked the phone (apparently Willow didn't see the need for a password or anything) and found Dean's pager number. She tried texting it, becoming impatient and calling it as well for good measure.

"Come on, Dean," she muttered, beginning to pace around the room. She knew she was likely freaking Willow out, but at the moment, this was more important.

"Terry, what's going on?" Willow asked. "Dean's probably still with Cassiopeia, what's wrong?"

She stared down at the phone, flipping through the list of apps while it continued to ring.

"Can this thing track our IDs?"

"I mean, probably," Willow said. "It was meant for Dean, after all."

Terry impatiently mashed the red end call button. "I have to go, I'm taking the phone with me. I'll take good care of it, but you need to stay here and tell Dean if you see him to track my ID with his beeper. I assume it can do that."

"Wait!" Willow shouted, grabbing her by the shoulder. "Can you at least tell me what's happening?"

She paused a moment, looking between Willow's face and the door she was blocking.

"I think Asher is going to cheat someone with my ID. I have to find him."

It didn't take Terry long to get to the bus station. Most of the foot traffic was heading away from the terminal, and she wove through them, only half paying attention to where her feet were

PurgaTerry

taking her. She continued to try Dean, unsure if her calls were making it through to his pager. With a frustrated groan, she hit the end call button again, now searching for the app that was able to track her ID.

She was at Angie's station before she knew it, and she barely registered her greeting as she watched the little dot on the phone's screen trying to locate her ID and Asher.

"Are you okay, honey?" she heard Angie ask through her focus. "What's wrong, anything I can do?"

As she was about to say that she was fine—even though she could tell Angie would see through that—the phone pinged, and the little dot on the screen zoomed in on a location. She didn't recognize it, but maybe Angie would.

Terry turned the phone around to show her the screen.

"Do you know where this is? What bus do I need to get on that will get me there now?"

"Sure, it looks like the Number Seven will get you there, but sweetie, does Dean know—"

"It's an emergency." Terry stowed the phone into her hoodie pocket. "I've been trying to contact Dean, but he hasn't responded or shown up. If he comes asking for me, tell him where I went."

Her eyes then locked in on the location of the Number Seven bus on the schedule, and without another word to the stunned Angie, Terry sprinted in the direction of the bus.

She made it right before the driver shut the door, relief flooding her then stopping short when she spotted the scanner. Crap, she didn't have her ID.

The driver turned to look at her, annoyance growing on his face. "You got your ID?"

She grimaced. "Listen, this is an emergency, so do you think, just this once, we can forget about having my ID?"

"No ID, no entry," he said flatly. "Get off, I've got places to be."

It was then that they both heard a tapping on the bus door. The man opened it to reveal Angie, out of breath from trying to keep up with Terry and waving her own ID to show the driver.

"I'll vouch for her. This is Dean's kid. She's dependable. If she says it's an emergency, then you should let her on."

The driver appeared to consider this before shrugging.

"All right, if you vouch for her, Angie. But just this one time."

The stuttered relief she'd felt earlier came flooding back, and she turned to mouth a grateful *thank you* to Angie, who smiled and waved as the door closed. She thanked the driver as well and found a seat closest to the front, tapping along the window pane anxiously as the bus pulled out from the station. She fished the phone from her pocket and checked it, ready to pull the cord above her the minute they were close.

It felt like forever before they finally reached a place close enough that Terry could exit the bus. Of course, whoever Asher was manipulating wouldn't be on the schedule, and as she walked in the direction of the area the phone indicated, she almost wasn't sure which house she would find him in; they all looked so alike. At last, the phone pinged again on the house at the end of a cul-de-sac. There didn't appear to be any cars in the driveway or the garage, so Terry hoped that meant Asher and his target were alone, and, therefore, it would be easier to stop him. She didn't know exactly how she would stop him, but she knew that she had to try.

Terry found the door to the house unlocked, which saved her the trouble of attempting to kick the door in, which she wasn't sure she would be able to do.

She dashed down a narrow hallway and up some stairs, but found no sign of Asher or his target in any of the rooms. There was nobody in the house but her. A dog barking from outside alerted her to someone in the backyard. She tripped over a table and knocked a framed photo to the floor. When she was able to find her footing, she gripped the windowsill for purchase and saw a tool shed in the back. Terry tried not to trip down the outside stairs as she made a beeline for the shed.

As she neared the open door, she heard the telltale click of some form of firearm. It clicked twice before she made it to the doorway, and then Terry winced as the gun went off.

The loud bang echoed off the surrounding houses and trees, causing the dog that was already barking to be joined by a chorus of other dogs farther away. Terry's insides froze, fearing she was too late. She steeled herself, preparing for what she was about to see when she entered the shed.

The gun was still smoking and the hand that held it shook as the young woman burst into a sob. A tiny bullet hole let a thin stream of light in from the ceiling.

As the woman wept, shaking even more violently, she nearly dropped the gun while opening the chamber to reload. A hand she didn't appear to notice through her tears placed the magazine within her reach, and as the hand retreated back into the shadows, Terry found Asher waiting in the corner, eyes fixed on the gun still in the girl's hand.

It took Terry two steps from the doorway to be beside her, and as she knelt down, she shot a glare at Asher.

The weight and pressure of the emotions pressed down on her, filling her mind with an urgency, and a palpable haze surrounded the woman, dimming the light that came in through the shed's doorway and windows. Terry recognized this feeling completely now; it brought back memories of another small house in the woods and an almost audible voice in her head bringing forth these emotions, magnifying them.

"It's no use, Pj's," Asher said without moving. "Carmen here is too far gone. All she has to do now is pull that trigger, and I can get out of this bullshit Purgatory for good."

"And where does that leave her?" she asked. "Do you even care how this affects her?"

"All I care about is getting out of my service so I can move on. Serena is waiting for me."

"We all have people waiting for us, Asher. But that's not the point. This isn't right, and you know it. What would Serena say if she knew what you were doing? Do you think she'd be glad you were taking advantage of this girl's vulnerability?"

As Terry knelt beside Carmen, it slowly dawned on her that the girl wasn't acknowledging either of them. She tried putting a hand on Carmen's shoulder to get her attention.

"Carmen, Carmen, can you hear me?"

The girl didn't look up at her. Her tears continued to fall as her fingers closed around the clip, hesitant to put the new one into the chamber.

Terry looked up questioningly at Asher, who waved Terry's own ID in his hand.

"I'm still emotionally influencing her. She's blocked out the world now, kinda like tunnel vision. She'll only listen to me now."

Asher pulled Carmen's ticket from his pocket, and Terry realized that Cassiopeia and Dean wouldn't be able to print it out from the Ticket Repository again without an override.

But they could still manage to override it. If she could keep Asher talking, she might be able to buy herself and Carmen some time.

"So, what happens now? How exactly does your time transfer to her?"

"She's already agreed to it, not that she'll remember."

"How?"

Asher then held her ID up to his face, speaking to it as if into a walkie talkie.

"You want an end to this pain, right, Carmen? All you have to do now is squeeze that trigger. I can end the pain for you, but you have to do exactly what I say."

Terry watched as Carmen—still sobbing—nodded her head absentmindedly. Her hand had finally reloaded the clip, and it was trembling as she brought the barrel closer to her mouth.

"That's how you got her to agree, by taking away her options?" Terry asked, disgusted. "But that's—"

Cheating, of course it was. Cheating the system, and cheating

PURGATERRY

Carmen out of her life.

"Asher, you don't have to do this," Terry pleaded.

He scoffed. "I've come too far now, Pj's. Ain't no way they won't send me Downstairs if I fail at this now."

Keep him talking, she just had to keep him talking. Terry silently pleaded for Dean to hurry.

"So, you used Delilah's ID to get her to this point and mine for your final attempt?"

"Stating the obvious isn't gonna confuse me or make me change my mind," Asher said. "But yes. I followed in the footsteps of Delilah. Her plan seemed solid. I'll bet if you try, you can remember how it felt when she did it to you."

This threw Terry off momentarily, because while she couldn't recall the specific memories, it wasn't difficult to remember how she had felt. That night in her car with the rain, she could clearly feel hopelessness magnifying every harmful thought. She could nearly hear it as a whisper along with a dull ache at the base of her neck. She couldn't see Delilah, but she had felt her effects, and maybe on some level, heard her?

"So, you were chipping away at her mentally. Is that why you were at the hospital that day?"

Asher's brows raised at this. "Surprised you saw me there. She'd just been discharged, and I couldn't have her improving and undoing all of my hard work."

"But look what you've done, what you're *doing* to her!" Terry shouted, rising and gesturing to the poor weeping girl. "She's already going through enough. She's already fighting her own demons, and she already feels like the world would be better off without her." Her face softened at the look on Carmen's face, tears beginning to fall on her own cheeks as well. "This girl can still back away from the edge, she can still try and find her reasons every day to stay alive. You know exactly how she feels right now. Why would you steal away her chance to make things better?"

Asher blinked at her, and for a millisecond, Terry saw him hesitate.

"Why would you help her steal away her life?"

Turning desperately back to Carmen, she placed a hand on the girl's head and began to whisper to her, even though she knew Carmen couldn't physically hear her.

"Carmen, listen to me. I know this feels like the only way out. I know you don't see an end to this pain. I've been there. You don't think there could ever be a way out of this, that your family will be better off once you're gone."

Terry knew her emotional manipulation wouldn't work without her ID, but maybe—just maybe—if she could get through to Carmen somehow, she could convince her to stop.

"I can't tell you to keep living for your family, or even for yourself. I don't want to give you false promises that it will absolutely get better. Sometimes, you'll fall again, and sometimes, it will feel like ending your life is the only option again. But I can promise that if you do this, there's no going back. There is no way to fix it, and there's no way to see if things *could* have gotten better. There are bad days coming, yes. But there are good ones, too. And if I could have the choice again—"

Terry's voice hitched as she choked on a sob of her own, thinking back to her last day on Earth, that last sunrise and her lonely walk through the woods.

"Well, I don't have that choice anymore, but you do. Please listen. Please take a second and consider. You're not a coward, and you're not a burden. You are you, and that may not seem like much at the moment, but one day—one day—I promise you that if you stay strong enough to see it—one day you will be so happy to be who you are. That you're still you, and that you're still here. I want you to make it to see that day, Carmen."

Terry sniffed, blinking through her tears and watching the gun still in Carmen's trembling grip. For one glorious moment, she thought she saw Carmen actually glance her way. She didn't know if she imagined it, but she still hadn't pulled the trigger.

"Please..."

Terry took a deep breath and was surprised that Carmen did

PURGATERRY

the same. Terry held it, waiting to see if that breath would be Carmen's last. But she exhaled with a half sob, half laugh, and not only did Carmen lower the gun, she threw it against the wall of the shed with a metallic thunk.

Her sobs continued, but now she would be out of danger, and Terry smiled through her own tears as she hugged Carmen without her realizing.

"What?" Asher said, coming out of the shadows, Terry's ID and the ticket still in hand. "How did you do that? I had the ID. I could control her."

"You could influence her," Terry said. "But she took control."

The phone began ringing, a tune breaking through the haze and the tension, and Terry's heart lifted at the sound of Dean's voice calling for her.

"In here!" she called back. She shot a look to Asher, who'd dropped her ID and began scrambling for an exit, only to be stopped by not only Dean, but Cassiopeia.

Terry didn't know what they were saying, or how the officials of Purgatory went about arresting people for cheating. She left it to them, tearing her gaze from Asher being manhandled by Dean back to Carmen, still shivering and sobbing, but still alive.

18. Terry's Final Question Answered

Hood up and eyes covered, Terry followed Dean through his managers-only portal door without being able to enjoy the experience since she couldn't see where they were going.

"You're sure you can't see anything?" Dean asked as he led her by the elbow. She shook her head, but the moment she assumed they crossed through, she thought she knew where they were anyway.

She heard the beeping of some form of machine—a heart monitor?—and the slightly muffled bustle of people. She had a hunch about what Dean was doing, and as ecstatic as she was, she wouldn't spoil this for him.

"All right, go ahead and look."

She lowered her hood and hands in one fluid movement, her eyes landing on the one person she had wanted to see most lying in his hospital bed, unmoving but breathing.

"Hatori." The name came out as almost a sigh, Terry's smile growing as she took in the sight of him. He looked a little older than in the memories she had seen. Someone had been taking the time to comb his hair and shave his face and even place his glasses on his nose, even though his eyes remained closed.

She was embarrassed by how much tearing up she had been doing in the past few cycles of Purgatory, but since it was just Dean, her, and her unconscious brother, it wasn't so bad.

She took a few tiny steps closer to the bed, turning back to Dean to make sure it was okay.

"Can I... talk to him? I mean, can he hear me?"

"Better than that, go ahead and use your emotion manipulation to tap into his feelings," Dean said.

Terry raised an eyebrow at this, but after a moment, she tested out touching his forehead and then pulled her power to the forefront. Immediately, she was no longer in the hospital room, but standing on the side of a cliff that separated a large expanse of wood from where she stood.

She could still feel her hand on Hatori's forehead, but when she lifted it off, the image of the wood disappeared.

"What was that?" Terry blinked and found Dean again, who only smiled.

"Whatever you just saw was what he's dreaming about," Dean answered. "You can talk to him in the dream, and he won't realize anything weird is happening."

Her hand whipped back to Hatori's head so fast, it might have been magnetized, and again, she found herself on the other side of the wide chasm. Hatori stood on the opposite side, looking lost and wandering.

"Hatori!" she called from across the chasm. Thinking quickly, she willed herself to join him on his side then appeared right next to him. Hatori turned toward her, relief washing over his face.

"Suki!" he answered. "I'm so glad I found you. I must've gotten lost when I took a walk from the campsite or something. Do you know the way back?"

Suki... was that her name? Her real name? She was so stunned about hearing her own name that she didn't register what he'd said at first.

PurgaTerry

"Hatori, we're not really camping, you're—dreaming," she had started to tell him about the coma, but decided against it. She didn't know much about how the brain functioned while in a coma, but it might be easier to wake him up if he thought he was dreaming.

His brows furrowed, regarding her contemplatively. "This is... a dream?"

She nodded. "Can you remember how we got here? Or who is camping with us? What's the name of the campsite?"

Hatori looked around, as if the answers were somewhere around them. Wind whistled through the dream trees, but no answers fell out of them.

"I-I can't," he said. "So, this is a lucid dream?"

"Um, sort of."

"That's so cool. I've never had one of those before. So, are you here to help me wake up?"

Again, she swallowed her true answer. She didn't want to tell him she was dead and only visiting to say goodbye, but maybe this could be her last gift to him, if she could indeed help him out of these woods.

"Yes, yes I am," she said with more confidence than she felt. "I'll guide you back to our camper, then maybe that will be enough to wake you up."

"Okay, great, lead the way."

They began walking through the trees and tree-shaped approximations that Hatori's mind could conceive. A few sounds of animals came through, but Terry couldn't see any hiding or flying above them.

They walked for a few minutes before Terry couldn't keep her questions in check. There was so much she wanted to say, to know, from her brother. And here she was, walking along beside him in some autumnal dreamscape. She just didn't know what she should say first.

"Hatori... " she started.

"Hmm? This must be a dream; you never call me by my full

name. You see me calling you 'Natsuki'?"

She perked up at that, scrambling to meet his steps. "So, I don't call you Hatori?"

"Nope, I'm just Tori to you."

"Okay, I'll try to remember that."

"It's fine, dream Suki."

He seemed rather chill in his dream form, or perhaps that was how Tori always was, and the sample set of memories Terry had seen were the exception and not the rule.

Terry supposed that if Tori thought this was all just a dream, all the better for her questions. None of them would seem odd if they were coming from what he thought was a manifestation of his own subconscious.

"I miss you, Tori," she said at last, feeling more comfortable sharing some of the feelings that had bubbled up inside her upon seeing him.

"I miss you too, Suk," he said with a smile. "I mean, I know I've been away for school and all, but I do miss you and the way we used to be."

"The way we used to be?"

"Yeah, before our whole falling out thing, before you changed and stopped going to therapy or taking your meds. You know, I never told Mom about that. You made me promise."

"I did?"

"Yeah, and I was pissed about it. Also when you dropped out of college, and then you couldn't hold down a job, and Mom was on your case about it all the time. It didn't sit right with me how she always seemed to use me as an example of how you should be. I mean, I know I stayed in school, but I'm far from perfect."

"I find that hard to believe," she said. From what little she saw of the times when they were younger in those files, he really did seem to be the perfect brother. It would only make sense for him to be the perfect son, too.

"I know you always saw me as somebody who could do no wrong, Suki. But I'm human, too, the same as you. I was messed up when Dad left and when Baba passed away. I didn't even get to see her before and say goodbye. You did. Who was the perfect child then, huh?"

Terry wished she could remember any of what he was talking about so that she could understand the full magnitude of these events. These pivotal moments that made up their shared history.

"How long has it been since we've talked like this?" she asked, kicking a dream rock and watching her foot go through it.

Tori seemed to think about this, and he frowned at the answer before speaking. "It has to have been at least a year. I don't think I've even seen you since Mom's birthday."

"When was that?"

"You don't remember Mom's birthday?"

"Hey, it's your dream. You must have forgotten it," she joked, mostly to hide the truth from him, and also because—now that they were talking—she could sense the ease between them, the sibling feeling of comradery and, even though she couldn't recall it, the shared history that she wished she could remember.

Tori laughed at this. "Yeah, I guess you're right. But that was in March? What month are we in now? I remember leaving Mom's house, and then I was on a muddy road close to the river, I took a turn too hard and started skidding—"

"It has to be about September," she answered quickly. She wasn't sure what would happen if Tori fully realized he was in a coma, but she didn't want to find out.

She had died in June, Willow's birthday was in August, and that was only a week or so ago, she thought. Purgatory timeline, and all.

"Well, we barely said anything to each other then," Tori said, looking up through the dappled light spilling from the trees. "I wanted to tell you about my new girlfriend, Marcy."

"But you didn't," she continued.

"I... didn't think you wanted to hear about my life. You didn't seem to care."

"I'm sorry," he said after a few minutes of silence. "I'm sorry if

I ever made you feel like you weren't good enough."

"It wasn't your fault," she said. "It was my own stuff I had to work through. I guess I failed at that, too."

"I never thought you were a failure," Tori said. "You beat yourself up enough that none of us had to do it."

They were nearing a clearing, and Terry thought she could see a couple of tents up ahead. They were getting closer the longer she walked with him. Terry wasn't sure if she was guiding him or if just talking to her helped him find his own way, but they were very nearly out of the woods. She just hoped that—for him—it was the literal and the figurative woods.

"Thanks, Tori," she said, and then added with confidence, "I don't remember a time when you ever did."

"I think I can see the camper," Tori said as he squinted toward the end of the trees ahead of them. "We're almost there."

She, too, saw the camper through the trees. She hoped that it meant this was going to work, even if it did mean that their time together was short.

"I need to tell you something," she said, not wanting to give much away, but more to prepare him for the eventuality that he would make a full recovery.

"When you wake up from this, just know that nothing was your fault, okay? You couldn't have done anything, because I had stopped accepting help. You couldn't have helped if I didn't reach out to mend the bridges first."

"I don't really understand what you're saying, but... okay," Tori said with a smile. "Dream logic, I guess."

"Yeah, dream logic," she agreed. "But seriously, I'm sorry things had to go like this. And we didn't get a proper goodbye."

"You can say goodbye to me now, I guess," he said. "We're almost there."

She stopped walking, causing him to do the same. Terry took a deep breath of the imagined crisp autumn air, then let it out slowly.

"Tori, don't forget about me."

"Of course not. Don't forget about me either, okay?"

PurgaTerry

"Can't make any promises," she said, laughing at a joke that he never would have gotten. "But just... see you around, Tori."

"See you around, Suki."

Tori held out his arms half-heartedly, and Terry took him up on the offer of an awkward sibling hug. She squeezed him like she might never get the chance again (which she didn't think she would), patted his back twice, and then let go, eyes shimmering now, threatening tears.

She stayed where she was as Tori ran for the camper, and a dream Mom and a dream girlfriend greeted him as he approached. He paused on the first step and turned back to see her. He gave her a wave, which she returned, and then went inside.

Terry then found her exit from the dream and came back to herself. She was still in the hospital room, still standing over Hatori's body and holding his hand. When the machines he was hooked up to started beeping faster, causing some of the nurses to come rushing in, Terry was already gone. She and Dean had swept out just as the hospital's team had swept in.

Soon, she found herself outside in the bustle of the hospital's parking structure, walking down the sloping driveway toward the street level.

"So, did you get your closure?" he asked after they had both been able to take a minute to reassess their surroundings.

Terry felt like she was waking up from a dream, and she hoped that meant that Hatori was waking up, too. They had passed their mother in one of the waiting rooms sitting next to a young woman she thought she might have recognized. Her straight dark hair and dark eyes were a contrast to her periwinkle-colored glasses.

"I think so," Terry answered. But... I can still keep tabs on them, like you do?"

"Of course," Dean said. "Willow will get you set up on all that social media stuff; you can cyber stalk them to your heart's content."

Terry sniffed involuntarily, something welling up inside her that she didn't want to release out in public.

"Can you— Can you make the door to take us back to Level Eight?"

"What's the rush?" he asked. "We can make a day of this. It's your reward, after all."

"Just do it, please." She nudged him lightly on his left side where she knew his beeper was. She didn't think it controlled the portal door, but she didn't feel like doing what she felt like doing in public.

Dean obliged, the elevator doors parting from nowhere, and he led her through.

He'd brought them to the entrance of their residence building. As good a place as any. Terry made certain to look around and make sure nobody was around. Once she was sure, she swiftly tackled him in a hug.

Dean stumbled a few steps back before he regained his footing, awkwardly stretching out his arms before realizing what she was doing, and then bringing them to rest around her, returning the hug.

"Well, this is unexpected," he said. "But a welcome surprise."

"Thanks for this, and, for, well—everything you've done."

"You've still got some questions left. Do you want to cash those in now?"

Terry pondered the offer. At the beginning of her time in Purgatory, she was desperate for answers, and though she had gotten some, it felt like the time for their deal had passed. Maybe she didn't need to know everything right now.

"You know what? I think I'm okay."

"I've got one more offer for you though," she heard him say as they ended their hug. "It's something I've been thinking about, and I want you to hear me out."

"Okay," she answered, a sense of dread beginning to settle in her stomach—the kind of dread that comes from an impending choice.

"I know I can't give you your life back. Death isn't exactly a two-way street. But I can do something to make things a little easier for you here."

He pulled from his jacket pocket a folded piece of paper, handing it to her. Terry unfolded it, her eyebrows raised. It looked like some sort of contract. And although she couldn't read all of the legalese, she caught the words "transfer of unaccounted years."

"Dean, what is this?" She looked up from the paper to see him smiling with eyes that looked much sadder than the casual air he was trying to convey.

"I've gotten the okay from Cass, so—if you're up for it—I'm willing to take on the years that Dels left you with."

Terry blinked, sputtered, and physically shook her head. "What? Dean, no, there's no way I can let you do that."

"Look, I wasn't there for you when you really needed me, before we'd ever met. I still feel that if I had just seen what Delilah was doing, I could have—"

"But you didn't," she cut him off. "You didn't know, and there is no way it was your fault. Delilah may have influenced me, pushed me, but in the end, it was all down to me. I could have done something. But neither of us can take it back now."

It took Dean a moment to absorb Terry's words. She hoped he understood that the answer was no. She couldn't allow him to do that for her. Even if it took her an extra forty years, she would do it. He'd not only helped her, but she felt inspired by his kindness to maybe pay it forward. An extra forty years of service didn't sound as bad when she thought of all the souls she could help in that time.

"How refreshingly mature." Dean tousled her hair, and she swatted his hand away with an awkward chuckle. He brought her into a shorter one-armed hug. "Nice to see you're learning. Keep that up when I'm gone, all right?"

Terry then pushed him away, looking up to his face, certain that she'd misheard him. "I'm sorry, what?"

Dean then took his own ID out of his jacket pocket and

handed it to Terry. Next to Dean's own Level Eight identification number—where there was the Px7 on hers—there was a Pxo.

"Dean," she said, blinking in astonishment, "does this mean you... you're—"

"Yup," he said, finishing her thought. "I'm on my way out of here."

"But if you've gotten all of your hours, shouldn't you be gone already?" she asked.

"Well, typically, yes," he said. "But you know how Cass just *loves* to bend the rules just for me." He smirked at his own joke. "But seriously, being a manager, I have to get my affairs here in order first. I put off a couple of things to make sure I could stay as long as possible."

"For me and Willow?" Terry asked.

Dean bobbed his head. "In part. I wanna make sure you two can't get up to any mischief after I'm gone. Cass said she'll keep a look out for you, and she has her own things she wanted to run by you personally, but I really just have one bit of unfinished business left to do."

When Terry didn't ask—only looked quizzically—he answered the question she hadn't asked.

"It's April. I had to get my trust sorted, because she's on her way out, too."

"Your daughter?"

"Yup. I've been checking, because Cass was sweet enough to let me know April's time was coming. So, I wanted to make sure that when my little girl's ticket gets punched, that I'm around to be the one to Shepherd her."

"Dean, that's—"

"I know, I know, ultra sappy. But what can you do? I guess I'm just an old sap at heart."

"But... I mean—" Terry stammered. "I could watch your family for you, along with my own. I can make sure Edie and her kids are okay for you."

"I couldn't ask you to do that," Dean said.

PURGATERRY

"No, no, I want to," she said. "I want to pay you back. You've done so much for me, and you were even willing to risk staying here for decades more on my behalf. You're more than my manager, Dean. You might be the best friend I've ever had."

"Better than Willow? I mean, she did get you something for her birthday."

Terry laughed, shook her head, and rolled her eyes. She would normally have told him to just take the freaking compliment, but by now, Terry knew that this is just how Dean was. With his own memories or not, his personality still shone through. And he would be getting them back soon, once he left Level Eight and Purgatory behind.

"Does Willow know that you're leaving?"

"She will once we tell her."

"She's going to want to throw you a going away party."

"I wouldn't expect anything less from one of my favorite girls," Dean said, putting his arm around her and leading her out toward the foggy, overcast day. "You're another one of them, in case that wasn't clear."

"Yeah, I got that," she said through a laugh.

Willow did indeed want to throw Dean a going away party. She wanted to take him back to Disneyland, but Cassiopeia shot that idea down, bemoaning that they were already doing enough "rule bending" for all of their after-lifetimes.

To Terry's surprise, Willow kept it small, just a cake and the five of them—because Cassiopeia had to attend, and so did Juliet, who clung to Willow's arm the entire time, still apologetic to Terry about the whole Asher situation.

Dean was touched, Terry could tell. He said as much about every five minutes of the whole thing. But the moment it was over—the very second the last slice of cake was spoken for and eaten—Cassiopeia rose from her chair and declared that it was time.

They all followed Dean to the bus station to see him off. Both he and Cassiopeia had told her that after he Shepherded his last soul and had run out the clock on his community service, Dean would immediately be pulled to his final evaluation. So, the goodbyes would have to be here.

Carrying no luggage, Dean walked toward the desk where Angie sat and gave her a heartfelt goodbye handshake. Angie then handed him his final schedule with a smile—his daughter's appointment papers.

Terry's stomach dropped lower and lower the closer the group got to the bus Dean would be getting on. She found her heart beginning to ache at the thought that he was really, truly leaving. He had so kindly and with such understanding taken her hand and guided her through this whole Purgatory thing when she was freshly dead, confused, and lost. She had been lost in more ways than one, she realized. And Dean was there to help her find her way, just like a true Shepherd should.

As Dean turned to look at each of them in turn, he sighed a humongous sigh and turned his attention to Cassiopeia.

"Cass, Cassio, my darling Cassiopeia," he said fondly as he took her hands in his, Cassiopeia tilting her head and rolling her eyes.

"Dean," she said, swinging their arms back and forth, looking like she was searching for what to say. "I'm not going to miss all the fudging of the rules you did or your unfinished paperwork you'd still hand in anyway." She then tried to hide her wand wiping away a tear by tucking her hair behind one ear. "But I will miss you."

Dean grinned back at her. "Aww, and you didn't think you could have human emotions," he said. "I'll miss you, too, Cassio." He then dropped one of her hands, pointing to his cheek and making a kissy face.

Cassiopeia laughed—actually laughed—for the first time that

PURGATERRY

Terry had known her and slapped his shoulder playfully. He dropped her other hand and turned to Willow and Terry.

Giving another sigh, he placed one hand on each of their shoulders, looking from one of them to the other.

"My girls," he said wistfully. "I don't quite know how much time you'll have together, but I want you to look out for each other, okay?"

Willow was not able to hold back her own tears for a single moment as she nodded through sobs, leaping into him and wrapping him in a hug. Dean was ready for this one, squeezing her tight and holding her just a second longer before Willow let go.

"You stay that little ray of sunshine, all right?"

"I will," she blubbered, then sniffed. "If you're allowed to stay in touch, send me a text or something, okay? So I know you made it there safe."

"I doubt they get cell service up there, Wills," he said. "But I'll see what I can do."

Willow then gave him another quick hug before backing up to stand with Juliet, who had given them their space.

Then it was down to Terry and Dean. Again.

"Oh, Scarecrow, I think I'll miss you most of all," he said, adopting an actually decent Judy Garland accent.

Terry was holding back her own tears as she let out a watery laugh. Her heart would have been about to explode if it was still beating. She didn't think she realized until this exact moment how much she was truly going to miss him.

"I think that should be my line," she said, a small quaver in her voice as those tears she tried to keep in check began to spill over.

"What, so I'm the one with no brains?" he asked. "You're the one who didn't have her memory."

Terry sniffed, wiping her tears with her hoodie sleeve. "That's fair. But, Dean, I just— I can't thank you enough, and I just want to say—" She tried to finish, but only tears came out as he wrapped her in a hug of her own. Dean allowed her to get her somehow running afterlife snot all over his nice pale-blue tie.

She savored the closeness, lingering even longer than Willow had. She couldn't help it, what she'd said to him was true. He was probably the best friend she could have in the afterlife.

"I'll miss you too, Kiddo," he said, a hitch in his own voice as he whispered close to her ear.

When they finally parted, Dean cleared his throat to hide his own tears. "Now, you take care of yourself, Ter."

"I will," she answered. "I'll take care of them, too, all of them."

He patted her shoulder, turning her attention back to Cassiopeia. "And Cass has a little something to offer you."

Cassiopeia walked back to them, holding a new manilla envelope in her hands and holding it for Terry to take. "I was going to propose this earlier, but Dean wanted to wait until right now for some reason."

"Why, to see the look on her face, obviously," he said. "When she hears the good news."

"What good news?"

Cassiopeia smiled at her even more broadly than Terry had seen her do to Dean. "I know that you turned down the offer Dean made for him to take on your extra years of community service. So, I wanted to give you a different offer. Normally, we don't give souls the option this early in their stay here, but given your past performance and the extenuating circumstances, I felt it was prudent that we go ahead and present you with the opportunity."

Now it was Dean's turn to roll his eyes. "Cass, get to the point, some of us haven't got all day."

"Since we will be in need of a new manager, I wanted to offer the position to you," Cassiopeia said.

Terry was taken aback, giving an actual—if small—gasp. "Me? You actually want me to be a manager? But—I mean—I broke the rules about as much as Dean has."

"And yet, he was still a manager," Cassiopeia said.

Terry blew air out through her nose in amusement. "True."

"It would appear that your progress has greatly improved, and on top of that, you've done something that was once deemed improbable."

"That being?"

"You were able to break through to the young woman Asher had targeted. I've never seen a Shepherd able to get through to someone that close to ending their life. By that stage, they're usually too far gone. And to be able to accomplish that without your ID, that is extremely unheard of."

Terry could only stare. She wanted to shrug, but she thought better of such a minimizing gesture. Even though she was the one to get through to Carmen, she didn't feel like the credit should go to her.

"I believe Carmen was strong enough to break free of Asher's influence," she said. "I just helped her find that strength." She thought back to her own death, wondering if she'd had someone to talk to her, if she would have found her own strength to escape from Delilah's manipulation.

"In any case, it is a skill that could be greatly beneficial if developed," Cassiopeia said. "You could do a lot of good for those in the same situation as you were."

She was right, Terry could do a lot of good. And what was more, she wanted to. Pay it forward, in a sense, in whatever ways she could here.

"You'll need to be trained for the new position, but I don't believe the higher-ups will have a problem with it."

It would probably take a while—a long while—but however long it took, Terry felt like she was up to the task. Becoming a manager would enable her to help even more people than only being a Shepherd. And she could think of no better way to work off all the extra years she had here.

Epilogue

Terry kept her head cushioned by her arm as she propped her elbow on the bus window.

She was alone, for once. Willow's next Shepherding was not scheduled until later. Besides, her destination was a place that Terry mostly liked to keep to herself. From her pocket, she pulled out an old wallet she'd found at a thrift store. She took a moment to admire her ID in the plastic rectangular window. It had been a while since that number next to the P had gone from a seven to a six, but she could much more easily believe that than her card's newest addition. Under her name and information where her old title had been were the words "Shepherd Manager." It still struck her that it was real, and new enough that sometimes she forgot about it. Once Cassiopeia finally gave her some trainees to whip into shape, though, it would be harder to forget.

The bus rolled to a stop, in the same place as usual, and Terry thanked the driver before departing. This was just one of the many things Terry found herself doing that reminded her of Dean. She smiled at the memory as she entered her favorite coffee shop: Brewed Awakenings.

The smattering of small circular and square mismatched tables were nearly full of people today, and the couches on the far end held a few patrons, too. Terry's favorite table, though, one with a collage of pictures under a glass tabletop, always seemed to be empty when she stopped by.

She passed the tables and reached the counter where a woman with dark hair pulled a shiny lever and steam erupted from a large espresso machine. When she turned with a steaming coffee cup in hand, she spotted Terry.

"Terry!" she called with a smile, then corrected herself. "No, wait, this drink is for Nancy, sorry!"

The patron came to retrieve their drink, and Terry stepped forward, greeted by the woman's bright smile.

"I'm glad you're here, Terry. Marcy has some big news to share," the woman said, wiping her hands on a rag. "I'll get your usual, and she'll come say hi in a bit."

"Thanks," Terry replied and headed back toward the tables. Hers wasn't the only table with a collage, but it was the only one with bottle caps glued to the edges, and for some reason, Terry just liked it. It made her stand out a bit, but here, she didn't mind a little extra attention.

The view outside wasn't anything spectacular, only a four-lane road and a gas station across the way, but that wasn't why she came. She pulled out her most recent notebook and started jotting down her thoughts about the last few scheduled excursions when another young woman placed her drink down in front of her and swiftly took the seat across from her. The name 'Terry Dean' was printed on the sticker on the cup's side.

She looked up to see Marcy, her bangs freshly trimmed and her hair in a ponytail, holding out her hands like she expected Terry to look at her manicure. But when she looked at her friend's fingers, one sparkled with a brand-new accessory as it caught the light: the gemstone sitting on a gold band on her left ring finger.

Terry's eyes widened.

PURGATERRY

"Is that— He didn't—" she stammered, trying to process the significance but not finding the words for her surprise. "When?"

"Last night!" Marcy replied, excitement brimming and spilling over from the two words. She described the proposal had happened after they'd hiked up to the top of a peak to see the stars. He'd had her close her eyes to make a wish, and when she opened them, there he was on one knee, ring in hand.

"That's so amazing," Terry exclaimed, matching Marcy's smile and hoping that if she noticed Terry's eyes getting watery that she assumed they were with joy (which they were, in part).

"Congratulations, I just know that you and Hatori will be so happy."

"I just hate that you still haven't met him officially. You always seem to come by when he's not here," Marcy said. "I think he'd really like you. From what he's told me, you remind me of his sister."

Terry laughed only a bit nervously. "She sounds like a cool person, then."

A sad smile appeared on Marcy's lips, but she didn't elaborate on the sister Terry knew must have still been a sore topic.

"Of course you will be coming to the wedding, right?"

"I'll try my best," Terry answered, pulling her drink closer to her to take a sip.

Marcy turned her head as she heard her name being called. "Well, I've gotta get back to work. I'm so glad you're here so I could tell you. Don't leave for a little bit. I'll be off work at three." She stood from the table, pointing at Terry as if to make sure she stayed put.

Terry waved her away for now, knowing that she'd be back, and they could talk some more. She loved hearing from her about Hatori, the life they'd already started to build together. Terry sniffed, looking back outside as she tried to keep the tears from falling and failing.

She wiped them away with her hoodie sleeve, taking a deep breath and letting it out slowly. She was still smiling, and a small whisper escaped her.

"Way to go, Bro."

She would wait until Marcy ended her shift, she would listen to the whole story of how Hatori proposed and what they were planning next, but even though her heart ached to see him, Terry knew she wasn't ready. Not yet. Dean had been allowed to see his daughter because she wouldn't have recognized him, and his descendants wouldn't, either. Cassiopeia had told her that she wouldn't be recognizable to her loved ones, but that only made Terry feel less inclined to give it a try.

He was still grieving Natsuki, and she was still grieving herself. It felt weird to come back into his life as someone else somehow, even at the fringes of his world. She was an anecdote that Marcy mentioned to him when she came home after a long day, and for now, Terry thought that was enough.

Her phone beeped, and she pulled it from the pocket of her hoodie along with her wallet. A text from Willow with several hearts and smileys. She unlocked the phone and checked her schedule to make sure she didn't have any work for a while. She had a couple duties slated for this evening, but that was all for the rest of the day. And in keeping with tradition, tomorrow, she had the day off.

She and Willow were going to Disneyland.

Acknowledgements

The seeds of ideas that became this book began to sprout in 2014, when I was at a very low point in my life. Now nearly a decade later, I'm so grateful to the people in my life (and the creators of the things) that helped me through those times. I would have never seen how good, bad, awful, and amazing the intrevening years have been without you.

Thank you to my family; my parents, brother, and his new beautiful family. You listened and supported me through all my ramblings even when you didn't fully understand them. To my extended family, who have been amazing cheerleaders on social media, to my blessed grandparents (now passed) who instilled in me values I cherish today.

To my friends IRL and online, thank you for being some of the first to hear about my characters and for lending me the names of some of your OCs.

Thank you to God for inspiration and for allowing me to be so very weird. Weird enough to call this story my 'heart book'.

And I'd never forget to send a million thank yous to the team at Tala Editorial (Nikki, Tara, Cheyenne, Kristy, Ben, and Juan) who were amazing and never got annoyed at how much I dragged my feet on those first edits. Thank you as well to Rob Batey for my lovely author photo.

Thank you to Bryan Fuller for the quirky shows about death I love.

And finally, thank you to the readers for giving this story a shot. I hope you were at least entertained and that if you needed to hear something helpful or life affirming, maybe you found some of it here.

There are probably a whole sea of people that I haven't included but if you aren't mentioned here know I thank you, too.

Thank you all again, my gratitude overflows so much it might soak your shoes.

And if after reading this book, you feel compelled to take action to help people in crisis, please consider donating to one of the gracious charities that support help for people with mental health conditions and those at-risk for suicide.

About The Author

Coming from teenage years spent in the land of fanfiction, writing stories has been an integral part of Celia Cleaveland's life for many years. After graduating from the Institute for Children's Literature in 2010. Celia honed her craft with many writing projects. This has all culminated in the creation of her debut novel *PurgaTerry*, the book you're looking at right now.

Find her on:

Twitter/X @ckatwriter

Tiktok @ckatmyla

Instagram @ckatwriter

Made in the USA
Columbia, SC
26 June 2025